Praise for the
  Poetic Death Mystery Series
  by Diana Killian

"Involving. It is the appealing summertime setting of Britain's Lake District, the enigmatic relationship between Grace and Peter and the possibility of a second suitor that give the book its charm."
—*Publishers Weekly*

"Fun to read… I just sat back and let things wash around me while I enjoyed them…. A true beach or airplane book."
—*Mystery News*

"A series to watch…. This well-plotted novel is certain to appeal to mystery lovers everywhere."
—*RT Book Club* (Top Pick of the Month)

"The landscape is filled with detail that will transport readers…. *High Rhymes and Misdemeanors* is a fun outing for literary mystery fans as well as an introduction to a new heroine who will be interesting to learn more about."
—*The Mystery Reader*

"A lot of fun and very witty and winsome. I was won over. Diana Killian knows her setting and Lord Byron's factual biography as well as lore. You don't have to know the poet to read and enjoy—never fear."
—G. Miki Hayden in *Futures* magazine

"A light, charming novel…filled with wonderful characters and with substantial information about the Lake Poets and their lives…. An entertaining romp through a beautiful part of Britain."
—*Dallas Morning News*

DOCKETFUL OF POESY

BY DIANA KILLIAN

The Poetic Death Mystery Series
  High Rhymes and Misdemeanors
  Verse of the Vampyre
  Sonnet of the Sphinx
  Docketful of Poesy

The Mantra for Murder Series
  Corpse Pose
  Dial Om for Murder

DOCKETFUL OF POESY

A Poetic Death Mystery

Diana Killian

PALO ALTO ■ MCKINLEYVILLE ■ 2009
PERSEVERANCE PRESS ■ JOHN DANIEL & COMPANY

This is a work of fiction. Characters, places, and events are the product of the author's imagination or are used fictitiously. Any resemblance to real people, companies, institutions, organizations, or incidents is entirely coincidental.

A Perseverance Press Book
Published by John Daniel & Company
A division of Daniel & Daniel, Publishers, Inc.
Post Office Box 2790
McKinleyville, California 95519
www.danielpublishing.com/perseverance

Distributed by SCB Distributors (800) 729-6423

Book design by Eric Larson, Studio E Books, Santa Barbara
www.studio-e-books.com

10 9 8 7 6 5 4 3 2 1

LIBRARY OF CONGRESS CATALOGING-IN-PUBLICATION DATA
Killian, Diana.
Docketful of poesy : a poetic death mystery / by Diana Killian.
    p. cm.
ISBN-13: 978-1-880284-97-1 (pbk. : alk. paper)
ISBN-10: 1-880284-97-9 (pbk. : alk. paper)
    1. Women teachers--Fiction. 2. Women screenwriters--Fiction 3. Motion
picture actors and actresses--Crimes against--Fiction. 4. Los Angeles (Calif.)-
-Fiction. I. Title.
PS3611.I4515D63 2009
813'.6--dc22
                    2008030205

Dedicated to blogmates Tasha Alexander,
Laura Bradford, Regina Harvey,
Sara Rosett—and Good Girls everywhere

ACKNOWLEDGMENTS

The author wishes to express her sincere gratitude to the Mystery Writers of America for the award of an MWA grant.

Thank you to the readers who coaxed, cajoled, and finally convinced me that there should be another Poetic Death novel. Thanks also to my husband for his love and support—and to my endlessly patient family. And, finally, thank you to the "Wednesday Nighters": Candace, Dorothy, Lynn, and Tanya.

DOCKETFUL OF POESY

PROLOGUE

Where there is mystery, it is generally suspected there must also be evil.
—Lord Byron

THE BITE of spade and shovel on stone echoed off the pillars of the Gates of No Return. Captain Stanley had ordered his men to dig up the courtyard flagstones to make a vault for the Governor's lady—found dead that morning on the floor of her chamber, an empty bottle of prussic acid clutched in her rigid hand.

The soldiers worked all afternoon while the tropical rains poured down.

It was after midnight when they lowered the coffin, wood scraping brick. The fort's chaplain read a few prayers—his words caught and tossed away by the salty Cape wind that sent the torches flickering. There were none to weep for her; her kith and kin far across the sea, the Governor himself too drunk to stagger down from the castle tower. Dark eyes watched from the shadows, and the whispers had already begun.

Was it an accident? Had she taken the stuff by mistake—one bottle might look very like another to a woman stricken. She was often ill with mysterious pains and complaints.

Her unhappiness was no secret. Lonely little London bird flown so far from friends and home. Had death come at her own hand?

Or the hand of another?

The soldiers bricked up the vault. The flagstones were laid in place once more.

The soldiers returned to their barracks. The slaves and servants crept to their beds. The light in the tower went out. The

13

rain poured down and washed the mud away, trickling through the stones, drip, drip, dripping on the sepulcher below. And Laetitia Elizabeth Landon—once known to the London literati as the poetess L.E.L.—slept in her chamber of stone, lulled by the hollow echo of the restless, beating sea.

CHAPTER 1

"A FILM?" Peter's voice echoed hollowly down the transatlantic line. "You're going... Hollywood?"

"I...um...believe it's straight-to-cable," I said.

Silence. Then, "And this is a documentary?"

"I think so."

"You think so?"

"Roberta Lom, the producer—" I winced, hearing my own slightly self-conscious tone as I spoke the word *producer* "—was a little vague. It was a short conversation. She was late for a meeting."

Another of those awkward silences. I glanced at the clock on the bedstand; ten o'clock P.M. Peter's time. I had been so looking forward to talking to him; I always seemed to call at the wrong hour: either he wasn't home or he wasn't able to talk. But now, after three and a half weeks of phone tag, I finally had him on the line—and it was almost as though I were talking to a stranger. He seemed so...far away.

Of course, he *was* far away—over five thousand miles of far away. Peter was in the tiny village of Innisdale in the English Lake District while I was in Los Angeles, so maybe I was letting my imagination make too much of a bad connection. Bad in more ways than one.

He said flatly, "I don't see why anyone would want to make a documentary of your book. Who, other than academics like yourself, would care whether or not Lord Byron fathered yet another bastard child?"

Now, I found that a tad irritating, but I'm the first to admit that when it comes to my passion—my passion for literature of the

15

Romantic period—I'm not entirely objective. So, striving for sweet reason, I said, "Well, first of all, how we determined that little fact makes a pretty good story, I think. I mean, I was kidnapped—three times—"

My gaze wandered past the assorted silver- and pewter-framed photos of my parents, me, and my brothers, Clark and Colin. Clark, four years older, had the blond hair and wide green eyes—behind the same horn-rimmed glasses—of our father. Colin had Mother's freckles and red hair. As the middle child it had fallen upon me to somehow manage a diplomatic combination of genetic traits: green eyes and auburn hair—and if there's one thing I'm good at, it's diplomatic relations.

"You can hardly count Allegra taking you to Lady Vee's as actual abduction."

Perhaps he was not defending yet another former girlfriend so much as being a stickler for accuracy. Still striving for sweet reason, but now through gritted teeth, I said, "I was held against my will. Never mind the fact that we were *both* nearly shot by that crazed—"

"A bit sensationalistic for a reputable documentary," Peter drawled in that annoying public-school accent, and if I didn't know better, I'd have sworn he was deliberately provoking me.

"I assume the documentary will focus on the academic aspects of our search."

Peter laughed. And now I was quite sure that he *was* trying to provoke me. "What academic aspects might those be?" he inquired as though genuinely interested. "As I recall, you were convinced we were searching for a lost manuscript."

Now that was one for the books—no pun intended. For once I, Grace Hollister, was at a loss for words. In fact, there was the oddest prickling behind my eyes—as though I were about to suffer a dreadful allergy attack. What was happening here? We were very nearly quarreling.

This, after exchanging no more than a dozen words or so since I'd left the Lakes for a brief visit home. Or what would have been a brief visit if it hadn't been for my parents' fortieth wedding anniversary, the holidays, the difficulty in arranging the subletting of my apartment, catching up with old friends and colleagues, and now this once-in-a-lifetime opportunity to see my first book made into a film.

I couldn't understand it. Did Peter regret the things—those lovely, romantic things—he had said before I left, nearly three... four...*six* months...earlier? Did he not want me to return to Innisdale?

Into my silence he said, "If this is a documentary, wouldn't I need to sign a release of some sort? You're planning to use my name, I take it?"

"Are you saying you would refuse to sign a release?"

The hiss in the long-distance line seemed ominous.

"No," he said quietly, at last. "I'm not going to stop you, if this is what you want."

Were we still talking about the proposed documentary film? There was something in his voice....

I said uncertainly, "Is everything all right there? Was there— you said you had something to tell me." I'd been so thrilled that he had called me, so excited about my news; I'd hardly given him a chance to get a word in until at last his pointed lack of interest had penetrated the bubble of my enthusiasm.

"It'll keep," he said.

Abruptly, I remembered the beautiful and dangerous Catriona— and the much less beautiful but equally dangerous Turkish prison guard Hayri Kayaci. I remembered three murder investigations and far too many close calls to count. Peter's past was checkered at best, and the publication of my first book alone had brought re-sults similar to poking a stick into a nest of cobras. Was it possible that he had valid reasons for not wanting this film made?

"Peter," I began.

"Look, Grace," he said at the same time. "Something's come up. I'll ring you later, shall I?"

"All right," I said reluctantly, but I was speaking to a dial tone.

Slowly, I replaced the handset, fearing that more than a phone connection had been broken.

■ ■ ■ ■ ■

"That didn't take long," my mother said when I entered the kitchen a few minutes after ending my phone call to Peter. She was chopping asparagus stalks for yet another of her highly nutritious casseroles. Mother is one of those women who does everything brilliantly; everything except cook. I had a sudden longing for one of Peter's butter-drenched, cream-soaked, cognac-laced specialties.

It was hard not to love a man who could cook as well as Peter, even taking into consideration all his unsavory acquaintances and the number of close calls I had experienced since becoming involved with him. Assuming "involved" was the right word.

"Something came up. He had to ring off," I said.

"Was he pleased about the documentary?"

"No." I met my mother's hazel gaze and shrugged. "He's a… very private person."

"Is he?" Mother added the asparagus and baby carrots to the small new potatoes already steaming on the stovetop. Nature camouflaged my mother's razor-sharp brain beneath feathery red hair and a playful smattering of freckles on a pert nose. But there's nothing feathery or pert about my mom—especially when she's grilling one of her susp—offspring. She studied me levelly for a moment, clearly choosing her words, and I felt one of those qualms that adulthood and autonomy had done nothing to shield me from.

"Grace, your father and I have made a point of never interfering in our children's lives, but I can't say we're pleased to discover that you're seriously considering committing yourself to a man with a criminal record."

Of course, I had known this chat was coming from the moment I set foot on American soil, and for one cowardly instant I wished I'd revealed a little less of Peter's background to my concerned parents. But I'm a firm believer in honesty being the best policy—besides, it was a sure bet that the visiting Detective Inspector Brian Drummond, whom I'd been seeing while he was in town, would have been only too happy to fill my family in on the more colorful aspects of Peter's history.

With the uncanny mind-reading ability that had terrified me and my brothers in our formative years—not to mention generations of students in her Women's Studies courses—my mother said, "What time is Brian picking you up?"

"A quarter to seven. The seminar ends at four-thirty."

Brian, an expert in art and antiquities theft, had arrived a few days early to attend an Interpol-sponsored international conference on cultural trafficking. The conference had been postponed several times, but finally his trip coincided with my visit home in a way that seemed fortuitous from his viewpoint and that of my parents.

Whether in reaction to Peter Fox's criminal past, or on the basis of his own merits, of which, true enough, he had many, Brian had already received the stamp of approval from my nearest and dearest.

That last sounds like I was being forced to see Brian against my will, and of course that's not true. I liked him—a lot. I found him very attractive and very good company.

"He's an attractive young man," Mother said. "Intelligent, presentable, politically conscious."

"Yes," I said noncommittally.

"He's certainly very interested in you."

"He's a long way from home," I said. I could feel my mother's gaze, but I kept my own glued to the flowered Harker Pottery casserole that had once belonged to my grandmother.

It was a very pretty dish, though not particularly valuable—something I had learned working at Rogue's Gallery Antiques with Peter. One of the more useful—and law-abiding—things I had learned. Another thing I had learned was the importance of family and treasured traditions. Which is why I didn't object when my mother continued, "I can't pretend that your father and I are pleased with some of the things you've told us about this…Peter Fox."

Even I had to admit Peter didn't, well, look good on paper. "If you were able to meet him…"

"Well, that would be up to him, wouldn't it?" Mother said. "If he's genuinely interested in building a life with you, I would think he would be willing to make the effort to meet your family."

There really was no answer to that; I would hardly strengthen my position by admitting that I couldn't picture Peter in this country or this house. Let alone this kitchen.

"How many criminal investigations has he dragged you into?" Mother continued.

"He hasn't dragged me into anything," I countered. "In fact, from the minute I met him he tried to discourage me from getting involved in these…these adventures. But if I hadn't gotten involved there would have been no book and no documentary, so it isn't all a bad thing."

My mother looked unconvinced.

And the truth was, I wasn't entirely convinced either. It had been roughly two and a half years ago that I visited the Lake District researching the Romantic poets for my doctoral thesis, and became involved in a bit of literary skulduggery. With that involvement had come involvement of another kind: a romantic liaison with Peter Fox, antiques dealer and former jewel thief. Peter claimed to have turned over a new leaf, but not everyone in his murky past seemed to have got the message. Which wasn't likely to endear him to my friends and family—and even I had to admit that the fact that Peter's kisses turned my bones to water and my brain to mush wasn't exactly an endorsement for sane and healthy living.

"I understand the power of sexual chemistry," my mother said in that voice as cool and clear as astringent, "but I speak from experience when I tell you that nothing is more important to a successful marriage than respect and shared interests."

I had a sudden, vivid childhood memory of lying in bed listening to the quiet murmur of my parents' voices—and the surprising sound of my mother giggling. "I know you and Dad have been very happy, and of course I want that for myself. I do respect Peter and we do share many interests."

"Amateur sleuthing?" my mother inquired tartly.

"More than that, Mother."

She had the grace to look down at the vegetable swamp.

"Are you able to share your work with him?"

"Yes. That is, he…listens."

My mother fixed me with her all-seeing gaze. "But does he share your passion?"

"For poetry? He understands it." As much as anyone who wasn't a fellow academic could understand my obsession for the written word.

"You know what Joubert said. 'Only choose in marriage a man whom you would choose as a friend if he were a woman.'"

The picture that conjured held me silent for the second time that afternoon.

■■■■■

"You look smashing!" Brian said a few hours later when I opened the front door to my parents' home.

Brian looked rather smashing, too, in his dark suit; I wasn't used to seeing him so formally attired. He generally wore jeans and a blazer on duty. Pristine jeans, mind—I even suspected him of pressing them—and beautifully cut tweed blazers.

"Thank you, sir." I accepted the peck on my cheek automatically.

Surreptitiously, I studied him. It's always interesting seeing that reflection of yourself in the people that your nearest and dearest want to set you up with. Brian was about my age, medium height and trim as a Marine. His hair was dark and his eyes were that shade of blue that looks mostly gray. In some ways he reminded me of Chaz, my other longtime, family-approved significant other. Brian was a bit edgier, and a lot more stubborn—er, forceful—than Chaz, but they shared similar values and world view. I suppose I shared those, although I'd hitched my star to a former criminal and ladies' man.

"New dress?" Brian inquired. He was very good about noticing that kind of thing.

I shook my head. "It's been in storage with the rest of my things."

"It suits you. Very feminine. The green brings out your eyes."

Yes, it was difficult; Brian made no bones about the fact that he was interested, that for him it was not just friendship. He never overstepped the boundaries, but he didn't pretend either. He wasn't a man for playing games. That was one of the things I liked about him. But then, I liked many things about him.

I watched him being pleasant with my parents, watched the warm welcome they extended him, and I couldn't help thinking how much simpler my life would be....

"So where are you taking me tonight?" Brian inquired as we walked outside to my car.

"Mélisse on Wilshire Boulevard. And, no, before you ask, it's not Mexican. Try not to be too disappointed."

"I *am* disappointed," he said. "I suspect some addictive substance in that salsa. But it's all right, I had tacos for lunch today."

I laughed, unlocking my car door. Yes, it was very easy with Brian.

Mélisse Restaurant is supposed to be one of the most romantic dining spots in Los Angeles, although this was not why I had picked it. At least I didn't think that was why I had picked it. While I would never consider myself a foodie, I had gained new appreciation and knowledge of food through my relationship with Peter—and I say this as a woman who has battled her weight since adolescence.

The food at Mélisse is traditional French with a California flair; the wine list is fabulous, and the setting comfortably chic. We were seated quickly. We ordered wine, and Brian asked, "How's the research coming?"

My mother's words in mind, I responded, "It's fascinating."

"Yes?"

"Absolutely. Maybe I'm crazy but I find research seductive. I think I enjoy it more than the writing, to tell you the truth." I was supposed to be starting work on a book about the premier female poets of the Romantic period, but so far I'd been unable to whittle down the list of potential candidates to a realistic size.

And right on cue Brian asked, "Have you settled on who you'll be writing about?"

"Not finally. It would be easier to go with the obvious choices: Felicia Hemans, Anna Laetitia Barbauld, Charlotte Smith…"

He'd heard this all a dozen times, of course. He said mildly, "You wouldn't want to do the easy thing."

"Ha. It's not just a matter of doing the easy thing. It's ground that's been covered, of course, but well worth re-examining. The thing is…"

I paused; Brian looked inquiringly.

"I feel terrible admitting this, but I don't feel inspired by these women the way I feel inspired by the works of Byron or Shelley or Keats. It seems disloyal to say it, but it's the truth."

"That's because you've a soft spot for villains."

I shook my head, and Brian said, "All right, remind me again why you're writing this book?"

I leaned forward on my elbows. Brian put a hand out to steady the table. I do tend to get a little carried away once I get going. "To begin with, it's incredible to me that as well respected and popular as these women were during their own writing careers, they're virtually unheard of now. As well read as I am in the Romantic period, even I'd heard of almost none of them before I began researching this book. They aren't even listed as minor poets. It's as though they never existed."

"Maybe their work doesn't stand the test of time."

"But it does. That's the thing. These are smart, talented, often courageous women who deserve to be remembered for their contribution to literature. They deserve our respect."

"Is respect a substitute for passion?"

I stared at him. "No," I said slowly. "It's not."

Brian looked a little puzzled, although he smiled. Our server came then and we ordered our meals, I opting for morel-crusted imported Dover sole, and Brian deciding on the dry-aged Côte de Boeuf Rôti.

"How was the conference?" I inquired after our wineglasses were replenished and our server had departed once more.

He settled back in his chair. "Today it was mostly discussion of the UNESCO and Unidroit multilateral treaties."

"Ah."

Brian grinned. "It's been interesting, but I admit I'm looking forward to going home. Any idea about when you're returning to Innisdale?"

Realizing to my surprise that I had come to a decision, I said, "I'm probably going to book my flight tomorrow." His smile caught me off-guard. "I—it's time I was getting back. I did hear this afternoon from Roberta Lom, the producer of *Dangerous to Know*, and she's invited me out to the set tomorrow. They're filming in Tehachapi, of all places."

"What's Tehachapi?"

"About as far away from the English Lake District as you can get—although it's apparently very green this time of year. I can't imagine a small indie film company has much of a budget, so shooting on location is out. I mean shooting on the *actual* location—not that anyone does anymore. I think everyone goes to New Zealand or Romania nowadays."

"Er…right," Brian said cautiously. "I thought they simply used computers."

"Maybe they do. I'm not exactly an expert." Noticing I was about to monopolize the conversation again, I turned our talk back to Brian's conference.

Our meals came, and for a brief time we were pleasantly occupied with food. Peter had taught me to give a fine meal the appreciation it's due, and in fact, he'd have been right at home in this place with its muted, romantic lighting, the gleaming Riedel flatware and Limoges china. Peter valued what he referred to as "life's little civilities" as much as he respected wonderful food, and my food that night was wonderful indeed: potato gnocchi, king oyster mushrooms, and *jus de cuisson truffée*. One melting bite of sole, and I realized that Mélisse's awards and reviews were well earned.

Blinking back the haze of foodie fever, I became aware that Brian was studying me with a rather odd expression on his face.

"Is something wrong?" I glanced at his plate. Potato-leek torte, wild mushrooms, braised Boston lettuce: it all looked perfect to me. It smelled perfect, too.

Brian's gaze met mine and sheered away. "I have something to tell you, and I've been trying to find the right way to say it."

A chill of premonition slithered down my spine. "What is it? Just tell me."

"I received a phone call this afternoon from Chief Constable Heron."

Over the past two years I had come to think of Innisdale's chief constable as a friend—or at least as close a friend as a copper could be to a woman whose intended was a former villain.

Staring at Brian's grave face I told myself that if something… bad had happened, Heron would call me directly. He wouldn't leave it to Brian to break truly bad news to me, would he?

But it was clearly not tidings of great joy about to be delivered.

My heart slamming against my breastbone in silent panic, I sat very still, very straight, waiting to hear whatever this was. "And?" I asked, dry-mouthed.

"Apparently someone tried to kill Peter Fox this morning."

Did the room's lighting suddenly dim? I managed, "Is he all right?"

Brian hesitated, and I barely felt the pain of my nails sinking into my clenched hands. It was all I could do not to scream at him. He said, after what felt like an eternity, "No one knows. He's disappeared."

CHAPTER 2

PURSUED CLOSELY by the black van, the blue BMC Mini swerved sharply, spun out, and skidded to a halt in the middle of the muddy side road. The van, narrowly missing crashing into the smaller car, rocked to a stop. Its doors flew open and two men wearing ski masks and waving semi-automatic weapons jumped out and ran to the Mini. They dragged the driver, a tall blond woman, out of the car.

"Where is he? Where's David Wolf?" yelled one of the masked men. He shook the woman.

Roberta had informed me that morning that because of possible liability issues all of the characters in *Dangerous to Know* were getting name changes. Peter Fox was now David Wolf. I was Faith Bolton. Needless to say, this was not a documentary. Maybe it was a dramatization, but I had the sinking feeling that any resemblance to living persons, places, or actual events was entirely coincidental.

One man loosed off a short burst of gunfire into the air.

The woman and the other masked man stopped tussling and stared at him in astonishment.

"*Cut!*" yelled a stocky, middle-aged man in a cowboy hat. Director Miles Friedman left the safety of a grassy verge well to the side of the action. "For chrissake, *cut!* Pammy, what the hell was *that?*"

Pammy Dickens, the assistant director, threw her hands wide in an open shrug.

Miles began to swear lengthily.

"Uh-oh," murmured Roberta Lom, standing next to me on our vantage point behind the silent camera. The rest of the cast and crew of *Dangerous to Know* milled about the trailers and equipment stationed on the wildflower-sprinkled hillside. Roberta, the film's producer, was a tall, sleek, gently aged brunette. She smiled at me—she had a flawless smile. "It's pretty tedious, isn't it? Making movies."

"A little," I admitted. They had been working since seven o'clock that morning, rehearsing each leg of the car chase at half speed, verifying the "choreography," then rehearsing again, and then finally shooting at full speed. It was four-thirty now, and as far as I could tell they were only about three-quarters of the way through the scene.

Of course all kinds of things could spoil a scene: the extraneous noise of a diesel truck changing gears on the freeway behind the hills, the cries of a hunting hawk—or things that affected the continuity of a shot like jet contrails in the sky.

"That's one reason I try to avoid visiting the set during shooting." Her eyes were hazel behind decorative cat's-eye glasses. She studied me curiously. "What's it like seeing a chapter of your own life acted out?"

"It's interesting," I said politely. What I was thinking was: *Are you serious?*

Never mind that it had been autumn and England—and this was winter and obviously Southern California. Never mind that my attackers had been wearing funny Halloween masks, and that the only gun in sight had been a handgun—terrifying for all that, but hardly the mini-arsenal the movie bad guys were carrying. No, what really irked me was that I, a medium-sized, thirty-something woman with auburn hair and a fairly decent brain, had been replaced by a tall, thin, platinum blond twenty-something whose dialogue mostly consisted of lines like, "But why is this *happening* to me?"

A documentary this was most certainly *not.*

"It wasn't so tedious yesterday," said the slim young man with the wispy goatee on my left. Walter Christie was the film's screenwriter; which was enough to jaundice my view of him. Interestingly, Christie seemed equally unenthusiastic about meeting me— and less inclined to hide it. "You heard about the brakes going out on Miles's car last night?"

"That was a close call," agreed Roberta. "I take it the Jag is back in the shop today?" She met my inquiring look. "That vintage Jag is Miles's pride and joy. He'd just taken it in for a tune-up, so you can imagine how livid he was."

"The brakes went out?"

"On the Grapevine. Not a road you want to try to tackle without brakes, but Miles was lucky. A trucker saw what was happening and maneuvered his rig in front of the Jag. He was gradually able to slow it down and then finally bring it to a stop."

"That *was* lucky."

The three of us watched the cowboy-hatted director shouting, "Ted, what are you doing? You're not supposed to fire that thing. Why the hell is it even loaded?" He continued to rant and rave.

"I thought it added to the scene," the hapless stunt man said.

The director went on yelling while other crew members scurried around looking harassed. "You're a stuntman. You're not an actor. You're not paid to think! For chrissake!" He relieved his feelings at length, ending, " Okay, people, back to one!"

Walter muttered, "Cinéma Vérité for Dummies."

"Now, now," murmured Roberta.

"How's the camera rig in that car doing?" Miles called, and one of the cameramen gave him thumbs-up.

Miles threw something uncomplimentary over his shoulder, striding back to where the rest of us stood. He pulled a silver flask out of his pocket and took a swig. The stunt people, actors, and crew resumed their positions.

"Miles," Roberta called, "what about all those skid marks where they practiced turning off the highway onto the dirt road?"

Miles put his flask away and turned back to the deserted highway streaked with myriad skid marks on the faded road. "Don't waste my time with that stuff, Robbie. We can fix it in post." He glanced upwards at the somber gray sky. High above, predatory black specks could be seen circling. "Perfect," he muttered.

"Miles is winging in the rain," Walter commented, sotto voce.

Roberta, who had stiffened at Miles' dismissive tone, smiled unpleasantly. Without looking at Walter, she murmured, "Remind me again of how many screen credits you have, Walter?"

He reddened, and shoved his hands in his jean pockets. Shoulders hunched, he moved away down the line of watching crew members, dollies, and lighting hardware.

"Twerp," Roberta remarked to no one in particular. Catching my eye, she said, "I guess we seem a little uncivilized compared to academia?"

"Oh no," I assured her. I didn't bother to say that some of my most treasured moments in academia made the World Wrestling Federation seem civilized.

"Places! Quiet!" shouted the assistant director. She spoke rapidly into her walkie-talkie.

Miles, who had been scowling through the lens of one of the cameras, straightened up. "I want to get some wide profile shots this time around." Catching my eye, he winked with practiced charm. "Enjoying yourself, Ms. Hollister?"

"It's a whole new world," I assured him.

Which was certainly true, if not exactly what the director was asking. I was trying to enjoy myself, but anxiety over Peter was a constant presence in the back of my mind. Brian's information had been sketchy. Two masked men with shotguns had burst into Rogue's Gallery in the middle of the afternoon, and opened fire. Luckily no one had been hurt—primarily because the gunmen had a specific target, and that was Peter Fox. They had ignored the screaming, terrified customers, going after Peter with deadly purpose. But Peter had made it to the stockroom in time, slid the bolt on them, and escaped through the passage concealed behind the shelving units. It had not taken the gunmen long to blast through the stockroom door, but long enough. By the time they burst in, it was empty; and whoever they were, they were unacquainted with the secrets of Craddock House and Rogue's Gallery.

The gunmen had departed, and not long after, the police had arrived. Eventually they had uncovered the entrance to the passageway, but there was no sign of Peter. He had simply disappeared.

"There was no sign that he was…hurt?" I had asked, swallowing on the word.

"Nothing to indicate it," Brian had reassured me.

And certainly Peter had sounded healthy enough when we'd spoken on the phone, and that call had taken place hours after the shooting at Rogue's Gallery.

I watched, unseeing, as the van and car reversed and disappeared down the empty highway, followed by a truck with a camera crane mounted on a platform.

"What the hell is going on? Has anyone here ever worked on a film before?" Miles cried. "Pammy, tell them to hold up, we don't need to reshoot that part!"

The assistant director chased after the truck, screaming into her walkie-talkie.

"What was it like?" Roberta asked suddenly. She nodded after the disappearing vehicles. "Being abducted, I mean."

"Terrifying," I said.

She eyed me curiously. "And it all happened like it did in the book?"

"Yes." If anything, I had toned down actual events for the book. The tentative beginnings of romance with Peter: that had definitely been missing from the book.

As though reading my mind, Roberta said, "And Peter Fox, the antiques dealer and ex-jewel-thief, that was all true, too?"

"That was true."

"Truth really *is* stranger than fiction?" There was something in Roberta's tone….

My eyes met hers, and Roberta licked her lips. "He sounds yummy," she said, and I blinked. It couldn't possibly work long-distance, could it: that magnetism Peter seemed to hold for the opposite sex?

"Uh, yes. He had his yummy moments," I said, and could have kicked myself.

"What does he think about this film?"

I said honestly, "I think he hopes it doesn't bring a lot of the wrong kind of publicity his way."

She seemed amused. "Is there a wrong kind of publicity? Not in our business."

We fell silent as the Mini screeched into view, made its turn—barely—and skidded to a stop, mud spraying from beneath its tires. The pursuing van banged into it—hard—and the little car bounced a couple of feet, the stuntwoman inside lurching forward.

"Jeeeez," one of the crew muttered.

Quietly, Miles ordered, "Keep rolling. Keep...the camera... rolling...."

As before, the van doors flew open and the two stuntmen got out, approaching the Mini. They dragged the blond stuntwoman out of the car again.

"Where is he? Where's David Wolf?"

And that was the sixty-four-thousand-dollar question, wasn't it? I had waited all day for my cell phone to ring with an update from Brian, but there had been nothing. No news was good news, right? I reminded myself of this—and that Peter was very good at taking care of himself.

I kept running our last conversation in my mind, understanding only after the fact what it was that Peter had called to tell me. And maybe if I had shut up about the damned movie—

But, after all, how could I know? It was Peter's responsibility to have made me understand, wasn't it? The fact that he had let me rattle on, choosing not to tell me that he had been the target of would-be assassins, surely said more about Peter's faulty communication skills than mine?

So now what? Would Peter contact me again? Would he disappear out of my life forever? I wanted to believe that he would never abandon Rogue's Gallery and the life he had built for himself in Innisdale, but he hadn't behaved like the normal, innocent victim of a crime—he had not gone to the police. Brian naturally took the dimmest possible view of this, but I could not imagine a situation where Peter *would* voluntarily go to the police, no matter how clean his own hands were.

"Aaaaaand print!" called Friedman, and I snapped back to the present in time to see Tracy Burke, the film's "Faith," moving to take the place of the stuntwoman. Booms and C-stands were shifted, grips moved, camera angles changed. So many people on a movie set—even for a little independent production like this one.

"It is effing fer*eeeezing* out here!" Tracy complained loudly, tossing her long platinum hair. Except she didn't say "effing."

It was a strange feeling not to like the person who was supposed to be portraying you in your own real-life adventures, but I did not care for Tracy. In fact, although I didn't want to admit it, so far I wasn't wild about anyone I'd met on the set of *Dangerous to Know.*

Not that I *dis*liked Tracy; she was fairly harmless, despite a mouth like a sailor (and that would not be one of the hands on the good ship *Lollipop*) and a strange tendency to shed her clothes at the slightest provocation. She stood now in black stovepipe jeans and a teeny-tiny pink midriff blouse, hip sexily canted while she waited for the gold-leaf reflectors to be positioned around her.

A few yards down, I spotted Walter Christie, his face pinched and red with cold. He was watching Tracy, and even I couldn't mistake the naked longing in his eyes.

"Let's move it, people! This light won't last much longer. Hell, this weather won't last much longer. We're losing our window of opportunity here," Miles called. I glanced up at the increasingly ominous skies. The assistant director began running around like a harrying Border collie, barking out directions, snapping orders. There were several groans and a smattering of language not approved for General Audiences.

"What will you do now?" Roberta asked.

I tuned back in. "About what?"

"Now that you're home for good. Will you go back to teaching?"

For a moment it was as though she were speaking in another language. It took a few seconds to translate. "I'm not home for good," I said. "At least…" At least I didn't think so. That had never been the plan, and the idea that it might play out this way was shocking to me.

"Oh, but I was under the impression…"

Why should she be under the impression of anything concerning me? It was my turn to study the other woman. Roberta did not fit my idea of a movie producer: she wore jeans and a leather jacket and those funky little rhinestone glasses. She looked like someone who should be in an *In Style* photo spread. I pictured movie producers—when I thought of them at all—as fast-talking, ulcer-riddled, wheeler-dealer types—usually male.

"I'm here to visit my family and tie up a few loose ends," I said. "My decision to stay in England was spontaneous—well, you know that from my book. I still plan on returning to Innisdale."

"When?"

Why in the world did it matter? But apparently it did. Roberta was staring at me intently.

"Actually, I was hoping to book my flight this evening. I'd like to fly out within the next few days." I closed my ears to the inner voice that questioned what I would do if Peter did not contact me soon—that perhaps there was no point in flying anywhere.

"Damn."

"I'm sorry?"

Roberta smiled ingratiatingly. "It's just that Miles and I had discussed asking you to take an active part in the project. Specifically, we were thinking about asking you to hire on as a consultant."

To my own surprise, my first thought was, *How fun!* Then I remembered the last time I had hired on as consultant to a theatrical production. I said, "Well, that's very flattering, but—"

"The money's pretty good," Roberta told me quickly. "Very good compared to a teacher's salary. Let alone what a writer earns. But then what isn't, right? You know how it is in this industry. We throw money away. And I don't guess you're exactly rolling in dough these days."

"Still…"

"And I'm sure you want this film to be right. All those little details. No one knows them better than you."

That was almost funny. Never mind the little details, the challenge here would be getting the major plot points straight.

"It's just that I've stayed quite a bit longer than I planned as it is." I was tempted, there was no denying it. After all, it was my book—my *life*—they were filming. Of course I felt a little possessive of it; and of course I wanted to see it done right. But…what about Peter?

Then again, I didn't even know where Peter was at the moment. He might not be in England. Wasn't the next move his? And wouldn't it be easier for him to make that move if he knew where to find me?

"Think about it," Roberta urged.

CHAPTER 3

BRIAN CRAMMED the last of the nachos into his mouth, washed them down with the final mouthful of Corona, glanced at his watch and said regretfully of the tortilla chips and cheese, "I shall miss those."

"And all the Mexican restaurants in the West Valley and vicinity will miss you," I returned. "I hope our local economy can withstand the hit."

He smiled, but distractedly. "I suppose I should be making my way to the gate."

"I suppose so," I agreed reluctantly. It was Wednesday evening. We were sitting in the crowded El Paseo café in the Tom Bradley International Terminal at LAX waiting for Brian's ten o'clock flight. I was sorry to see Brian go. Not because I was falling for him, although I did find him awfully attractive, but because he was a living, breathing link to my life in Innisdale. Brian took it for granted that I would be coming home, that for me "home" was now the English Lake District.

Rising, he gathered his Mac and his briefcase, and laid the tip on the table. We moved together from the restaurant, Brian taking my arm—which reminded me of Peter, of all those little Old World gestures, the tiny courtesies that had initially grated on my independence but which I had come to think of as separating the men from the boys.

"What are you going to do about this film?" Brian asked. "Have you decided?"

I shook my head. "I could use the money of course, but the filming could go on for months—likely will. I don't want to delay my return too long."

"No," he agreed, and the glint in his blue-gray eyes was warming, although I didn't want to encourage him unfairly. If it weren't for Peter—but there was no point even acknowledging that thought because Peter was a fact, and I wouldn't have it any other way. That much I was sure of, although as certainties went, it wasn't much to base a future on.

I said, "You'll let me know as soon as you hear anything?"

"Of course I will. I'll call you as soon as I've arrived."

That was well beyond the call of duty—and more than I wanted, really.

We had reached the security checkpoint. Brian began the inevitable removal of watch, pocket change, shoes, tossing them into the gray plastic bins and setting them on the conveyer belt.

Even in his socks, Brian had dignity as he turned one last time to me.

"I'll say good-bye then."

"Good-bye," I said. "Safe trip."

Brian's hands closed on my arms, bringing me forward and kissing me gently but definitely on my mouth. As kisses went, it was rather nice, Corona and nachos notwithstanding. He'd obviously had a fair bit of practice. As he released me, he seemed to be waiting for some reaction.

But I found myself at a loss for words.

"Take care, Grace." He smiled. "See you soon, will I?"

I nodded, surprised to find myself unexpectedly choked up.

Brian let me go, turning away and taking his place in line. I stepped back behind the roped-off dividers, watching until he was through the security checkpoint. Shoes on, he picked up his briefcase and Mac, and turned to wave a brief final good-bye.

I waved back, watching 'til Brian vanished in the press of people. Feeling strangely adrift I started back for the arrival hall, avoiding the usual obstacle course of suitcases on wheels, potted palm trees, and Starbucks-sloshing travelers. I went down the escalators, wriggled my way through the serpentine lines of check-in, and walked out through the glass double doors into the smoggy night.

Even at this time of night the sidewalk was crowded with people and their luggage. The noise of voices and car engines bounced off the concrete. The air was thick with exhaust as cars, taxis, shuttles screeched up to the curb.

My attention was caught by a recognizable set of shoulders on a tall, lean man moving a few yards ahead of me through the crush of people. I stared.

Surely not?

Apologizing, I pushed and twisted my way forward, gaze pinned on the back of a well-shaped head that seemed as familiar as my own—more familiar, truth be told.

If he would just turn so that I could see his profile…

For a moment I lost track of him behind what appeared to be a just-arrived Zulu dance troop. Mountains of luggage and many exotically garbed tall and willowy people called to each other in a foreign tongue, managing to block my way. I began to fear that this was going to turn into one of those scenarios from my favorite suspense writers—a Mary Stewart moment, perhaps—and that the man with Peter's haircut would vanish into the teeming mass of humanity, leaving me uncertain as to whether I'd really seen what I thought I had.

It would have to be an awfully amazing coincidence. Not that coincidences didn't happen, but—

The blond man moved swiftly, purposefully through the crowd. Stepping to the curb, he raised his hand to hail a taxi, and I caught a clear glimpse of his features.

"Peter!" I shrieked.

He didn't seem to hear me as a cab squealed to the curb.

I abandoned courtesy, shoving through the crowd, yelling, "Peter! *Peter!*"

And to my relief, he paused, turned, and spotted me. Just for a moment I thought his expression lightened, but it was hard to tell in the artificial glare.

"What are you doing here?" I demanded, reaching him. Almost tentatively I reached out to touch his sleeve. He didn't disappear and I didn't wake up.

There was something funny about his smile. "Grace."

It was unbelievable. It really *was* Peter. In the flesh—and a very nice bronze-green Burberry mac. Peter in Los Angeles. It seemed...fantastical. Like finding a unicorn galloping down the 101 Freeway.

He looked tired, little lines of weariness radiating from his so-blue eyes, the glint of golden bristle on his unshaven cheek— but he looked so *good.* I'd forgotten—and how could that be?—how sharp-edged and vital the reality of him was: those intense eyes beneath the dark V of his eyebrows, the contrast of gilt-fair hair— looking unusually ruffled this evening—the thin, sensual mouth that was curling into a smile that was half pleasure, half...something else.

"Thought I'd see for myself what was keeping you," he said, and he sounded perfectly casual, as though picking up the thread of a previous conversation.

I looked past him to the taxi driver who was leaning on the hood of his cab, waiting for us to get the reunion over with. "I've got my car," I said. It occurred to me that he was not taking me in his arms, not kissing me hello; in fact, there seemed to be an invisible force field between us—and I was pretty sure I was not the source.

"Right," he said, and nodded to the driver who raised his shoulders and got back into his cab.

I glanced around for his luggage, and he said, "I didn't stop to pack a bag."

And there it was, right out in the open. "What *happened?*" I asked. "Brian told me—"

"I imagine he would," Peter said, and his hand cupped my elbow, guiding me towards the crosswalk. I looked up, trying to read his face, but it had never been an easy face to read.

"I'm in parking lot three," I said, pointing the way. "And, anyway, it's not like it's the kind of thing you could hide: armed men bursting into the shop and opening fire on you." I wanted to stop and put my arms around him, reassure myself that he was all right, that he was still in one piece, that he was still...mine. But he hustled me along, hurrying me through the cars that barely slowed down to permit pedestrians safe passage.

And then we were in the chill, sickly artificial light of the concrete parking structure—and I was still talking—and still not getting any answers.

"I can't believe you're here. Why didn't you tell me you were coming? Why didn't you let me know you were all right? I was so worried!"

"Were you?" His smile was a little wry.

"Of course I was. What does *that* mean?"

He shook his head. "Where are you parked?"

I led the way to my Honda Accord and unlocked the door. Peter folded his lean length into the passenger seat with a sigh of relief.

"How did you get out of the country without your passport? Or do I want to know?"

"I have my passport. I keep a copy in a safe place for emergencies."

"Of course you do," I said grimly. He gave me a cool look.

"I've a reservation at the Hyatt Regency," he said as I pulled out onto Century Boulevard.

I opened my mouth to object, and then closed it again. Even if I were convinced that Peter or my family would be comfortable rubbing shoulders, I couldn't invite a man who might have some kind of team of international assassins after him to stay at my parents' house.

"Do you have any idea who tried to kill you?"

"No, I don't." He met my eyes. "I'm as startled as you, believe me."

I wouldn't exactly have described myself as "startled." Horrified maybe. Worried, definitely.

I asked delicately, "Had anything…happened…recently?"

"Happened? Not that I recall. And I should think I'd recall my doing something liable to result in someone actively pursuing my removal from the bloody planet."

Unsurprisingly, Brian believed that the attack was the result of Peter resuming his former criminal activities—and perhaps attempting to double-cross his newest confederates. I didn't believe it. Not only because I didn't want to believe it; after two years I felt I knew Peter well enough to be certain he had no interest in returning to a life of crime. For one thing he worked far too hard at Rogue's Gallery.

It seemed more likely that yet another of Peter's former criminal associates had resurfaced with a grudge—real or fancied. I couldn't think of a tactful way to suggest that, however, and the thought was bound to have occurred to him in any case.

It took about half an hour to reach the Hyatt Regency on the Avenue of the Stars. Peter's reservation was confirmed, he checked in without complication—did he keep spare copies of his credit cards as well? That couldn't be a good sign, could it? Surely there was such a thing as being *too* prepared?

"I can't believe you actually made a hotel reservation," I remarked, as we got into the elevator.

"Don't you make hotel reservations when you travel? A woman as well organized as yourself?"

"I'm usually not fleeing one step ahead of a hit squad."

"You underestimate yourself. Besides, two goons with shotguns don't make a hit squad."

"I bow to your superior knowledge. What are they supposed to be? Unhappy customers?"

"Possibly." He yawned, and then smiled apologetically. It was the smile that undid me; it was so unguarded, so genuine. He was dead on his feet, that much was clear.

Reaching his room, Peter unlocked the door, felt inside for a light switch.

I stared about the spacious, well-appointed room furnished in soothing cream and earth tones. Peter's eyes went straight to the enormous king-size bed.

"Are you staying?" he asked simply, and it was clear he was thinking in terms of sharing precious sheet space and nothing more.

And to my surprise, I—for once—didn't have to think about it. "I'm staying." I hesitated. "That is, if you want me to."

He had moved to the picture window, staring past the private balcony to the Los Angeles skyline. Beneath the starry skies, the myriad city lights twinkled, and a river of headlights flowed slowly through the gleaming towers; streetlights, office lights, porch lights, and the lights of several million windows glittered in the night.

"You're joking," he said without turning. "Of course I want you."

Oh. All right. That was reassuring. It could have been said with a little more enthusiasm, granted, but still...

"Do you think they followed you?" I asked his back.

Peter did turn then. "I don't think they were professionals. They came in guns a-blazin' in the middle of the afternoon when the shop was full of customers."

"Do you think it was some kind of a threat? Could it have been a—a hoax?"

"Not that, no. I think they'd have been happy to top me. They certainly gave it their full attention. But I don't think they were pros."

He drew the drapes shut. "I think I'll have a shower. Break open the mini-bar, will you?"

"Shall I order you some kind of dinner from room service?"

"Just drinks for me. Order yourself whatever you like."

"Why do I suddenly feel like Nora Charles?"

"Whom?"

"Mrs. Thin Man."

Peter winked at me and disappeared into the gleaming bathroom. I went into action. I phoned home, leaving a brief message for my parents who were dining out that evening, then I flipped through the hotel services booklet and called down to room service, ordering from their selection of desserts. I took Peter's room key, got ice from the machine down the hall, and returned to ransack the contents of the mini-fridge.

Peter strolled out of the steamy, deliciously scented bathroom a little while later, and stopped short. The bed was turned down, the lamps cozily lit, a tempting selection of desserts sat on a side table.

"Cheers," said I, handing him a glass of Chivas Regal. "And don't worry, I wiped that tumbler myself."

"I…wasn't worried," he said, looking around bemusedly. "What's all this in aid of?"

"Turn about is fair play."

He stared at me for a long moment, his eyes very blue, his hair falling over his forehead in damp, gold strands. He had shaved and he was wearing one of the hotel's guest robes. He smelled distractingly of herbal soap and himself.

"I like the sound of it. I just have no idea what that means."

"It means…it's my turn to…take care of you." I wished I sounded less defiant and more…seductive. But I wasn't used to seducing men. Actually, I wasn't used to taking care of men, either.

"Ah. The chocolate mousse is for medicinal purposes?" His mouth was twitching with that old secret amusement as he brought the glass of whisky to his lips, and despite myself, my heart sped up.

"They didn't have chocolate hazelnut cake."

"What sort of establishment *is* this?" Peter demanded, glancing around with great displeasure.

I bit back a laugh. "Do you remember what you served me the afternoon I arrived at Rogue's Gallery to tell you I thought someone was trying to kill you?"

His face changed. Softened. "Tea and cake. What a sentimental girl you are, Miss Hollister."

I hoped I wasn't blushing. "I figured you'd prefer whisky to tea."

"You figured correctly." He tossed back the rest of his drink, set the glass aside, and took me unhurriedly into his arms. "You're glad to see me, then?"

I was not a woman given to rolling my eyes, but I rolled them then. "Need you ask?"

"Sometimes, yes," Peter said quite seriously. He kissed me then, his mouth warm and smoky with the taste of whisky; and I understood, as much as I liked Brian, as attractive as he was, what the difference was. And, alas, it had nothing to do with still wanting Peter for a friend had he been born a woman.

"So what happens next?" I asked, after Peter released me, and went to find another mini-bottle in the well-stocked fridge.

"I'm wounded," Peter said. "I'd hoped you might still have some faint recollection of those few precious—"

"Not *that*," I said, trying not to laugh. "Of course I remember that. I meant, what will you do next? Are you planning to return to the Lakes?"

"Yes. Are you?"

"Yes."

"Sure about that? You haven't been in a tearing rush to come back."

"Things…kept coming up."

"Yes, I'd noticed that." His gaze held mine.

"I always intended to come back."

I was surprised when—abruptly—he let it go. "Lovely. Now we've got that settled…"

He had another drink. We sampled the desserts, chatted, and Peter brought me up to speed—although he would have loathed that term—on how everyone was back in Innisdale. I filled Peter in on my impressions of the *Dangerous to Know* production.

"You're sure you won't regret passing up your chance to make movies?"

"Maybe a little, but to tell you the truth there's a weird vibe on that set. I can't put my finger on it. Maybe I'm just not used to Hollywood types."

"Perhaps." He surprised me then. "You've got good instincts, though. How's the book coming?"

"I think I'm narrowing down my list. Have you ever heard of Laetitia Elizabeth Landon? She was sometimes called the 'female Byron.'"

"'While lingers in the heart one line, the nameless poet has a shrine,'" Peter quoted, surprising me.

"That's her, yes. Letty Landon. Anyway, it suddenly occurred to me that in many ways *she* embodies the poets I want to write about. The ones who really are forgotten, nameless now."

"I don't think L.E.L. has been utterly forgotten. The mystery surrounding her death guarantees her a certain immortality."

"For all the wrong reasons. Think about it: at one point she was one of the most popular writers in England, male or female, but I don't feel I've read anything that begins to capture who she really was. It doesn't help that all the information on her is so contradictory and confusing."

I didn't want to admit that part of what fascinated me was the idea of this brilliant young poetess giving up everything and everyone familiar, journeying across the ocean to a distant and foreign land—all for love of a man she barely knew. He was liable to find the parallels a bit...much.

Peter's mouth tugged into a reluctant curve. "So what's your theory? Was it murder, suicide, or accident?"

"I don't have a theory. The real tragedy to me is that the drama of her death overshadows her literary legacy. It's a shame, because I find her a compelling figure. Maybe because she was so ordinary, so...everywoman."

"Every woman is not an influential critic, poet, and celebrated literary figure by the age of twenty."

"True. Anyway, I can't wait to get home and really get to work."

He smiled; I listened to the echo of my words, and smiled, too.

It was well after one in the morning when we finished nibbling and drinking. Peter shrugged off the hotel robe and dropped onto the bed with a small groan of relief. Much more self-consciously, I undressed to my panties and bra and slipped in beside him.

His arms closed about me, drawing me close, and it was like coming home. The geography of the heart, I thought. Home was not Los Angeles; it was not even the Lake District. It was here with this enigmatic, but still dear, man.

I wrinkled my nose at the sheer sentimentality of that thought, but there was no point in lying to myself. This was what I had wanted, what I had been waiting for, longing for. It didn't make sense, but I felt that all was right with my world again.

I could feel his body relaxing as he slipped into slumber. His breath was light and cool against my face. I listened to the steady, reassuring thump of his heart beneath my ear, the even tenor of his breathing.

A thought suddenly occurred to me. "Did they say anything?" I asked, and I felt him start into wakefulness.

"Who?" He sounded half-drugged.

"The men who attacked you."

"As I recall…bang, bang," he murmured. A few moments later I could tell by his breathing that he slept.

CHAPTER 4

"GUESS WHO'S coming to dinner?" I said, speaking softly into the phone receiver. The shower was still running in the hotel bathroom, but I lowered my voice anyway.

"The mysterious Peter Fox?" my sister-in-law, Laurel, inquired gleefully. "I heard. I can't wait to meet him!"

"How are they taking it?" By "they" I meant my mother. My dad was the epitome of the relaxed and occasionally absentminded professor of literature—an excellent foil for his highly strung spouse. Not that Dad was a pushover; there was never any doubt who wore the pants in our family.

"The house is now in session. Nora called for a quorum—which unfortunately took place behind closed doors. I'd have loved to have been the fly on *that* wall. Your dad seems to be taking it all in stride, but you know Frank. When will you be here?" Laurel was married to my older brother, Clark. The mother of active twin girls, not much threw Laurel off her stride. In fact, most things amused the heck out of her, including, apparently, my love life.

"Not till this evening. I've got a slew of things to do today."

"Chicken. Oh, your movie producer friend called. Apparently you're having lunch with the guy writing the screenplay of your life. And here I thought you were just making it up as you went along."

"You couldn't make this stuff up," I told her. "Did Roberta leave a number?"

Laurel recited the number and I jotted it down. "Not that I mind," I said, "but how is it you're answering my parents' phone?"

"We had a date to go jogging, remember?"

"No. I'm happy to say I totally forgot about it."

Although I had learned to love walking during my stay in the Lake District, I was never going to be a fitness nut, and as far as I was concerned, jogging was an activity mostly popular in one of those inner rings of hell.

Laurel made *tsk*ing sounds.

I asked, "Where's Mother?"

"She's busy grinding the glass for tonight's dinner. Is there anything your Mr. Fox is allergic to? I'm sure she'd be happy to add it to the menu."

I laughed nervously. "You're going to be there tonight, right? Just for moral support?"

"Gracie, we're *all* going to be there. I'm surprised Callie isn't filming it for one of her sociology courses." Calliope was the college girlfriend of my younger brother, Colin. "Does that poor man have any idea of what he's getting into?"

"He's very brave," I said.

"He must be. Turkish prison will seem like a picnic compared to interrogation by Nora."

I was not a woman giving to squeaking, but I couldn't help the sound of distress that escaped me. My heartless sister-in-law only laughed.

■■■■■

If one more sales associate told Peter he had "such a cute accent" I was going to commit murder.

After the first hour I had decided that clothes shopping with the great love of one's life should be an exercise required of any and all couples intending...coupling. Given Peter's care and attention to details great and small, it shouldn't have come as a surprise to me that he was not willing to just grab any old thing off the shelves of such fine establishments as Brooks Brothers and Bloomingdale's.

Actually he rather reminded me of me—and is there anything more annoying in one's Significant Other?

It was not that he didn't know his mind or fretted over prices; he knew exactly what he wanted, and he didn't even look at price tags. But he seemed to be on a kind of quest for the Holy Grail of men's wear. In fact, the only quick and painless purchases of that morning were a couple of pairs of Levis.

On the other hand, he was pleasant and polite with sales staff, and left a legion of charmed salesgirls—and boys—in his wake.

To distract myself I did a little shopping as well, justifying it by the fact that I could hardly go to my lunch meeting in yesterday's jeans and T-shirt. When I reappeared in Ann Taylor skirt, blouse, and heels I got a slow, approving smile from Peter. I told myself firmly that I was not dressing to please a man; pleasing the man was a mere happy coincidence.

Peter reached over and untucked the tag I'd overlooked in my collar. Just that brush of his hand against my neck reminded me of that morning, of the sleepy pleasure of waking up together for the first time in many—too many—months. He snapped the plastic tie between his fingers; because he was so lean, so graceful, it was easy to forget how strong he was.

"Thank you."

He smiled briefly and turned away, selecting a khaki cotton shirt from a crisp stack.

"Do you think you should contact Chief Constable Heron?" I asked. He was frowning. How much could there be to object to in a simple khaki shirt?

Finally Peter transferred his intent gaze from the hem of the shirt to me. "To what purpose?"

"Well, to let the police know you're alive."

"They know I'm alive. Even that lot can hardly fail to have noticed they didn't find my body."

This seemed a very un-public-spirited attitude to take—and not terribly logical. "They probably want to question you. In fact, I *know* they want to question you."

"That will wait," Peter said coolly, and seemed to make his mind up about the khaki shirt and—miraculously—an olive pin-stripe, too.

"But they could be finding these men instead of allowing them to get further and further away."

"Chief Constable Heron couldn't find his arse with both hands and an hour to spare," Peter said bluntly. "And your pet plod DI Drummond is worse."

Which pretty well concluded discussion on that topic.

While Peter paid for his purchases I tried calling Roberta Lom once more, and this time managed to get through to her. Roberta confirmed my lunch date with Walter Christie—which I'd been half hoping would be canceled.

I tried hinting that it was not a good day for power lunches, but Roberta seemed set on the meeting. "It's the least you can do, Grace, if you're going to turn down the technical advisor gig. Walter's very talented but he's a little out of his depth in this project—and, after all, it is *your* life." She made it sound like it was my fault that they were all stuck making this movie. I wanted to point out that any resemblance to my own life was pretty much coincidental, but I refrained.

In the end it seemed easier to agree to meet with Walter Christie.

I disconnected the call and turned to Peter, who somehow managed to look both comfortable and masculine holding shopping bags.

"Something wrong?" he asked.

I sighed. "I have a lunch meeting with Walter Christie. He's the scriptwriter for *Dangerous to Know*. The producer wanted us to... get our heads together—" I paused at Peter's expression, knowing exactly what he thought of the term "get our heads together." The fact was, there was no way to say any of this without sounding like a "right prat" as Peter would put it—and probably *would* put it before long. "Apparently he's having problems with the screenplay. Or I guess, more accurately, everyone else is having problems with it, so they want me to..."

"To—what?"

"I'm not exactly sure, to tell you the truth. I think Walter is supposed to ask me about some of the things that actually happened and then see whether he can incorporate them into the script."

"Isn't the script based on your book?"

"In theory. Anyway, would you want to come along?" I tried to sound optimistic rather than desperate.

"I would, actually," he said, surprising me. "I'd like to hear more about this so-called documentary of yours."

"Oh, it's definitely *not* a documentary," I said. "No mistake about that. In fact, it's not even a dramatization really. At most I think it's a 'based on.' And it's probably going to be as bad as those kung fu films where the dubbing is off and the sound of fists and feet on flesh resembles wooden blocks hitting each other. That's right, go ahead and laugh!"

He was not exactly laughing at me, but his eyes gleamed with wicked amusement.

"But they really *are* making a movie. I was out there watching them film yesterday. They've got sets and catering trucks and stunt people and… Even a terrible, cheap film costs a small fortune to make. From what I gather they've sold it to one of those women's-interest TV channels."

"I suppose it's a good sign that someone somewhere believes women would want to see a film about a female obsessed with poetry rather than shoes and sex," said Peter.

"Oh, by the time this film is made I'm sure they'll have given me a much more glamorous job than a teacher. I'll be a freelance publicist or a museum curator or a former FBI profiler. Besides, there's no reason a woman can't be obsessed with poetry *and* shoes and sex."

"That's true. You do have an inordinate number of shoes now that I think of it." He checked his watch. "Right, then. Let's hear what your Mr. Christie has to say for himself."

■ ■ ■ ■ ■

But Walter Christie had little to say for himself, apparently no happier to be breaking bread with me than he had been to meet me on the set of *Dangerous to Know*.

We met him at a trendy watering hole, Pizzeria Mozza on North Highland Avenue, and it was clear that Walter had already been partaking heavily from the Italian wine bar. Brief introductions were made and Walter peered owlishly into Peter's face. "So you're Peter Fox. At least they got you right."

"Sorry?"

"Todd Downing. He could pass for your brother." Walter glanced at me. "You haven't met Todd yet."

"No," I agreed. "Todd Downing is playing you in the film," I explained to Peter. "Or rather he's playing David Wolf. I guess the names have been changed to protect the innocent, or maybe to protect the guilty. Anyway, Downing has been back east doing some kind of off-Broadway thing."

Peter's expression changed at the mention of Todd Downing; I had no more than registered this when Walter spoke up again.

"You," he said accusingly to me, "don't look anything like Tracy."

"Shouldn't Tracy look like me?"

From Walter's expression that was obviously a dreadful idea. Peter met my gaze with raised eyebrows, and I smothered a laugh as we moved to the last table in the filled-to-capacity dining room.

"Have you worked with Tracy before?" I asked for the sake of something to say.

"No. You're a foodie. Try the duck," Walter advised Peter.

"I'm a what?"

"An epicure," I supplied.

Peter didn't look particularly thrilled about his epicurean status.

"She wrote a lot in the book about what you ate and drank," Walter said, nodding at me. "I'm not sure what it had to do with anything."

"She was very hungry, as I recall," Peter said.

"I'll have the chicken cacciatore," I told the waitress, ignoring their exchange.

Peter and Walter ordered, and Walter turned to me. "Sorry to be rude, but I don't see the point of this."

"Lunch?"

"This meeting." He finished off the wine in his glass. "I know

Roberta and Miles have been talking to you, but I read the book. It was okay. It's got the bones of a good story, but it's a little too Nancy Drew, if you know what I mean."

"Not really," I said. "The book is nonfiction." I glanced at Peter who was sipping Sangiovese-Merlot with the air of a man who knows better than to stick his head up while a sniper is on the loose.

"Whatever," said Walter. "The thing is, our audience is looking for something with more of an edge, something fresh, something...*real*."

I interjected sweetly, "More real than nonfiction?"

Peter cleared his throat.

Walter said, "I mean, sure it's women's interest and all, but what I'm trying to do is give it the feel of a thriller and less of a fem-jep, which really limits our target audience."

"Fem-jep?" I asked.

"Female in jeopardy."

"Isn't it already sold to one of the women's networks?"

"Well, yes, but..." When Walter stuck his lower lip out he reminded me of my little nieces when things weren't going their way—which, when you're five, is a lot. He began to talk about the importance of purity of vision, the profundity of imagery versus realism. He was just warming to his theme when our meals arrived.

I took advantage of the lull. "May I ask how many screen credits you have, Walter?"

Walter's eyes narrowed. "I've co-written some things. *Alien Dogs*, that's one of mine. *Fire is for Burning*."

It wasn't easy, but I think I managed to control my instinctive reaction. "I can see that this screenplay is important to you, and I'm glad about that. But...this movie is based on my life. Not just something I made up, my actual *life*, so it's hard for me not to take it seriously, too. It's bad enough that a blond bim—that the person selected to play me in the film isn't remotely like me."

"I didn't have anything to do with hiring Tracy Burke." He gave me a hostile look. "She's a wonderful actress, though. You're lucky they could get her. She's going to be *big*."

"I realize that, and I hope that you can realize that it's important to me that everything else not go too far into alternate reality."

His face took on that sulky look again. "I'm not sure what you're getting at."

"I looked over the screenplay at the request of Roberta and Miles, and some of the scenes…well, for example, the high-speed car chase that takes place in London: not only did nothing like that happen, even *I* know that would be extremely expensive to film."

"There are ways around that."

"And the fact that you have me and Peter—I mean, the film's Faith and David—falling into bed together every couple of pages—"

Peter interjected. "Might I have a look at this screenplay?" He was ignored.

"Look," Walter gave me a patronizing smile. "I understand where you're coming from. You had your professional reputation to think of, and you probably worried your parents or your grandparents or the headmistress of the orphanage you worked at were going to read the book, but no one is going to believe that two normal, physically healthy, single people didn't have sex for a week."

"For a *week*? We didn't have sex for nearly two years!" *That* drew some interested glances from our fellow diners—those not currently engaged on their iPhones and BlackBerries. Uncomfortably, I met Peter's blue gaze.

He remarked, "Anything I might say at this point would be a serious mistake."

I swung my sights back on Walter who was wiping hastily at the strings of cheese attached to his goatee.

"And turning my friend Monica into a gay man—*and* an interior decorator—"

He glared at me. "The character dynamic works really well."

"—and her husband into a gay Reggae musician. Calum Bell is an Oxford don. Monica and I are *teachers*."

"Nobody wants to see a movie about Oxford dons or teachers,"

Walter informed me, tossing his napkin aside. "Unless the movie was made in the sixties, or is about an ex-Special Forces guy kicking some serious teen butt—or stars Michelle Pfeiffer."

"Are you serious?"

"Do you have any clue how unsexy poetry is?" Walter asked almost pityingly. "I don't think so."

"Speak for yourself!"

"I am speaking for myself. And every other person in the viewing audience. Someone has to. *Poetry?* Not even modern poetry. Not even...Maya Angelou. No, it's all about dead white guys with you."

More so than he might think.

I said, "I believe it was Audre Lorde who said, 'For women, then, poetry is not a luxury. It is a vital necessity of our existence. It forms the quality of the light within which we predicate our hopes and dreams toward survival and change.'"

If I'd thought quoting a black lesbian feminist was going to shut Walter up, I thought wrong. He said flatly, "Did you notice none of the major characters in your book are people of color? Did you notice there were no persons of alternate sexuality? Everybody in your book is white bread. Sexually, racially, politically—"

"It's nonfiction," I said.

"Boy, *that's* convenient!"

Disbelieving, I turned to Peter, and realized he was struggling not to laugh.

Was it funny? Somehow it didn't feel very funny. Maybe I was losing my sense of humor. I was turning this over in my mind when our waitress, apparently in a hurry to get to her next audition, appeared at our table, asked if everything was all right, and before getting an answer, dropped off the check and vanished.

I said, "You know, this lunch was not my idea. Miles and Roberta seem to feel there are some problems with the script as well."

Walter's face twisted into a sneer. "*Miles and Roberta?* This is Roberta's first film, and Miles hasn't had a hit since *Virtual Ninja.* Miles and Roberta better take another look at their contracts if they think they have the final say on *anything.*" He drained his wineglass once more, reached for his napkin, and mopped his face.

"Well, this has certainly been instructive," I said, reaching for my purse and pulling out a handful of bills. "I'll let Roberta and Miles know we met."

"Cool. Thanks for lunch," Walter said, rising.

I opened my mouth to protest being stuck paying for Walter's lunch, then let it go. It really wasn't worth it.

Peter murmured, "I've got it. I wouldn't have missed this for the world."

I started to argue, but Walter, who was appraising Peter closely, interrupted. "Is it true about your being a former jewel thief?"

"To my shame, yes," Peter said, not sounding ashamed at all.

"*You* probably have some stories that would be worth adapting for the big screen. Did you ever think about that?"

"Never." Peter offered one of those lazy, charming smiles, and glanced my way. "All set?"

"Yes," I said tersely.

Walter, however, didn't take the hint. His concerns about having to pick up the lunch tab assuaged, he waited while I attempted to out-argue a pained-looking Peter over the check, continuing to hover while Peter paid the bill, and then accompanied us outside still trying to inveigle Peter to share his life story for the entertainment of viewing audiences everywhere. He was still chattering as we walked to where I had parked—or rather, wedged—my car on the crowded street.

Peter took my keys as Walter followed us out into the road. "Just think about it," he was saying as Peter unlocked my door and pulled it open. "It could make an incredible feature film. I've seen *Midnight Express* like eleven times at least."

The car seemed to come out of nowhere: a battered Datsun 280zx hurtled down Highland Avenue straight at us—and for a moment it seemed that all the world fell silent, moving in excruciatingly slow motion as the car bore down.

Then Peter shoved me inside the Honda and sprang onto the

hood—quick as a cat—and the Datsun shot past, catching my car door—and Walter Christie—on its right bumper. Christie flew up in the air like a broken doll, landing face down a few feet in front of the Honda.

I screamed. The Datsun's engine gunned as it sped around another car, just missing oncoming traffic. Cars were honking, brakes squealing, people on the street shouting as the Datsun screeched away and disappeared around the corner.

CHAPTER 5

"AND YOU can't tell us anything more than that?" asked the plainclothes police officer for the third time.

I shook my head. I had stopped shaking, but it was still an effort to control my voice. "The car seemed to come out of nowhere. It bore straight down on us—I don't see how he could have helped but see the three of us standing here—"

"You said 'he,' but you didn't actually see the driver?"

"I didn't see much of anything. Peter—Mr. Fox—pushed me inside the car just a second before—before the accident." My eyes went to the sheet-covered form in the avenue. Walter Christie had died instantly. My gaze moved to the uniformed officers cordoning off the street from traffic and bystanders—and then on to where Peter was being questioned by another detective.

It was Peter who had checked Walter's bloodied and crumpled body, and then shook his head, meeting my horrified gaze as I crawled slowly out of my damaged auto.

Knowing Peter's antipathy toward law enforcement, I would have been disappointed but not entirely surprised had he disappeared following the accident, but he had waited with me for the police and paramedics to arrive.

"But you recognized the make and model of the vehicle?" the officer asked.

"My brother had the same car in college. A Datsun 280zx."

"Anything else you can think of? Anything at all?"

I shook my head.

He took my contact information, thanked me, and moved away. Despite the plainclothes detectives, LAPD was treating

Walter Christie's death as a traffic accident. And maybe it was an accident; certainly I would have loved to believe it was just an accident. After all, the three of us had been standing in a very busy street during a time of high traffic, and Los Angeles drivers were not famed for their courtesy or care.

If it just hadn't been for the fact that someone had tried to kill Peter forty-eight hours earlier...

I looked over at Peter, and apparently his interview was over as well. He walked around the police tow truck where two attendants were busy hitching up my poor mangled Honda, which was being impounded as evidence.

"All right?"

I nodded, and he put his arm around my shoulders. I leaned against him, glad of the support. That was one of the perks of having someone—although if the car had been aimed at Peter, it was also one of the downsides of having someone.

"We can go," he said, and he nodded at a waiting taxi.

Once we were on our way to Peter's hotel he said, "You've had a shock. Did you want to cancel dinner with your parents?"

"Nothing less than your death or mine would be sufficient excuse," I answered. I wasn't really sure why I was on my way back to Peter's hotel. I should have been heading home, bearding the lioness in her kitchen, preparing for battle with the arsenal of cosmetics in my makeup drawer—and my own full-size hairdryer. But instead I was acting on the almost superstitious dread that if I let Peter out of my sight, I'd never see him again.

"She can't be that bad," Peter said in the tone of one thinking aloud. And it was clear who he meant.

"She doesn't like charming men," I said. I met Peter's gaze. "Well, excepting my father."

"Right. I'll try and remember to spit on the floor at regular intervals."

Against my will, I laughed.

"And remember to call her Dr. Benson-Hollister," I said.

He gave me a long, level look.

■■■■■

I'm not the kind of woman who typically fortifies herself with alcohol, but I had a drink while Peter shaved—as Peter remarked upon when he wandered out of the bathroom, razor in hand.

"You really are nervous."

"I don't know if I'm nervous," I objected. "I'd just prefer to be as relaxed as possible tonight."

His brows rose. "This sounds promising."

"Not that relaxed," I amended, smiling. I was thinking that even a few weeks ago it would have been hard to picture this scene of comfortable—well, mostly comfortable—intimacy. Peter seemed comfortable enough, anyway, but he was probably used to women littering his hotel rooms. I was not *un*comfortable, which was promising, considering how little we knew about each other. Oh, we knew the important things—but I meant the getting along together day-after-day things. Things like who preferred which side of the bed, whether alarm clocks and/or wake up calls were really necessary, whether it was still permissible to make love after the alarm clock or wake-up call had rung—those little details had yet to be worked out. Admittedly, the working out was part of the fun.

Studying him now: a white towel around his lean waist, electric shaver—which I had already learned he detested—in hand, I said, "If you don't mind, I don't think we should mention Walter Christie's accident to my family."

Peter arched one winged brow. "That's quite an oversight."

"I know. It's just that my family might think that this accident...wasn't."

"Wasn't an accident?"

"Right."

I didn't trust that smile of his. I said carefully—there was really no diplomatic way to put it, "They—well, my parents—actually, my mother feels that you're—"

"A bad influence?"

"Dangerous to know."

He was still smiling. "She has a point, doesn't she? Three murder investigations aren't likely to endear me to the maternal bosom."

"No."

"How does the paternal bosom feel?"

"Dad tends to take the long view."

"How long a view would he prefer? Me on the other side of the Atlantic?"

I laughed. "He hasn't said. He's not as quick to judge people."

"Ah."

"Remember to call her *Doctor* Benson-Hollister. Don't call her Mrs. Hollister. And *don't* call her Nora."

"Got it," he said quite mildly. "Both times."

"I know." I added uncomfortably, "It's not like it sounds. I love my mother. I admire my mother. I *enjoy* my mother. We usually get along beautifully. It's just hard for her to understand some of the choices I've made in the last two years."

"But then it's hard for you to understand some of the choices you've made," Peter said gently, and I stared after him as he sauntered back to the bathroom, relaxed as ever.

■■■■■

It was raining by the time we reached my parents' house. "I think it's a good omen," I said to Peter as we got out of the taxi.

"Remind me not to have you tell my fortune," he replied, and maybe he had a point. It was one of those California cloudbursts: hard, driving rain that the streets and gutters weren't built to handle. Despite my protests, Peter was already shrugging out of his mac, and holding it over me as we splashed up the sidewalk past Colin's Jeep, and then past Clark and Laurel's minivan parked in the driveway.

Lights shone brightly behind drawn curtains in the trim 1940s-style cottage. I could hear voices from behind the door. When my family gets together it's a bit of a crowd.

Rather than using my key and walking in on a conversation I might not want to hear, I rang the doorbell.

"This is the house you grew up in?" Peter asked, glancing out from the shelter of the brick portico.

I nodded.

"Has the neighborhood changed a lot?"

Compared to a small English village at the back of beyond: radically. For Los Angeles County? Minutely. "Not a lot. New neighbors on the left and across the street. That's about it," I said slowly. "You never talk about your childhood or your family."

A little muscle tightened in his jaw. "I don't, do I?" He flicked me a quick look from under his lashes. "Mine aren't happy memories." His gaze turned to the door although I hadn't heard anything. "I'll tell you one day."

The door opened and my father stood there. He hugged me, and then turned, offering Peter his hand.

"Peter. Good to meet you."

"Sir," said Peter, sounding about as formal as I had ever heard. My father was smiling, though—his usual wide, warm grin—and as I met his eyes, he winked.

That was the first of a succession of fleeting images that made up my memories of that evening: Peter meeting my brothers; Callie's and Laurel's faces; Peter studying the photo gallery of me and my brothers growing up; Peter meeting my giggling nieces, Amelia and Charlotte—proving that women under the age of ten were just as susceptible to his charms; Peter meeting my mother— proving that she really had managed to immunize herself against those same charms.

Not that Peter had turned on the charm. Not to full blast, anyway. He was probably the most reserved I'd ever known him to be. Pleasant, yes, but a little…distant. For the first time I realized how very far from his home turf he was. He was on defense. A restrained and understated defense, but defense all the same.

"What will you have to drink, Peter?" Dad asked. "I've got a very nice pure malt scotch."

"Are you interested in the study of Romantic literature, Mr. Fox?" Mother inquired.

"Scotch. Neat, thanks." And to my mother, "Interested, yes. But I'm not an academic."

"Did you attend university in England?"

"Briefly." Peter's eyes met mine and returned to my mother. "Where did you—?"

"Liverpool."

"Liverpool!" I said, before I could stop myself. I had to hand it to my mother: she'd elicited as much information from Peter in two minutes as I'd managed in two years.

My father handed Peter his drink. "What drew you to the antiques trade, Peter?"

"I like beautiful things," Peter said, and just for a moment my parents' eyes met.

No, he did not fit in. Not like Brian had fit in. And yet—

"Oh. My. *God*," Calliope whispered behind the kitchen door as she and Laurel dragged me away from the battlefield. "*He's* beautiful."

Laurel breathed, "Wow."

"I don't want to leave him too long—"

"It's all right; the boys will look after him."

And when I was at last able to escape back to the living room, Peter was sipping scotch and making polite conversation with my brothers about his recent buying trip to France.

After what felt like eons of careful small talk, we moved into the dining room to sit down at the long table where my family had eaten Sunday and holiday dinners for as long as I'd been alive. It felt surreal to look down the line of well known and loved faces and see...*Peter Fox?*

In honor of the occasion Mother had prepared something she called Five Spice Chicken—although I could only taste one spice: turmeric—and a lot of it.

I watched Peter take a bite. He met my eyes and chewed. Once. I smiled brightly—hopefully. He chewed carefully and swallowed even more carefully, but somehow I could tell by the glint in his eyes that this was something we were going to laugh over later. It was a reassuring thought.

"Turmeric, ginger, garlic, Chinese five-spice, and...toasted anise?" Peter inquired of Mother when he had recovered from that first bite.

She *almost* defrosted. "Why yes, that's correct, Peter," she said, and the rest of us tried not to indicate anything amiss as she at last let go of the chilly "Mr. Fox" with which she'd been addressing Peter all evening. "Grace mentioned that you're an accomplished cook."

At last something my mother strongly approved of: men taking their turn in the kitchen.

"I enjoy cooking," Peter said. "It focuses the mind wonderfully."

My mother smiled politely, clearly skeptical of whatever Peter might be focusing his mind on.

■■■■■

After dinner I caught my mother sending my father pointed looks, and a few moments later, with a hint of awkwardness, Dad invited Peter into his study. Mother commandeered me to serve dessert.

"Will we be staying for dessert?" I asked, once safely behind the swinging kitchen door. "What's going on? Don't tell me Dad is grilling Peter about his intentions?"

Mother ignored this. "I read a review of a new book on Felicia Hemans this afternoon," she said, dishing up a lemon upside-down cake that appeared to have turned inside out. "You might find it interesting. Personally, I'm not a great fan of Hemans, but one can't discount her popularity or her influence on the premier poets of the day—male and female. Granted, her domesticated imperialism—sentimental militarism—is a little unsettling. Especially in today's political climate."

"To tell you the truth I've been thinking about focusing more on some of the lesser-known women poets."

My mother said tartly, "That pretty much covers every woman who put pen to paper during the Romantic period."

"But some are better known than others. There's been a resurgence of interest in Mary Robinson, Joanna Baillie, and Hemans—there have been one or two well-received biographies and an annotated bibliography as I recall."

"Hemans is far too important a literary figure to ignore."

"'The boy stood on the burning deck,'" I quoted sententiously. "She's hardly ignored. In fact, she's about the only female Romantic poet to get any serious press these days."

I had lost enthusiasm for Hemans after reading that the poetess had cut off correspondence with an admiring Percy Bysshe
Shelley whom she deemed a "dangerous flatterer." I suspected it
had more to do with Shelley's disapproval of Hemans's fascination
with "fatal sanguinary war." There was nothing I loved more than
a good debate, and Hemans's reluctance to engage Shelley—one of
my favorite Romantic poets—disappointed me.

I said tentatively, "I think L.E.L. is due to be rediscovered."

"Letty Landon?" Mother shuddered. "I don't see that as an improvement. I thought you were going to focus on women poets of
the Lake District?"

"There aren't enough of them. Besides, you have to judge
Landon's work by the literary aesthetic of her age. It would be
hard to find a poet, male or female, who more embodied the spirit
of Romanticism—both in her work and her personal life."

"Grace, if you want your work to be taken seriously, you'll focus
on a more worthy subject than Letty Landon. Next thing, you'll
be wanting to write about Sara Coleridge or Caroline Lamb or the
Countess of Blessington."

And since I had indeed been considering both Coleridge and
Blessington, that seemed to be the end of that.

■■■■■

Peter and Dad returned to the living room as the rest of us were
finishing up our cake. I couldn't tell anything from Peter's expression, but it seemed a very bad sign to me when, having manfully
downed his dessert, he said he was going to make it an early night.
I saw him to the door a short time later, and asked, "Did something happen?"

"Of course not. I've had a strenuous couple of days, and I could
use a decent night's sleep."

"But what was that all about?"

His smile gave nothing away as he tucked a strand of my hair
behind my ear. "Don't you worry yer purty little head, Gracie girl,"
he said with an appalling Texas accent.

"What does *that* mean?"

From down the hall Callie yelled, "Grace…phone!"

"I'll call you tonight," I said quickly.

"I'll talk to you tomorrow," Peter said at the same time.

We gazed at each other, mutually discomfited.

"I'll talk to you tomorrow," I said.

Peter drew me close and kissed me, a press of warm mouth on mine, the hint of coffee and lemon and something uniquely Peter.

"Tomorrow," he agreed, and turned away to walk down the tidy brick path.

I darted back into the house, cheeks flushed by more than the cold, and picked up the phone. It was Roberta Lom and she sounded flustered.

"Grace, Miles just called me with the terrible news about Walter."

I made polite sounds of acknowledgment and commiseration. I was very conscious of my mother, Callie, and Laurel moving about the kitchen, tidying up and chatting in that desultory way that indicates the conversation is merely cover for listening in on other people's phone calls.

"And according to the police you were actually there when it happened! You must be in shock!"

"It was pretty shocking," I agreed. I was trying hard to find a way to communicate that shock without letting my loved ones know I'd been witness to—not to mention nearly the victim of—a horrific traffic fatality.

Roberta ran on for a few minutes, long enough to confirm that she didn't apparently have anything more to say than I, and then she said, "Grace, the reason I called—I mean, besides wanting to make sure that you're all right—is to ask you to reconsider your decision about signing on with us. This project really needs you. *We* really need you."

"It's not that I don't want to—"

Roberta didn't wait for me to finish. "But you've *got* to help us out now. We're already filming; we can't start over trying to find a new screenwriter."

"But you've already got a script."

"But you've *read* it."

It was hard to argue with that. And I *wanted* to be part of the project; I really did. It was my book, my life. I said, "I wish it were possible, but Peter and I are flying back to England within a few days. We just have to book the flight."

"Peter! Peter Fox is *here*? In America? In Los Angeles?"

"He flew in last night. I thought you realized. He was with me when Walter…when Walter died."

Silence.

"My God," Roberta said. "This is fate. This is kismet. It's too good to be true. Promise me you'll bring him to the set tomorrow."

"Roberta, I'm not sure that's possible, and even if Peter wants to visit the set, it's not going to change anything. As I've said, we're leaving in a day or two."

"But that's just it! That's what's so perfect about this. We're moving production for *Dangerous to Know* to England. We're going to be filming on location in the Lake District!"

CHAPTER 6

"I AM GOING to *murder* Miles!" Roberta yelled.

"He promised he'd be back after lunch," Pammy, the harassed A.D., assured her. "It's the Jag. It's back in the shop. Something to do with its brakes."

"Brakes again?" I couldn't help remarking.

Roberta gave me a chiding look, waving this off as she ushered me before her. "There's something wrong with his brakes all right, but it has nothing to do with his car, and everything to do with not being able to keep his pants zipped up."

Not for the first time that Friday morning I wondered what the heck I'd let myself in for. Anyway, it was too late now. I had agreed to help out as script doctor—for a truly embarrassing amount of money—with the production of *Dangerous to Know*. It had been a little difficult to refuse when Kismet Productions was going to be filming in my own Lake District backyard.

I waited as Roberta paused once more to answer questions about Walter Christie.

If Walter's untimely and violent death was causing anyone heartache—or even inconvenience—I couldn't tell. It seemed to be business as usual on the set of *Dangerous to Know*.

In fact, Peter's presence seemed to elicit a lot more excitement than poor Walter's absence. Granted, Walter had not been a particularly strong or pleasant personality, whereas Peter knew how to make himself charming, and was doing so with minimal effort and maximum results.

Tracy Burke, for one, could hardly take her eyes off him. "So we're supposed to be in love," she said when they were introduced.

She tossed her platinum hair and fluttered her thick doll-like eyelashes at Peter.

"It's a foregone conclusion," Peter said, and Tracy preened.

Catching Roberta's gaze, I managed a frosty smile and allowed her to edge me along to the next set of introductions—leaving Peter to fend for himself.

On this morning the Kismet Production Company was filming inside an old, abandoned house in West L.A. Crowds of sightseers had gathered out front, held at bay by one sheriff's car and two bored-looking deputies. The usual equipment trailers and trucks, generators, catering van, and vehicles of cast and crew clogged the street outside the boarded-up mansion.

Inside the house, which looked nothing like the structure where I had been briefly held captive in real life in England, hot white lights blazed, the camera was positioned and repositioned, and many, many people wandered around—aimlessly, as far as I could tell.

"Everyone showed up today," Roberta said ruefully, leading me down a long hallway paneled in carved wood that someone had spray-painted graffiti over. "It's because of Walter. Everyone loves a tragedy."

"Did Walter have many friends among the cast and crew?"

"None that I know of," Roberta replied. "But then he was an arrogant little snot."

He had struck me much the same, but it seemed heartless to say so now. "He didn't seem…experienced," I said.

"At what? Getting along with people or writing scripts? You're right on both counts." Roberta met my gaze. "As I'm sure you've noticed, we're not exactly big budget. Walter wouldn't have been my first choice, but his price was right."

I recalled Walter's scathing comments about Roberta and Miles not having final say on anything to do with the project. I wondered if Roberta saw things that way.

The hallway led to a giant, old-fashioned kitchen painted in a grisly green that would have worked well for a slasher movie. The appliances and cupboards had been ripped out long ago, the enormous deep sink was stained with rust, the linoleum was peeling. A large Coleman camp coffeemaker sat on the counter, and a tall, vaguely familiar woman was complaining that there was no green tea available.

"Come on, Mona, where's your sense of adventure?" Roberta admonished.

Mona gave Roberta a long, level look—and I abruptly knew where I'd seen her before: starring in the popular seventies TV series *Blue Angel*. Mona Hotchkiss had played tough and sexy policewoman Corky Simmons.

"There's adventure and then there are suicide missions," Mona returned.

Roberta chuckled, and introduced me to the older woman.

"I read your book. What an interesting life you lead," Mona remarked with a wide grin and a firm handshake.

She was very tall and very thin; what must have been sylph-like elegance in her twenties was now merely gaunt. Her skin was radiant, though. I hoped my skin looked nearly that fabulous at sixty-something. Mona's hair was waist-length and iron gray. She wore crystal earrings and a crystal necklace with a black T-shirt that read NO LANDMINES.

"It is," I agreed. And while I knew that wasn't what Mona meant, my work fascinated me and colored my life. Sometimes I took it for granted; the truth was that I was very lucky to be able to spend my time doing the work I loved.

"Mona is our Lady Ree," Roberta said, and I nodded. To avoid potential litigation, Lady Vee (Lady Venetia Brougham) was now called Regina Croydon in the screenplay.

"I'm hoping I'll have a chance to meet the original," Mona commented, unscrewing the cap to a small silver flask. "She sounds like a real *charactaah*." Privately I thought it was hard to imagine anyone less like that old fossil of the feudal system, Lady Vee. I watched Mona tilt the flask, take a quick drink, and shiver. Catching my eye, she winked. "My own concoction. Korean white ginseng, juniper berries, red clover, plum flower, and alfalfa leaves."

"It sounds...very healthy."

"I wouldn't drink it otherwise. It's horrible."

"Wouldn't that defy the whole theory of the space-time continuum?" We were joined by a nice looking dark-haired young man. "I mean, you and the original model sharing airspace," he said to Mona. I caught a whiff of breath mint and alcohol—mostly gin.

"Grace, this is Norton Edam," Roberta said. "He's playing Gerry."

"Gerry" or Geraint Salt was the character named after the real-life Ferdinand Sweet. For legal reasons, blah, blah, blah. I was getting a little tired of having it explained to me—as though I would possibly object to having a firewall of fake identities placed between me and this project.

"Apparently I've become typecast," Norton said. "I've played the least likely suspect in my last three films." He was slightly pudgy with gentle brown eyes. Attractive in a pleasantly nondescript way—the type that frequently got cast as either the most expendable victim or the killer in low budget straight-to-cable films.

"At least you've had three films," Mona said. "Has Tracy done anything besides shampoo commercials?"

"Meeeow," Norton murmured.

"Mona," Roberta cautioned.

Mona put a hand up. "I didn't say a word."

Roberta seemed satisfied. "Coffee, Grace?"

I nodded, and Roberta poured coffee in two Styrofoam cups. She dumped the appropriate powders in as requested, and handed a cup to me.

"So we're off to jolly old England," Norton said. "Cheers." He raised his cup in mock toast.

"That's right. Hopefully everyone's passports are in order."

Mona said dryly, "Tracy's is. But I overheard her worrying about her immunization shots."

Norton swallowed his coffee the wrong way, and moved off making strangled sounds. Roberta shook her head. "You're terrible, Mona."

"I'm just reporting the news as I heard it." Mona glanced at me. "Speaking of news. I heard you were with poor little Walter when he died."

"Yes," I said.

Mona nodded, but to my surprise didn't pursue it.

"Did you know him very well?" I asked.

Mona laughed and turned to Roberta. "She really *is* an amateur sleuth."

"I was just…making conversation," I protested guiltily. I was relieved to see Peter appear in the doorway to the kitchen.

"Yowza. Now who is this?" murmured Mona. I had to admit that Peter did look like *somebody*. He had whatever it was that managed to make jeans and a tailored shirt look like Savile Row.

"They're about to start shooting your incarceration," he informed me.

"Been there, done that," I remarked, and the others laughed.

"Coffee?" Roberta inquired of Peter, and once again she did the honors with the artificial creamer and sweetener.

We drank our coffee and chatted, and then Roberta shepherded us off to be introduced to the remaining cast members who were not immediately involved in shooting the current scene. Everyone seemed nice enough, if preoccupied. Most commented on Walter's death, and everyone had questions about the decision to shoot on location in Britain.

"I was wondering about that myself," I said, as Roberta finished discussing the day's shooting script with the assistant director. "Why *are* you moving the shooting to Great Britain?"

"I think it's a *fabulous* idea," Roberta enthused. "It's going to make all the difference to this film."

Peter's eyes met mine. I knew what he was thinking. I said, "But isn't it going to be incredibly expensive, moving an entire film production overseas? All these people? All this equipment?"

"Location, location, location," Roberta said breezily. "It's the way they used to make movies in the good old days. Think of Hepburn and Bogie filming in the Belgian Congo, Grace Kelly in Monaco, Audrey Hepburn in Rome."

"But isn't this just a little, cheap, made-for-cable film?" Not that I wanted to belittle the filming of my own real-life adventures but…well…wasn't it?

Roberta gave me an odd look. "It works out nicely for you, doesn't it? For you and for Peter?"

"Well…yes."

"Then I wouldn't worry about it. The head of Kismet Productions has decided this could turn out to be a commercially successful project after all. He's willing to pump a lot more money into it. That's great news for all of us."

I'd assumed Roberta was the head of Kismet Productions. Apparently not.

She caught sight of Miles coming in the side door.

"Miles!"

A momentary flash of irritation crossed the director's weathered face, but then he walked toward us with a rueful smile. Mindful of Roberta's earlier comment, I studied him curiously. Miles Friedman was not exactly handsome, but he was certainly attractive in a well-lived way. Medium height, stocky but muscular, very fit. His eyes were a light, striking green in his tanned face.

"I know what you're going to say, Robbie. I don't need to hear it right now." He turned to me. "Hey there, Grace. Roberta gave me the good news last night."

I must have looked blank because he said, "About you agreeing to join our project. The news about Walter was a shock, of course."

"And this is Peter Fox," Roberta said shortly.

"The man, in the flesh," Miles said cheerfully, shaking hands with Peter. "What do you think of our fair city?"

"Smog, traffic, concrete buildings: its charms are nearly irresistible." Peter was smiling, but there was no question he meant what he said. True, he had only seen a few of the charms the city had to offer, but if it had crossed my mind that we might spend part of any future together in the States, I gave the idea up then.

"Hey," Miles began. "We'll get together one night and—"

"Miles!" called Pammy. "Places, people! Time is money. Miles, we need you on the set now." The plump, red-haired assistant director moved off, listening intently to one of the technicians.

Miles excused himself. Peter indicated he would stay to watch the filming, and with a dark look I followed Roberta, who was gesturing a little impatiently. "Of course it's a tragedy about Walter. So young, so talented." Roberta sounded like she was reading from a script. And not a very good one. The speech was clearly for the benefit of the rest of the cast and crew. "It must have been horrible for you."

More horrible for Walter, I thought. I said mildly, "It was pretty awful."

"And they didn't find the driver?" The cat's-eye glasses turned my way.

"Not that we've heard. And I suppose we would have because we'd have to testify at any trial."

Roberta hesitated, and then asked, "Do you think there's any possibility that it wasn't an accident?"

I stared at her. "Why would you suggest that?"

Roberta appeared to be fascinated by the filming going on across the long echoing room. "Well, murder does seem to follow you, doesn't it? Walter was a pain in the ass, but I can't see anyone finding him so annoying they decided to kill him."

"Well, people may find me annoying, too, but hopefully no one's decided to kill me."

"I wasn't thinking of you so much as him." Roberta indicated Peter with a nod of her head.

For a moment we both observed him—and observed Tracy muffing her lines and giggling his way. I said, "Peter's trip was on impulse. I don't see how anyone could have known he was here."

Still not looking at me, Roberta smiled. "I notice you don't argue that someone might want to kill him."

"He's made enemies."

"Haven't we all?" Roberta did face me then. She smiled. "But some enemies are more dangerous than others."

■■■■■

Peter and I were booked to fly out Sunday. I was packing my books Saturday night when my mother stopped by my bedroom.

"Hi," I said, zipping up my suitcase. "I'm just about finished."

She sat down on the foot of the bed and picked up my copy of Feldman's *British Women Poets of the Romantic Era*, idly flipping through it.

This was the room I had grown up in: walls of the palest pink, the ornate black iron bed I had slept in since high school, violet-sprigged drapes and fluffy white duvet. I had grown up loved and sheltered in this house. My parents had provided every comfort, advantage, and protection they could afford.

I looked at my mother's bent head in the gentle lamplight. There were glints of silver in the red I'd never noticed before. Seeing them gave me an odd feeling.

"I remember when you went away to college," she said suddenly, looking up and meeting my eyes.

I sat down on the bed next to her. "I remember too. You came to my room the night before I left and told me that if it wasn't what I wanted—if I wasn't happy—I could always come home."

"Yes." She smiled wryly, set aside the Feldman, and picked up the silk-bound copy of *L.E.L.: A Mystery of the Thirties*. She smoothed the cover with an absent hand. "But there was really no question that you were making a wise choice and that you would be happy. And you have been very happy—and very successful."

"You and Dad gave us the confidence to…make the right choices."

She nodded. "Are you sure you're making the right choice now?"

Was I? There were never any guarantees when it came to the future, and of course I had qualms about leaving my family, friends—homeland. But I had no doubt that this was what I wanted to do. Didn't that count?

"Yes," I said. "I am." And I reached to hug her. She hugged me back—hard.

When she released me, there were tears in her eyes.

"I'm glad," she said. Her gaze held mine as she handed me the copy of Laetitia Landon's biography. "But if you decide this isn't what you want—that Peter is not the man you think he is—don't be afraid to admit you've made a mistake."

CHAPTER 7

THE WORDS of Ann Radcliffe's "To the River Dove" drifted into my thoughts as I watched the swans in the river below glide silently beneath the arch of the stone bridge where I waited for Peter on Monday morning.

Lulled by the summer breeze, among the drowsy trees...

The Nora Roberts of her day, the author of *The Mysteries of Udolpho* and *The Romance of the Forest* is chiefly important—and best known—for her influence on the Gothic romance. Jane Austen's *Northanger Abbey* was a parody of Radcliffe's work. But she was also a travel writer and a poet.

Unfortunately for my purposes, Radcliffe had lived and worked in almost total seclusion. She was well educated, conservative, married, and apparently quite happy to avoid the limelight. At the height of her fame and popularity, she inherited a fortune from her father and abandoned writing—much to the lurid speculation of her public, who preferred to believe the writer's tales of Gothic horror had unhinged her own mind.

Oh stream beloved by those with fancy who repose...

Nothing had changed, I thought with something like relief, watching the lazy blue water glittering in the shifting afternoon sunlight. Innisdale still looked like the illustration in a children's story—or perhaps a very expensive coffee table book. The white cottages with their dark slate roofs, flowerboxes blazing with flowers, elegantly untidy gardens lining the narrow streets. Gentle chimes tolled the eleventh hour from the church down the lane.

It seemed a million miles from Los Angeles—geographically and spiritually—but I knew from personal experience that murder lurked in the most unlikely places—and hearts.

Before leaving Los Angeles I'd called LAPD to see whether there was any new information on Walter Christie's death—and to make sure there was no problem with my leaving the country. The detective in charge of the case said that the Datsun 280ZX involved in the accident had been found abandoned several streets away. The car had been stolen from a used car lot on the other side of town; the prevailing theory was that the car had been stolen by joyriding punks, and that Walter had simply been in the wrong place at the wrong time.

The detective hadn't had a problem with me and Peter leaving the country, provided we were prepared to return to testify or provide depositions if and when needed. He seemed doubtful that the need would ever arise.

And that was that.

Movement at the other end of the bridge caught my eye, and I turned to watch Peter's approach. He strode along, long-legged and unconsciously graceful, his expression preoccupied, and I wondered how his meeting with Chief Constable Heron had gone.

I yawned. The flicker of light on water and the honeyed warmth of March's variable sunshine made me sleepy despite faithfully popping Airborne and No-Jet-Lag tablets on the long, long flight from Los Angeles; I'd been fantasizing about bed and breakfast—in that order—since we'd landed at Heathrow many hours earlier. Peter had been intent on getting home, and I, to my surprise, had felt much the same.

It was the first time we'd really traveled any great distance together, and I'd found it an eye-opener. For one thing it was the first time I had ever flown first class.

"How did it go?" I asked, as Peter reached me.

"As you'd expect."

I tucked a limp strand of hair behind my ear. "Well, that's cryptic."

"Your would-be swain DI Drummond seems to feel that any attempts on my life are the result of my misspent youth—and probably well deserved."

"He didn't really say that."

Peter's mouth tugged into a smile. "Oh, but he did. Very direct, your Brian. No beating about the bush. No tactful hints, no time wasted on diplomacy—"

"He's not 'my' Brian," I felt obliged to point out.

"No, but he wishes he were." Putting his arm around me, Peter dropped a light kiss on the bridge of my nose. "You look very peaceful standing here watching the river."

"I'm half-asleep. Do they have any leads? Any ideas about who the shooters were?"

"It didn't sound like it."

"But didn't the witnesses in your shop see anything?"

"It's difficult to notice details when guns are going off around you."

I quoted Kipling's "If." "'If you can keep your head when all about you are losing theirs…'"

"You probably don't fully understand the situation," Peter concluded dryly, and I laughed.

We walked the short distance back to Peter's Land Rover and headed through the woods to Craddock House. Peter was silent during the drive, and I wondered exactly what had been said in his meeting with the police.

The woods were still somber despite the first daffodils. The bronze tints of the dead bracken and yellowed moss hinted at the coming warmth of spring and summer, but the winter grass was still deep and the blue shadows were long across the lane as we sped in and out of sunlight.

When Craddock House at last appeared before us I was reminded of the first time I had seen it—and for a moment it looked untouched. It was still the most beautiful house I'd ever seen: dormant vines and a few budding flowers stark against whitewashed walls and silver slate roof. Weathered brick chimneys stood sharp against the clouds, diamond-shaped windowpanes glinting in the fitful sunlight.

It did indeed seem as if I were coming home. But as we pulled up outside I noticed the ground floor windows boarded up, and the crime scene tape.

I followed Peter up the flagstone walk, waiting while he unlocked the door, watching him disarm the security system. My gaze kept straying to the bullet holes pockmarking the walls, the broken pottery, the knocked-over furniture. I could easily imagine the panic, the terror of those few moments when the gunmen had burst in and started shooting.

"Who reset the alarm system?" I asked, talking myself away from the mental image.

"Mrs. Mac."

Mrs. Mac was Peter's charwoman. She wasn't exactly my idea of a reliable employee, but she did seem manically devoted to Peter and his interests. But then he was the kind of man who inspired mania in all kinds of people. For all kinds of reasons.

"You really don't have any idea—?"

He said, suddenly angry, "No. I've no bloody idea why someone wants me dead. D'you think if I did, I wouldn't have dealt with it by now?"

What did that mean? It sounded a little ominous. I didn't have a chance to comment—assuming I had a suitable comment—because Peter looked up at the ship's figurehead hanging from the tall vaulted ceiling.

"Goddamn it."

I stared at the splintered hole blown in the mahogany mermaid's midriff.

"Oh, no…"

He strode through the aisles of furniture, taking swift inventory of the damage. I followed more slowly, wincing at the destruction. Some of it had been done by the gunmen, some of it had probably occurred when Peter's customers had scrambled for safety, and some of it had probably happened during the subsequent police investigation. Peter was not popular with the local law.

The door to the stockroom was blown open, and I shuddered looking at it. It was obvious that Peter had escaped with only moments to spare.

"It's a miracle that no one was hurt."

"Yes."

He met my eyes. "Bullhead Drummond is right about one thing. It's probably not a good idea for you to stay at Craddock House 'til this is sorted out." He looked away.

I stared at his profile. "What does that mean?"

He gestured to the ruined door and the wreckage beyond.

"If you don't have a higher opinion of my courage than *that*—"

"Grace—" He bit off what he started to say. Instead, he said quietly, "This has nothing to do with your courage or my opinions."

"I see."

"No, you don't. Not if your tone is anything to go by." He was smiling one of those practiced smiles, clearly hoping to avoid a quarrel, and I took sour pleasure in not responding. He sighed. "I know what you're thinking, and you're wrong. This isn't me wriggling out of anything. Drummond's right. Whoever shot up Rogue's Gallery might try again."

"So you don't want me to work here either?"

"It's not a matter of what I want. They hit the shop in broad daylight. I can't guarantee that it mightn't happen again—and I don't want you in the line of fire."

He was making perfect sense; I knew that. I did. If only I didn't have the uneasy feeling that perhaps he was glad to delay our moving in together. I had wondered at how calmly he seemed to face the prospect of giving up his bachelor's idyll.

I said shortly, "Great. But according to you the police haven't made any progress with their inquiries?"

"No. That seems to lie at my door as well. Had I been here to personally tell them I have no idea about why someone would want to kill me, it might have made all the difference."

It wasn't funny; it was awful, but I had to hide a smile at Peter's acerbic words.

"Apparently no one saw anything—beyond the fact that the two masked men disappeared in the woods."

My eyes moved to the blasted door, and I shivered. He put his arm around me, drawing me close.

"What's the plan then?" I asked muffled against him. "We just keep our distance until…what? They try again or they don't try

again? And if they don't try again, how long will it take for you
to decide that they aren't trying again? Are we supposed to wait
weeks? Months? *Years?*"

"It's not like you won't have plenty to keep you busy," Peter said
bracingly. "You'll be working on this film—working on your next
book—you wouldn't have time to help out at the shop anyway."

I pulled away and stared at him. "I'm not actually worried about
keeping myself occupied. I thought the idea was, we were going
to…well, make a go of it."

"Live together, you mean?"

"Well, yes."

"We are."

"We are? Together but separately?"

"It's not for long." He wasn't meeting my eyes. "I'm going to
make a few inquiries of my own."

"Great." I moved away to the bow window that looked out over
the banks of rosebushes and hedges to the velvety lawn beyond.
"You know, if you don't want to—if you're not ready—"

"Grace." He pulled me back against his side and dropped
a quick kiss on the top of my head. "I'm trying to do the right
thing."

"I hate it when you try to do the right thing."

Peter laughed. "Lucky for you then, it doesn't happen often."
He let me go, moving towards the door. "Let's see if we can get
you a room at the inn where your posh movie star friends are
staying."

"Gee. That sounds like fun. A slumber party with the Holly-
weirdos. Have they already started arriving?"

"Oh yes." There was a wealth of unsaid commentary in those
two words.

I could just imagine local opinion. I gestured to the havoc
around us. "You don't want my help cleaning this mess up?"

"You're exhausted, love; and frankly, so am I. I'm not touching
anything tonight."

Apparently that included me. Was this any way for a famed
roué to behave? Apparently it was. He moved to the front door,

holding it wide, and I followed him out into the overcast afternoon.

■■■■■

Innisdale had three inns. At my insistence we started with the
least expensive one only to learn it was booked up with crew members of the Kismet Production Company. No room at the next inn
either.

That left the Hound and Harrier, a three-hundred-year-old
former coaching inn locally renowned for its six highly prized *en
suites*, cozy restaurant, lovely mountain views, and beer garden.

"I can't afford to stay here." Even as I protested I was trying to
calculate whether being foisted on Peter against his will was really
the move I wanted to make.

His brows arched. "What an appallingly mercenary wench you
are."

"It's easy to take a lofty view when you're not worried about
your finances."

"There's nothing for you to worry about. Naturally, I'll pay."

I stopped mid-step and Peter reached out to keep the door
from swinging back on me. "Why would *you* pay?"

"Must we have this conversation?" He sounded truly pained.
He nodded for me to continue inside, but I balked.

"Yes, I think we must." I gestured vaguely at the glimpse of
gleaming wooden floors, stained-glass windows, and watercolor
paintings before us. "I can't just…allow you to…pick up my tab."
That blank, blue stare was having the most ridiculous effect on
me. I knew I was in the right, yet I felt gauche, rude for pointing
out what was surely obvious.

"I thought we were going to 'make a go of it'?"

"Well, we are." I was annoyed to have my own words thrown
back at me.

"Then why are you prattling about—"

"I'm not *prattling*—"

He said flatly, "There are no balance sheets—no account
books—in love."

Love? That shut me up—as it was surely intended to do. I was abruptly reminded of a newspaper article I'd read on the plane coming over. NO LOVE FOR THE SUB-PRIME BORROWER had been the heading. You'd have thought a suitable quote from one of my favorite Romantic poets would have occurred.

I said, "Do you realize how much this place costs? You either really do love me or you're desperate to get rid of me."

"Yes. And yes," he said. And before I had a chance to question that second yes, he had ushered me inside. And inside was a madhouse. A well-run, genteel madhouse, but it was obvious that the proprietors of the Hound and Harrier had no idea what they had rolled out the red carpet to.

Luggage was piled everywhere. The lobby was crowded with weary and irritable Californians.

"*Hi!*" Tracy Burke called across a small mountain of Tumi bags. She was beaming hello, but it was for Peter's benefit not mine.

He gave her one of those professional smiles, and waved a greeting to Mrs. Zinn, the hotel proprietor. Mrs. Zinn greeted him with even more enthusiasm than Tracy, and Peter moved off to speak with her, leaving the rest of us waiting in line to check in.

"Do you know they have only six bedrooms with adjoining baths?" Tracy inquired sourly. "And apparently they're all booked!"

I made a commiserating face.

Peter returned a few moments later. "It's all arranged. I'll take your bags up."

"How on earth did you manage this?" I asked eight minutes and two flights of stairs later as he unlocked the door to a lovely room with dark wood furnishings and yellow rose-patterned draperies and easy chair—and a door leading into a private bath.

"It's what you'd call the home team advantage," he said.

Fresh flowers, chocolates, color TV, and a big, plush toweling robe. I was apparently being treated to the deluxe package.

"I don't know what to say." And for once I really didn't.

"Say thank you." He kissed me. "Say you're all right now."

"I'm all right now. Thank you."

"I'll see you tonight for dinner." And with that he was gone.

Resisting the temptation to dump myself into bed and forget about everything for a few hours, I unpacked my bags, took a quick shower, changed into jeans and a T-shirt, and headed downstairs. I found Mona, Pammy, Roberta, and Tracy in the hotel bar drinking Irish coffee. Pammy was all in black, as usual. Roberta wore white cowboy boots and white rhinestone glasses. Mona wore a fringed cowboy jacket. Her hair was in two long braids. Tracy was wearing her usual skinny jeans and a flimsy blue beaded blouse—more beads than blouse. They couldn't have looked more "Hollywood" if they had set out to make a statement.

"Where's Peter?" Tracy asked, spotting me.

I pretended not to hear her in the fuss of taking my chair and greeting the others.

"Where's Peter?" Tracy asked again once I had got myself settled.

I met her wide blue eyes and decided I really didn't like her. "We're meeting for dinner later this evening."

She nodded, smiled, as though she knew exactly what I was thinking.

I ordered an Irish coffee and listened to tales of other shoots and other films. It was interesting of course, like hearing a discussion of life on another planet.

"Are you planning to make a lot of changes to the script?" Mona asked me, catching me studying one of the framed *Punch* cartoons on the nearby wall.

"Me?" I turned back to the table to realize they were all looking at me. "No. I might simplify a few things. Fewer explosions. Fewer car chases—" I caught Roberta's gaze. "No sinking the Derwent Water steamer."

"Poor Walter," Mona murmured. "Such an unhappy soul."

"Was he? I never noticed," Tracy said, absently staring out the stained-glass window at what could be glimpsed of the street outside.

Roberta said, "I don't know how you could have missed it. He followed you around like a puppy."

"No, he didn't."

The other three laughed—not unkindly, but Tracy said defensively, "He didn't. Whatever you're thinking is way off base. He was just...sweet. And shy."

"Shy?" Mona seemed to consider this. "He was probably just cautious about trespassing on Miles's territory."

Tracy's head snapped up. She directed a cold look at Mona. "What's *that* supposed to mean?"

"Come on," Pammy said. "He never took his eyes off you. Walter, I mean."

"That is *not* true," Tracy said shortly. "Just drop it, will you? I never said more than a dozen words to the guy."

None of them said anything for a minute, and then Mona and Roberta caught each other's eyes and started giggling in a way reminiscent of the little darlings at St. Anne's Academy for Girls. Pammy joined in a moment later. I wasn't surprised when Tracy told them—without particular heat but in anatomical detail—what they could do to themselves, and left the table.

Mona, Pammy, and Roberta eventually dried up. "You must think we're awful," Mona said to me, while Roberta sipped her third coffee.

"Oh, no," I said cheerfully. They could lampoon Tracy for all I cared. "Are Miles and Tracy in a relationship?"

"Define relationship," Roberta said. "If you mean has Miles slept with her, yes. I can't think of a woman on the set Miles hasn't slept with." She added belatedly, "Except you, of course, and that's probably only a matter of time."

"I don't *think* so," I replied. What I was thinking was, *Roberta? Mona? Pammy? All* of them?

"Oh, Miles can be *very* charming when he tries," Mona assured me. She winked.

Roberta giggled at whatever she read in my expression. "In fact, he reminds me of your delicious Mr. Fox. Brothers under the skin."

I considered this thought without pleasure. "Has Miles ever been married?" I asked.

"God, no," Roberta said.

"Actually..." Mona said, and Pammy and Roberta stared at her. "He was married. Years ago. When he was first starting out."

"You're kidding. I never knew that," Pammy said.

"Her name was Elise..." Mona frowned, trying to remember. "I don't remember the last name, but she was an actress, naturally. It lasted about a year and a half. She gave up acting—and Miles—and went back to the midwest."

"Wow," Roberta said. "That's amazing." Meeting my gaze, she said, "Miles is sort of a legend in Tinsel Town."

"Wow is right," Mona said. But she was staring at the doorway to the taproom.

We all looked at the man who stood there. For a moment I thought it was Peter. Then he turned our way, waved, and moved toward us. It was not Peter, but he could have passed for Peter's brother. Peter's twin brother.

"Wow," I said.

CHAPTER 8

"TODD?" PAMMY said doubtfully, half rising. She waved to the man weaving his way through empty tables with that easy grace so like Peter's. "Todd Downing?"

"Thass right, luv." He nodded at all of us. Up close the resemblance was less striking. He was actually classically better-looking than Peter, but his face lacked the character, the intelligence of Peter's. I could have been a little biased, though.

Roberta leaned across, offering a hand. "Roberta Lom. I'm producing *Dangerous to Know*." She made the rest of the introductions quickly. Todd Downing—as if we couldn't have guessed—was playing Peter/David in the film.

"*Dangerous to Know*. Great title, that. Sounds like a sexy thriller," Todd said. This was a sore point with me. I had wanted that very title for my book, but the publisher had determined it was overused *and* that it sounded too much like a sexy thriller, and had gone with *Daughter of Time* instead. Which meant my work was going to be forever ordered in mistake by readers looking for the famous mystery by Josephine Tey.

Todd grinned broadly at all of us. "Sorry, luv. Didn't catch your name," he said to me.

"Grace Hollister."

"The bird who wrote the book!"

I nodded. He didn't seem like the type to spend his free time reading, so perhaps he simply had an excellent memory.

"But what are you *doing* here?" Roberta asked.

"Live here, don't I?" The voice, the accent was entirely different from Peter's. The differences were fascinating because, if I didn't

86

look directly at him, if I watched him out of the corner of my eye, I could have sworn it was Peter standing there.

"You live here?" I questioned. I was pretty confident I'd have noticed if Peter had a doppelgänger. Surely I hadn't been gone *that* long?

"Thass right, luv. Well, not *here*," he hastened to add. "London."

"But I just left word with your agent yesterday," Pammy said, exchanging a look with Roberta.

"Thass right."

"But...I'm confused," Roberta said finally, and she was speaking for all of us. "I thought you were in Vermont or Maine or somewhere doing local theater or off-Broadway. I thought you couldn't join the production for another week or two."

"Dunno know why you thought that. Summer's over, luv," Todd informed her kindly. "Been on 'oliday, 'aven't I?" He looked around, rubbed his hands together. "Who's ready for another?"

Todd went to get drinks while Roberta said, "I had no idea he was English."

"Neither did I," Pammy said.

"You didn't?" I questioned. That seemed odd to me. But then perhaps producers and assistant directors didn't have much to do with the casting. Maybe that was just up to the casting director? I really had a very limited understanding of what function each member of the production company served.

"He's definitely English," Mona said. "You could cut that accent with a gardening trowel."

"He doesn't sound anything like Peter," I said.

"Doesn't he?"

"About as much as Ringo Starr sounds like Cary Grant did."

"Yes. Well, his showing up early is one piece of good news, anyway. We can get moving on his scenes right away. That will make Miles happy." Pammy turned to ask me about possible changes to the shooting script. I had to admit that if we were going to move ahead with Todd's scenes, I'd want to make a few changes. That was putting it mildly. Walter's surreal vision of my life started the minute "David" entered the picture—literally.

Todd returned with a tray of drinks, which he distributed cheerfully. Pulling a chair next to mine, he smiled winningly. "So tell me the story of your life, luv. The rest of it, I mean." He smiled broadly—very unlike Peter's crooked grin. There was something appealing about Downing, something cheeky but inoffensively friendly.

We chatted more about the films he'd made, most of them low-budget indie—extremely indie—productions.

"Do you mostly work in the States or here?" I asked.

"Hmm. Here mostly." He laughed cheerfully. "Always enjoy a free ride to the good old U.S. of A. though, don't I?"

"How did you find out about the part in *Dangerous to Know*?"

"Me agent. They contacted us."

"Who did?"

"Kismet Productions."

I nodded. I had no idea how that worked.

"Bit of a lark, them moving the filming back home," Todd said. "'ere I was rushing to get ready for a few months out of the country, and it turns out—" He raised both arms indicating the now-packed taproom. Cast and crew members were crowded up at the bar with locals. Tables were filled. Voices and laughter, the scrape of chairs and tables rang off the dark wooden beams above us.

"How long have you been back?" I asked.

"Just got back Friday."

Which would have been Thursday in the States. The day Walter had been killed, I thought vaguely. Or was I getting confused with the time difference? I wondered if he'd heard about that yet. My question was answered when he said, "I 'eard you lived in the States now?"

"No, I…I plan on making Britain my home base from now on."

But Todd wasn't looking at me. He was staring at the doorway to the bar, and as I followed his gaze, I saw Peter scanning the room and crowded tables. He spotted us and moved forward.

"Blimey," Todd exclaimed. "It's Pierce!" He jumped up and offered a hand as Peter reached our table. "'ow've you been, mate? Where've you been keepin' yourself?"

Peter blinked, and then like someone in a dream, offered a hand. Todd pumped it. "Great to see you, mate!"

"Yes," Peter said faintly.

"Pierce?" I said. Mona, Pammy, and Roberta echoed me like an out-of-step Greek chorus.

"Pierce Fitzroy," Todd supplied. "Did some modeling together back in the good old days, eh?"

"Pierce?" I repeated as Peter drew a chair from another table and sat down next to me. He smelled wonderful. He'd had a shower and he was wearing the aftershave I loved, a sort of spicy bay-rum scent.

"It was my...er...stage name."

"I can see why you'd want to reserve your real name for your life of crime," I murmured loud enough for only him to hear.

"What makes you think Peter Fox is my real name?" he murmured back.

I admit that shut me up for some minutes. When I tuned back in, Todd and Pierce were reliving the highlights of their lives as models. Or rather Todd was reliving them and Pierce endured with stoicism that would have put those old arrow-riddled martyrs to shame.

"Do you have acting experience, Peter?" Roberta asked.

"Hey, maybe you can double for Todd while he plays you in the film," I suggested.

His eyes slid my way, but he withheld comment.

"Whatever happened to Chantal?" Todd inquired.

"Er—we've rather lost touch," Peter said vaguely.

Todd shook his head. "Terrific girl. Terrific." He met my eyes and winked. "Scottish bird Pierce used to go with. Did a bit of modeling herself."

"I believe we've met," I said. Catriona Ruthven, Peter's psycho former girlfriend—and partner in his life of crime—was a homicidal Scottish lass with, from what I'd heard, some modeling experience. It wasn't likely something I would ever be discussing with her. Catriona and I would probably not have been destined for best friends even if Peter had never been part of the mix.

"Aren't we going on for dinner?" Peter asked me as Todd rose and asked the table who wanted another round. More cast and crew from the film production company were packing into the taproom along with the locals who had turned out in hopes of catching a glimpse of a few movie stars—or who had heard the news that the production company would be hiring extras.

"We could order food and eat here," Roberta suggested. "They must have a pub menu."

"Oh, why don't we!" Mona agreed. "That sounds like fun. I wonder how the vegetable pot pie is?"

"I'm sure it's wonderful," Roberta said. "I heard somewhere that the best food is always pub food."

"Thass because you're too drunk to care what you're noshin'," Todd informed her, taking his place on the other side of me.

Feeling Peter's look of inquiry, I shrugged. I'd learned more about him from Todd Downing in five minutes than I'd learned in three years from the man himself. Besides, I admit the reminder of Catriona/Chantal hadn't exactly filled my maidenly breast with fond affection—especially when I recalled how eager and determined he'd been to unload me at the nearest hotel.

After the usual debate we ordered a selection of pub food and more drinks, and the talk turned inevitably to the following day's filming.

There was some question as to whether Miles would arrive in time, as his flight had been delayed in Washington, D.C. And apparently some cameras and other equipment hadn't arrived, but the plan was to forge ahead if possible under Pammy's direction.

"What would you think about letting us shoot the exterior of Craddock House?" Roberta asked. She had been drinking Irish coffees all afternoon and was enunciating *very* carefully.

"Well, the interior's certainly been shot enough," I said.

"Very droll, Miss Hollister," Peter said—but I could see he was making an effort not to laugh. He said to Roberta, "I'm afraid that might prove to be disruptive to business."

"Oh, we'll pay for any inconvenience," Roberta said.

They debated politely, and I listened in on the local conversation flowing around us. It was all the usual kind of thing: the results of the annual flower show—I was delighted to hear that Sally Smithwick, my former landlady, had taken a first in the fiercely competitive roses division; the news that a woman MP had bought a house in the area, and the word that police were attempting to crack down on recent instances of underage drinking and littering. The attack on Peter's shop was the worst crime in Innisdale since...well, since I'd first arrived nearly three years earlier. Coincidence? I hoped so.

Our meals came and I ate meat pie and mushy peas in a fog of weariness. Lack of sleep and Irish coffees—viewed askance by the locals—were catching up with me. I stopped listening to the chatter around me, only vaguely aware when Peter finally agreed to the filming of the exterior of Rogue's Gallery. Mona excused herself, and finally I conceded defeat and said I was going up to my room.

Peter excused himself as well and walked me upstairs.

"You know, you *could* stay the night," I said as he unlocked the door to my room. "Think how nice it would be not having to worry about villains breaking in and shooting you."

"It would be nice," he agreed. "But I've got a hell of a lot to get done before I can open tomorrow morning. It'll be easier this way."

"For whom?"

He drew me close, kissed me lightly, and put me away from him. "Sweet dreams, Esmerelda."

It had been a while since I'd heard that pet name from him. "Sweet dreams," I echoed gloomily. I could see the sense of what he was saying, and in fact, I was going to have to take a look at tomorrow's shooting script before I could turn in, but it didn't make me feel a lot better. Somehow I hadn't pictured my first night home in Innisdale with me cuddled up by myself in a hotel bed.

I closed the door, locked it, and undressed. Climbing into bed I briefly examined the pages Walter had written, made a few changes, and faced the fact that barring rewriting the entire script from beginning to end, I was going to have to live with the portrayal of my life as some kind of cheap romantic suspense flick. I put the script aside, and sorted through the books stacked on the night table, including the two novelized biographies of Laetitia Landon: *Letty Landon* by Helen Ashton, and *L.E.L.: A Mystery of the Thirties* by D.E. Enfield. I picked up Enfield's book and flipped through it sleepily. The politely smiling portrait of Landon flashed past.

There were also two mysteries inspired by Landon's life, but I'd been unable to find copies of them so far: *Eight Weeks* by Clyde Chantler, and *The Golden Violet* by Joseph Shearing, better known as Marjorie Bowen. That was one the many pen names of the prolific Gabrielle Margaret Vere Campbell, a fascinating if somewhat enigmatic figure in her own right. Novelist, biographer, dramatist, children's writer, Bowen wrote over one hundred and fifty novels, many of them tales of Gothic horror and the supernatural.

Landon seemed the perfect subject for an author who also seemed unable to find love and unerringly chose the wrong man again and again. Bowen, however, had managed to sublimate the personal for the professional satisfaction of her writing career.

That night though, I didn't have the patience for women making tragic choices in their personal lives, so I picked up Feldman's anthology and browsed the treasury of poems inside until my eyes grew heavy....

■■■■■

I woke to the sound of muffled talking. The hall light shone beneath the door, and I could hear two voices, male and female. I lay there for a moment blinking sleepily, trying to make out the words. Although I couldn't figure out what was being said, the tone of voice the two were using was not casual—in fact, something about their intensity got me out of bed and over to the door before I'd really thought about it. Yes, by now the snooping reflex was well ingrained.

Pressing an ear against the wood I could hear much more clearly.

"You worry too much," a male voice said. American, deep, vaguely familiar. Miles? Norton Edam? Neither of them had arrived as far as I knew—unless it was after I'd retired.

The second speaker responded, "And you don't worry enough. You just figure everyone else will clean up the mess." That was Roberta. I recognized her husky tones immediately even though she was keeping her voice low.

"Don't lose your head, Robbie. There's a lot at stake here—for me *and* you."

Quite shamelessly, I went on eavesdropping as Roberta answered, but I couldn't make out what she said.

The man answered, "Of course it was an accident. What do you think it was? Murder?" His voice faded.

I eased open the door and peeked out into the hall. It was empty.

I waited a few minutes more but heard nothing. I was just starting to close the door when I heard footsteps on the stairs. I waited, watching the head of the stairs, and Tracy appeared. She was wearing jeans and a short, tight leather jacket—the most clothing I'd seen on her yet.

Feeling very silly I stood motionless, afraid to close the cracked-open door and bring attention to the fact that I'd been spying into the hallway. Tracy never noticed.

She yawned widely, unlocked her room, and went inside. The door clicked shut behind her.

I closed my own door and went back to bed, though it was some time before I drifted back to sleep.

CHAPTER 9

WE BEGAN filming the exterior of Rogue's Gallery at seven o'clock on Tuesday morning. By nine o'clock I was sure that show business was no business—for me.

The day's shooting started with watching the stuntwoman drive a Mini identical to the one used in the States down the lane, and pull up under the trees in front of Craddock House. I'm sorry to say it was no more fascinating in the English Lake District than it had been in Tehachapi—although the scenery was certainly nicer.

At least everything was moving swiftly. The stuntwoman was timed and then the drive was filmed. Then it was Tracy's turn. She replaced the stuntwoman in the car and practiced getting out of the Mini and walking up to the front door of Rogue's Gallery. She walked like a model strutting down a catwalk, and even though I told myself it didn't matter, it drove me nuts. No one was going to mistake Tracy for a high school English teacher—unless she was a teacher who supplemented her income in ways guaranteed to go unapproved by the PTA.

"You're sniffing," Peter remarked, joining me at the picture window of his living room where I gazed down at the scene below. He handed me a cup of tea.

"I'm what?"

He gave a little disapproving sniff. "Like Jane Eyre when Mr. Rochester was telling her things she didn't like to hear."

I laughed reluctantly. He sipped from his own cup. Having spent the previous night getting Rogue's Gallery in shape to open this morning, he had only risen a short time before the camera crew arrived. He wore only Levis, despite the chilly morning. His hair was ruffled, and he smelled tantalizingly warm and male.

"Who's that?" Peter nodded at Miles Friedman striding through the immaculate front garden, cowboy hat on his head, shouting orders as he went.

"That's the director."

"He looks like it."

Miles had arrived during the night—and as I watched him talking to Tracy, I thought I had a good idea whom Roberta had been talking to in the hallway at two o'clock in the morning. "Apparently he's a Hollywood legend, but not for his filmmaking."

He drained his teacup. "I've got to get dressed. I've an appointment with the aide to the Right Honourable Angela Hornsby."

"Who?"

"Our new neighbor; you can't have missed the talk last night about our new lady MP. She's taken the old Monkton Estate."

Actually, between jet lag and Irish coffees, it seemed I *had* missed one or two points of interest. "My goodness, that house sees a lot of traffic. The estate agents should install a revolving door."

"Apparently the Honourable Angela is planning to furnish the old place with antiques supplied by local dealers. Very politic of her."

"Very. Is she still campaigning or something?"

He ignored this, giving me a quick kiss and disappearing into his bedroom. I returned to watching the circus below while I listened to Peter moving around, opening and closing drawers and the armoire door.

I thought again of that odd, disjointed conversation I had heard between Roberta and Miles. *Of course it was an accident. What do you think it was? Murder?* It seemed to me that the only thing they could have been talking about was Walter's death. Apparently Roberta feared that it might be something beyond the accident it appeared to be—she had intimated as much to me back in Los Angeles. Could Walter's death have been the terrible consequence of someone's attempt to eliminate Peter?

From the little I'd learned about Walter he didn't seem the kind of person to inspire murder in the hearts of his fellows. Mostly he just seemed to inspire irritation.

But unless someone had actually followed Peter to Los Angeles, no one could have known he was there—certainly not in time to arrange to kill him. I knew Peter hadn't told anyone about his arrival, because I'd been with him from the moment he left the airport. And why would someone bother trying to make an attempt on Peter's life look like a traffic accident when they hadn't bothered to make the previous attack look like anything but what it was?

The police certainly hadn't seemed to find anything suspicious in Walter's death—at least, nothing more suspicious than what it was on the surface: a hit-and-run.

So…really, the strangest part of all this was that Roberta would leap to the conclusion that Walter had been murdered. Surely that wasn't the normal first conclusion to draw when hearing of someone being struck by a car? But thinking back on my fading recollection of that overheard conversation, that did seem to be what Roberta feared. Unless I had entirely misunderstood her, but what else could she have been talking about? Surely a discussion about Miles making advances to his female stars or equipment malfunctions wouldn't involve the mention of murder?

I finished my tea, noticing that production seemed to have halted. Miles and Roberta were in conference again, and it looked like another animated one.

"I'm going downstairs," I called, and Peter called back something vague.

Todd was the first person I met in the front garden.

"What's going on?"

"Bad news," he informed me briefly, his mouth full of some kind of pastry. "The bird playing the Honourable Jacinda 'ad some problem with her passport. She can't get into the country."

"What will they do?"

A little gust of crumbs flew my way. "Hire local talent, I s'pose." He didn't seem worried about it.

We stood around a while more—a great deal of making a movie seems to involve standing around and waiting—and then Miles and Roberta seemed to come to some agreement. Roberta looked around, spotted me, and approached. The tinted glasses veiled her eyes, but I thought I recognized that expression, and braced accordingly.

"Grace, do you think if you were to ask Peter very, *very* nicely he might consider letting us shoot inside Rogue's Gallery?"

"I don't think I have that much niceness in me," I said.

She waved that aside. "It would save us so much time and money because either we've got to scout another suitable interior location or we've got to build a set, and none of them are going to be nearly as perfect as...well, the real thing."

"But you already knew that." I was genuinely puzzled. Though they were ostensibly on a shoestring budget, Kismet Production Company seemed to have unlimited funds when necessary for things like moving the filming overseas. Roberta and Miles seemed to be reasonably experienced in some ways, but in others...they seemed to be making it up as they went along. It was all so *odd*.

"Yes," Roberta said. "And we can make it work if we have to, but it would be so much nicer all around if we could actually shoot in there."

"Peter will never go for it," I told her.

"Why not? We pay well. *Very* well, as you can testify."

"Money isn't an issue for Peter."

She smiled a tight little smile. "Money is an issue for everyone. Take it from me."

We fell silent as the filming recommenced. I could feel her buzzing with unspoken annoyance at my uncooperativeness, but I didn't have to ask Peter to know that never in a million years would he okay filming inside Rogue's Gallery. He hadn't been thrilled about them filming the outside.

"Oh, for chrissake!" Miles suddenly yelled. "Cut!" He began shouting as a red Mercedes drove down the lane and pulled up beneath the trees on the other side of the road. "Pammy! Pammy, you're supposed to have these cowboys under control!" And to the cowboys in question, "You're not crosswalk attendants for chrissake! You're supposed to be *blocking* traffic! What the hell's going on?"

Pammy clicked off her walkie-talkie and trotted over to deal with the latest crisis.

"We couldn't stop him!" yelled Ted—one of the crew who also functioned as a stuntman. "Says he's working for the government."

The entire set stood in silence as an elegant young man carrying a briefcase got out of the Mercedes and walked quickly up the flagstone steps toward the shop, deprecatingly eyeing the cameras, crew, and milling cast members staring back at him. Bells jingled as he stepped inside the shop.

"Get that road blocked *off*!" Miles roared. "I don't care if you have to park one of the vans across it. This would *never* happen in L.A.!"

"We've got it under control, Miles," Pammy called over her shoulder.

The crew moved to cordon off the road, and I winced, imagining Peter's view on *that*.

While the crew was busily cutting off all access to the shop, the assistant director ran inside, verified that no one would come out, and Tracy and Todd began filming a scene where Peter and Grace argue over who knew what, and then fall into a long passionate kiss. Originally the scene was supposed to take place within Rogue's Gallery, but the decision had been made to move it to the front garden.

Tracy began running her dialogue—most of it things I would never have said if my life had depended on it—finally ending, "But you can't just let these miscreants take what they want. You can't give in to them!"

"Miscreants." As *if!* Walter Christie had formed the most singular notion of the way I talked.

"I admire your spirit," Todd said in character as Peter. He cocked a brow—and for an instant he truly seemed to be channeling Peter. "In fact, I admire many, *many* things about you, Faith Bolton!"

He swept Tracy into a passionate embrace and they began kissing each other in a way that frankly looked more like space aliens devouring an enemy species.

The rest of the cast and crew observed silently until finally Todd broke away gasping for breath. "Blimey!" he said, and there was laughter and a smattering of applause. Miles yelled, "Cut," and everyone looked sheepish. Tracy was grinning widely.

It was strange to me how disjointed the filming process was. Going by what Roberta had told me, half the scenes were to be filmed out of order. And imagine trying to act out an intimate moment with a giant camera just a few inches away—not to mention all those lights and all those interested observers. It was amazing to me that any actor could keep his focus or that any film had even a semblance of ambience or mood.

Tracy and Todd went through the scene again, kissing each other with nearly as much fervor the second time around. Miles yelled irritably to cut and print, and it was time to break while the cameras and equipment were repositioned on the far side of the garden. Tracy and Todd each had a costume change. Todd disappeared inside one of the trailers being used to haul equipment.

Tracy, her next outfit draped over her arm, tapped on the door of Rogue's Gallery. She tried the handle and the door swung open with a cheerful jingle of bells. "Hello?" she called. "Anyone at home?" She slipped inside and closed the door.

I looked down at the shooting script. I reminded myself that it would be silly to be disturbed by Tracy's transparent behavior; Peter had had a lifetime of that. If anything, he'd likely find her a pest.

"Grace!" someone shouted from behind me.

I turned—accurately, we *all* turned—in time to see a young, very blond woman in thigh-high boots hoofing down the road, eluding the crew members trying to keep her back.

I had to admit it was the voice I recognized, because the woman looked like no one I knew.

"Grace!" she yelled again, sprinting away from her pursuers. "It's me!"

"Cordelia?" I hurried across the lawn, waving off the crew members moving to intercept my young friend. "What are you doing here?" A foot or two from her, I blinked, taking in the long blond hair, Egyptian-style eyeliner, and scarlet leather boots. On the bright side, she wasn't wearing anything with skulls on it, and that was an improvement from the last time I'd seen her.

"I heard you were back!" We hugged. "I'm down for the weekend."

"Down from where?"

"Chiswick. London. I'm attending the Arts Educational School until I'm old enough for RADA in July."

"RADA? The acting school? I thought you were going to be a writer?"

"I am. A writer and an actress." She offered a sunny smile.

It was hard to imagine Lady Vee sanctioning a career on the stage, but at the same time she had never had a lot of time or energy—or patience—for her seventeen-year-old great-niece. Which is how I'd ended up spending so much time with Cordelia Dumas. At first it had been something along the lines of paid—well, bribed—chaperone, but eventually I'd grown fond of the kid. She was smart and funny—insecure and boy-crazy too, but those were things I planned on helping her grow out of.

We chatted for a few moments and then I noticed that Tracy had still not come out of the shop, and I suggested that Cordelia and I go inside so we could continue catching up upstairs.

I spotted Tracy immediately. She had changed into a very short, pink, gauzy dress—rather pretty if you didn't mind wearing your slip in public. She looked up from a display of Victorian chimney pots as Cordelia and I entered. I nodded politely. She smiled with her mouth, but her eyes stayed cool.

At the far end of the shop I could see Peter with the elegant young man seriously discussing a human-sized pair of plaster, scrim, and horsehair angel wings mounted on the wall. The wings were from an old abbey, and Peter had them astronomically priced. It looked to me as if he finally might be about to make a sale. I moved down another aisle with Cordelia where I could keep unobtrusive watch on both Tracy and Peter.

"Who's that?" Cordelia whispered, nodding to where Tracy stood still frowning over chimney pots.

"That, my dear, is the new and improved Grace Hollister."
Cordelia giggled. "I love what you've done with your hair."
"Speaking of which…"
"Oh, it's for a role in *Uncle Vanya*. But I like it."

I protested—knowing I sounded like I'd been boning up on the Official Guide to Adulthood, "But your own hair is so beautiful."

Cordelia tossed her head—and the artificial golden locks. "I know. I feel like a change. It's a woman's prerogative."

"So are tattoos and permanent makeup, but I'm telling you now, not every prerogative is worth exercising."

Cordelia just giggled. "Who are we spying on?" she whispered. "Him or her?"

"We're not *spying* on either of them," I whispered back. "What an idea!" I could hear the elegant young man talking to Peter about dates. Apparently the lady MP was getting married in the near future. Peter jotted down some notes. He was being more polite than usual, so I knew the MP was going to be the proud owner of some very fine and *very* expensive pieces of furniture in addition to the magnificent angel wings.

The door opened with another silvery swing of bells and Pammy poked her head inside requesting Tracy's presence.

Tracy threw a long look at Peter who—utterly oblivious—was glancing over a list handed him by the young man. Reluctantly, she withdrew from the field of contest.

"Can we go outside and watch them film?" Cordelia inquired hopefully, and I nodded.

We followed Tracy down the winding flagstone path to the garden, and I introduced Cordelia to Roberta and Todd.

Roberta was distracted but gracious. Todd was personable. In fact, Todd was very personable—if not quite as avuncular as I'd have liked. I could see Cordelia's dark eyes beginning to sparkle in that way that never boded well.

"Nah, RADA's for snobs, innit?" he was saying as I stepped away to glance over the newly revised shooting script that Pammy had just thrust into my hands.

The shooting script is a detailed description of characters, locations, actions, sounds, camera angles. It's everything from dialogue to the most elaborate technical points like camera heights and angles. The day's shooting script lets the cast and crew know exactly what and who are needed during any given day's work. In theory, anyway. The practical application seemed to be a little more…fluid.

I absently flipped through my copy. We were still mostly working from Walter's script, as little as I liked it. The dialogue, in particular, was squirm-making, but I was focusing my efforts on the later scenes. As I had received permission to scrap the original plan of sinking the Derwent steamer, I had to come up with a suitably thrilling, but more feasible, climax for the film. So far nothing brilliant had occurred.

When I noticed the two men in black ski masks advancing toward us from the woods behind Craddock House, my first reaction was exasperation. I began flipping through the script trying to see where they fit into the scene.

They didn't.

They weren't anywhere in the day's shooting schedule. I glanced over at Roberta and Miles, who were in conference again. No one appeared ready to resume filming. Crew members were still adjusting lights and cameras and reflectors.

"Hey!" shouted Pammy, spotting the approaching men. "Hey, there!"

I turned back in time to see the two men come from behind the house. They raised shotguns and began to fire—at us.

I heard Pammy shriek. She threw herself flat on the grass.

I'm not sure how I managed to shake off that moment of paralyzed shock, but without thinking about it I ran forward, grabbed Cordelia, and yanked her down with me behind the boxwood hedge. Around us people were running for cover and screaming. Todd Downing had ducked down and was crawling swiftly along the shrubbery. It would have been funny if it hadn't been so frightening.

I started to follow—and then a terrible thought occurred to me. I stayed put, heart hammering—and made Cordelia stay as well. She was shaking beneath the fierce grip I had on her arm, and swearing in a high breathless voice. I ignored her, watching Todd.

He slipped out from behind the banks of rosebushes and scurried, hunched over, across the lawn, making for the blue Mini parked beneath the trees across the road. The gunmen advanced down the hillside, pumping their guns and firing at the car.

I realized to my horror that they were closing in on him—that they must have thought he was Peter. And at that moment Peter landed in the grass next to me. He was holding a pistol—black, compact, deadly-looking—holding it with the assurance of someone who was used to handling guns. And that in itself was very hard to wrap my mind around.

"They're going to kill him," I told him. "Todd. They're going after him." I could hear the bewilderment in my voice as though I were listening to someone else—someone I heard from a distance.

Peter's eyes met mine. Then he reached across, ruffled Cordelia's hair, and said lightly, "Is it true about having more fun?"

She gulped. We both flinched at the repeated sound of shots.

To me, he said calmly, "Stay low. The garden gate is unlatched and the back door is open. Get her and yourself into the storeroom passage. Don't come out until I tell you."

"*Wait*. What are you planning to do?"

His smile was wry.

"Peter." I grabbed his hand. "You're not trained for this kind of thing—"

"I don't think people train for this kind of thing." He linked fingers with me quite casually and then released my hand. "I've rung the police, but they'll likely be too late. Move."

Cordelia was already crawling swiftly across the grass.

"She doesn't know where she's going," he told me.

"Peter—"

"It'll be all right." And then he was moving along the edge of the shrubbery.

"*Grace!*" hissed Cordelia, looking over her shoulder.

I turned her way, turned back toward Peter, but he was gone. What choice was there? I began to crawl towards Cordelia.

And then it sounded like World War Three had started. Automatic weapons, bursts of gunfire, explosions...

I couldn't help it. I had to see what the hell was going on. Cautiously, I poked my head up, then ducked back down at the thuds of feet in damp earth. The men with the shotguns sailed over the hedge—one of them landing a few feet from me. I froze but he never looked my way, taking off with his companion, racing for the back of the house, the lake and the woods beyond.

The firing and explosions died away, and I realized that the screams and yells of fright had turned into cheers and whoops. I stood and saw several members of the production team armed with enough guns and assorted weapons to run a small war.

Prop guns. *Props.* Make-believe.

Miles scrambled to his feet, snatched his cowboy hat off his head, and smacked it against his thigh, exclaiming, "Now *that's* Hollywood!"

CHAPTER 10

"NO SIGN of 'em anywhere, sir," a young uniformed constable reported to Brian. "We've got tire tracks in the woods that look promising. They might have parked there before walking across the meadow."

"Thank you, MacMillan," Brian answered. He turned to me. "Well, well. Your Mr. Fox has got up someone's nose."

I opened my mouth for an automatic, *He's not my Mr. Fox*, but then I recalled that, oh yes, actually, he *was*. Instead, I said, "What a charming phrase. I'll add that to my list of favorite Briticisms. It's right up there with *snogging*."

"You have a problem with snogging?" Brian inquired, interested.

Tearing my gaze from the emergency services van where the various minor injuries received by the cast and crew were being patched up, I answered, "Not with the act itself, just the term." *Snogging* was British slang for kissing, and a more unromantic word for it I would personally be hard pressed to find. (Possibly *suck face*, but that's almost too ghastly to contemplate.)

"You're a fascinating woman, Miss Hollister," Brian stated, although I suspected he meant "fascinating" in the way a scientist might observe insect colonies going about their business. I made a face at him.

"One thing's clear," Brian said. "If they'd wanted people dead, there would be people dead. They were firing shotguns, for godsake. It's a miracle this garden isn't awash with blood."

Now there was a jolly thought. But Brian was right. It was obvious the men in black had interest in one target and one target alone. True, they had got the target wrong, but how were they to know Peter had a near-double on the premises?

The police had arrived at Craddock House shortly following the attack on the Kismet Productions film crew, and several constables had set out eagerly across the fields searching for the gunmen—to no avail.

Chief Constable Heron was now in deep conversation with Peter; I could see from Peter's expression that it was not an enjoyable encounter. And the Chief Constable didn't look much happier. There were police and their vehicles everywhere; probably every law enforcement officer in the county—if not the neighboring counties as well—was present. Before last week nothing like this had ever happened in Innisdale. In fact, nothing like this had probably happened in the entire Lake District.

The police were methodically taking statements from the rattled cast and crew members. Granted, they weren't as rattled as the natives would have been—Hollywood is a rough town—but a lot of flasks and a lot of Valium vials were unobtrusively making the rounds. I'd already given my version of events to Chief Constable Heron—and then again to Brian. Not that there was a lot to tell.

Brian said abruptly, yanking me back to awareness, "You do realize you might've been killed?" His eyes were slate gray, his face grim. There was no sign of my former agreeable escort.

"I realize, yes. So could have every person here. Including Peter."

"Yes. Todd Downing for example."

I nodded noncommittally. After hearing that Todd Downing had been targeted by the men in black, it hadn't taken the police long to put two and two together—and their conclusion was not flattering to Peter. For the first time I got an inkling of why Peter had so little trust in the justice system. While no one actually came right out and said the attack on the production company was his fault, the implication was there.

"Fox knows these villains. And if he doesn't know them, he surely knows why he's on someone's hit list."

"I'm telling you he doesn't. I know you think I'm blinded by some romantic fantasy, but if he knew, he'd…" I stopped at Brian's expression. I finished mildly, "He'd go to the police."

Brian snorted. "Right."

Cordelia wobbled up in her high red boots. "I am *so* bloody late! Bri, can I go? Auntie is going to murder me!"

That was the beauty of being young. Cordelia was already over her fright and even sort of enjoying her recent brush with murder and mayhem.

Brian raised his eyes to heaven. "Go," he said.

Cordelia turned to me, the heavily made-up eyes studying me hopefully. "I'll see you tomorrow, Grace?"

"If you can't think of anything better to do."

She grinned, and departed on those ridiculous spiked heels. Brian stared disapprovingly after her coltish figure as she took the flagstone steps two at a time.

"She shouldn't be hanging about here. Neither should you."

"I agree with you about Cordelia, but the worst thing would be to deny her access. Don't worry. Making movies is surprisingly dull. It's mostly about standing around and waiting. I'm hoping she'll soon get bored and find something else to amuse her."

(True, my idea of a splendid time was poring over research materials or spending hours in a dusty archive somewhere….)

Brian turned away, spoke briefly to a constable, and then turned back to me.

I said, "Do you think it means anything that they used shotguns? I don't really think of professional hit men using shotguns."

"Do you think a lot about professional hit men?"

"More than I used to."

His mouth quirked but he didn't allow himself a smile.

I tried another angle. "Just a thought, but is it possible these goons might have thought the new MP Angela Hornsby was at Rogue's Gallery?"

Brian stared at me. "An assassination attempt? Is that what you think?"

Not really, but I did wonder if the police were entertaining any theories beyond the idea that Peter had brought all this on himself.

I replied, "I don't know. You get these cranks sometimes who have different political views and take them out on public figures. Is Ms Hornsby very popular?"

"She's not unpopular. Not *that* unpopular. You've been in the States too long. Besides, your theory wouldn't explain why these same men tried to kill your Mr. Fox a week ago."

"If they were the same men."

"True," Brian said equably. "He may have legions of people eager to kill him."

"Funny."

"Not really. Someone could have died here today. It's a miracle no one was really hurt." He was right. Apart from a few scrapes, sprains, and some minor injuries from shotgun pellets, Kismet Productions had escaped virtually unscathed.

"Yes, I know that, Brian." I watched Peter turn away from Chief Constable Heron, and even at this distance I could see that the lines of his face were tight with anger.

"Can we have dinner one night?" Brian asked suddenly, and I turned back to him.

"Well, the thing is—"

"Why should it matter? We're friends, aren't we?"

"Of course. But Peter and I are moving in together."

"Are you?" he inquired blandly. "Because I'd heard you were staying at the Hound and Harrier with all the other celebrities."

I overlooked the "celebrity" crack. "That's because Peter doesn't want me staying here until it's...safe."

"I'd like to think he had that much conscience—or common sense." There was no smile on Brian's face. "He'll never do it, Grace. I don't care what he tells you. Or even himself. He'll never have you living here with him—let alone marry you. I know him. I know the breed."

I reminded myself that Brian was a friend, and that he was saying these things because he truly cared for me. I said carefully, "I know you mean well, Brian, but in order for us to stay friends you're going to have to accept the reality of my relationship with Peter."

"I accept that you love him," Brian said. "Would you like to have dinner one evening—merely as friends?"

I thought it over. Irritated at the moment though I was with Brian, I did like him, and—cynical as it sounds—he was the closest thing I had to a police contact, and I wanted to keep track of how the hunt for these gunmen progressed.

"May I call you?" I said. "I'm not sure of my schedule yet."

He nodded, and then was called away by a couple of the crime scene technicians.

Miles was finishing up a short speech to cast and crew, trying to reassure everyone that there was no danger and that all was well under control. He made it convincing, but that was more due to the force of his personality than the logic of his argument. Although it was still early in the afternoon, he concluded briskly, "All right, people, I think that's a wrap for today. Let's head back to the hotel."

"Drinks on me and Miles," Roberta agreed, and there were a few halfhearted cheers.

The crew was still packing up as everyone else began piling into cars for the brief drive back to the village. I went inside Rogue's Gallery. There was no sign of Peter. I went upstairs to his flat. Tapped on the door, which wasn't quite shut.

"Come," he called, and I pushed it open.

He was sitting on the sofa, graceful yet somehow wary, whisky glass in hand. He didn't drink a lot of whisky, so perhaps that in itself meant something.

I sat down on the ottoman across from him. "I want to stay tonight," I said.

He laughed. Shook his head, took a swallow of whisky.

"Look, I'm an adult. We've been through plenty of dangerous situations before. You say we're going to make a go of it, but—"

"No."

I stared at him. That flat single word was so unlike him.

I said, equally curt—and a lot chillier, "Really? Any particular reason?"

"Use your imagination."

I studied him for a long moment. I wanted to give into the luxury of anger, and I probably would have if I hadn't understood that he was pushing for that very thing. Nothing like a good old-fashioned lover's quarrel to keep me at a safe distance.

"All right then," I said finally. "I obviously can't insist." I stood up. "Oh, I almost forgot. Roberta wants to know if they can film inside Rogue's Gallery."

There was a long, speaking silence.

"That's what I thought," I said. "Well, I expect I'll see you around." I was nearly out the door before he spoke.

"Grace—"

Hand on the doorknob, I paused. He said, unusually awkward, "I'll ring you."

I said tartly, "I look forward to it."

■■■■■

"Thought I was a goner for half a mo," Todd said cheerfully for the sixth or seventh time, and drained half his pint in a gulp.

We had gathered in the bar of the Hound and Harrier. The entire cast seemed to be crammed into the room, along with a number of locals who had heard the exciting news of the attack on the production company—and were now hearing each member of the cast relive where they had been at the moment the bullets started flying.

"They did seem to focus on you," Mona said thoughtfully. The others examined him with interest.

"Reminded me of the good old days when I used to wager a few bob on the ponies," Todd admitted, and everyone laughed. Shaken Todd might be, but I had to admit he was remarkably collected about his close call. "Thought for a moment or two I was done for," he said yet again.

"You!" Pammy exclaimed. "I thought we were back in East L.A. for a minute!"

We were all getting a bit tipsy reliving our collective close call—there was nothing like shared danger to build a bond, though; and there was a real sense of camaraderie that evening. Or I'd had more to drink than I realized.

"All those yoga lessons finally paid off," Roberta told Mona. "I've never seen anyone outside of a circus wrap herself into such a tiny ball."

"I think I invented a new move," Mona admitted. "The Praying Yank."

This got another round of laughs, especially from the locals.

"Of course this is old hat to you," Roberta said to me.

"Not really!"

And Mona said to Roberta, "Could someone shooting at you ever become old hat?"

"I just can't imagine what they would have wanted," Roberta said. "Other than Todd dead." She eyed me speculatively, and I knew she had not forgotten Todd's striking resemblance to Peter. I was relieved she didn't comment on it.

"Is the production insured?" I asked.

"Of course."

"You're not thinking this is somehow tied to the film?" Mona questioned.

"Not really, no."

"Although we *have* had a string of bad luck," Mona added.

Roberta didn't answer. I followed her gaze to a small table in the corner where Miles and Tracy were sitting together, their heads very close. True, the room was crowded and noisy, but there was something in their body language that indicated more than audio difficulties.

Mona noticed the focus of our attention and turned as well. "Why am I not surprised? She's just the type he likes."

I almost said, "Female?" but managed to bite my tongue in time.

Roberta smirked. "You mean she looks like you a few years back?"

"A few years? Don't bother being tactful, dear. It doesn't suit you." Mona met my eyes and grinned. "That's right; Tracy could almost pass for my kid sister."

"Or daughter," Todd offered helpfully—not noticing the little blink Mona gave at this unsolicited candor. He pointed a finger at each of us, counting us off apparently. "Who's ready for another?"

"Me," Pammy said. "I'm getting plastered tonight. Don't anyone try to talk me out of it."

"I've had enough," I said. "I need to get some work done tonight." Although, frankly, the last thing I was in the mood for was to go upstairs and start reading about how Laetitia Landon had thrown away a successful writing career for a man who didn't want her—and might have ultimately murdered her.

Todd rose unsteadily, making his way through the crowd to the bar. I excused myself and left the taproom.

In the lobby I spotted Norton Edam, the actor playing the Gerry Salt/Ferdy Sweet character, checking in. He caught sight of me and waved me over. He had the dazed and haggard look that comes from a transatlantic flight with efficient cocktail service.

"I heard there was a shooting on the set today." He fumbled his wallet over to the girl behind the front desk, spilling out credit cards and photographs on the counter. "Was anyone hurt?"

I shook my head. "Fortunately, no. How was your trip?"

He described it in exhaustive detail, shuffling his cards and photos back into his wallet. The girl pushed the room key to him, and he turned away.

"You missed this one," I said, picking up the snapshot that had slipped between the edge of the desk and Norton's sleeve. I showed him the picture of a young woman. He glanced at it and nearly snatched it out of my hand—which made me look at it a little more closely. I wasn't sure, but I thought it was a picture of Tracy. She did seem to have a powerful effect on the gentlemen. I didn't understand it myself.

Starting up the stairs, I was surprised to find Norton at my side. At my questioning look he said, "What I really want now is about eight hours of lying flat on my back without some kid screaming his lungs out two rows behind me."

I shuddered in sympathy.

"The girl at the desk told me the bathroom is down the hall from my room."

"That's not unusual in these older hotels," I said guiltily.

"This country!" he said, and that was his last comment until

I paused to let myself into my room, whereupon he muttered, "Good evening," and went on his way, suitcases banging against the dark wooden paneling in the narrow hall.

Locking the door, I switched on the light. The room was pretty and cozy—and about as lonely as the planet Venus, which I could see twinkling between the drapes. I moved over to the window, gazing out at the blue-black night.

Not exactly the way I'd planned it when I'd decided to return to England and Innisdale. I sighed and moved over to the little writing table where I'd stacked my books, picking up my notes on Laetitia Landon and thumbing through them.

At sixteen, Landon had first come to the attention of the reading public as the anonymous author of a poem called "The Michaelmas Daisy" in the popular *Literary Gazette*. More poems followed by the mysterious lady L.E.L., and the *Gazette*'s subscriber list grew by leaps and bounds. The public couldn't get enough of her, and Landon was in the first flush of creative fever. Her output was tremendous. In addition to her weekly appearances in the *Gazette*, she published in reviews, annuals, and periodicals. She produced numerous volumes of her own poems—as well as several novels. By the age of only twenty she was famous—considered one of the premier poets of her day.

At thirty-six she was dead.

And now she was virtually forgotten. Two dismissive fictionalized biographies and an enormous body of work no one remembered were all that remained of L.E.L.'s passionate literary legacy. And sadly, her story was not unique. Most of her female contemporaries, hailed in their own day, had suffered the same fate.

I thought of the stanza from "Lines of Life" written at the height of Landon's popularity when she was twenty-seven:

I think on that eternal fame,
The sun of earthly gloom,
Which makes the gloriousness of death
The future of the tomb—

CHAPTER 11

"THE SHOW must go on!" Miles announced with ruthless cheer Wednesday morning.

He strolled among the crowded tables of the dining room where most of his morose cast sat hunched over their breakfasts, wincing at Miles's booming greeting, coffee and teacups clutched in trembling hands.

The Kismet Production Company had made quite a night of it, and when I had fallen asleep sometime after midnight their voices and laughter were still filtering up through the floorboards of my room.

Needless to say, no one was particularly bright-eyed and bushy-tailed this morning—and one or two faces actually lost their color at the offer of kidneys and black pudding along with more recognizable breakfast fare.

I drank my tea and absently spooned up my hazelnut yogurt, reading over the day's shooting script. Today we were filming scenes with Todd, Mona, Tracy, and Norton. The writer and collector Aeneas Sweet had been entirely eliminated from the screenplay. Roberta had explained to me that Lady Ree's character was actually a composite of Lady Vee/Venetia Brougham and Aeneas Sweet, which I supposed sort of explained what Mona as Lady Ree was doing in some of the final scenes of the script. It didn't explain why she was apparently going to be taking part in a shoot-out, but I was beginning to realize that unless I was prepared to rewrite Walter Christie's screenplay front-to-back, I was going to have to accept a fair bit of poetic license. To put it politely.

Once again we were going to be shooting outdoors, and I reminded myself to grab a sweater before we left the inn. It was what the Irish call a soft morning, silvery with dew, flowers and grass glistening, and a gentle white mist rolling across the fields and meadows.

"Chop-chop, people," Pammy called, briefly poking her head in. "We've got a movie to make!"

A few rude comments were addressed to the empty doorway.

"Has anyone seen my flask?" Mona asked.

This was greeted by amusement.

"Do you think someone's after your secret ginseng and juniper berry elixir?" Roberta inquired, surfacing from behind a several-days-old issue of *Variety*.

"I don't know how you can drink that crap," Tracy offered. In deference to the drop in temperature she was wearing a long-sleeved cotton shirt that still left her flat, goose-pimpled tummy bare to the elements. She was wearing quite a lovely belly-button ring, and I sincerely hoped that Cordelia would not immediately want one of her own.

"The body is a temple, my child," Mona retorted breezily.

"Thank God I'm an atheist," Tracy said, reaching for her coffee.

"Is Pammy keeping you up-to-date? Does the script look okay?" Roberta leaned across to ask me.

"Uh…yes," I replied, reflecting that "okay" was really relative. We talked briefly about the day's schedule, then I got up to fetch my sweater, nearly bumping into Norton on his way into the dining room.

"When are we leaving for location?" he asked.

I peeked at my wristwatch. "I think we're leaving now," I told him. "But if you ask Mrs. Zinn, I'm sure she'll wrap something up you can eat on the drive."

He nodded and continued through the doorway. I headed along the corridor. Lost in my own thoughts I noticed too late that I was about to walk in on an argument between Miles and someone else in the anteroom off the lobby.

"What exactly are you insinuating?" Miles was saying in a dangerous voice.

"'s not like you 'aven't 'eard it all before, mate." Todd. I'd recognize those dropped aitches anywhere. Though that was the first time he'd used that insolent tone.

"Yeah, I've heard it," Miles said. "But not from someone who wants to remain part of any project I'm directing."

I stopped outside the anteroom. I was actually trying to think of another way upstairs, because I really didn't walk into the middle of that scene. But Todd chuckled, and something in that laugh raised the hairs on the back of my neck. I found myself listening closely.

"I'm not worried, mate. We both know who's callin' the shots. Or rather, we both know who *isn't* callin' the shots. And that would be *you*."

He was coming my way. I backed up quickly, stepped into the nearby alcove, and picked up the phone as though I were making a call. And because Todd did indeed walk into the hallway, I started dialing.

He walked past me and nodded pleasantly. I nodded back. A couple of numbers later, Miles strode past me with a curt inclination of his head. I bobbed my head in acknowledgment—but inattentively. I had automatically dialed Peter's number, and the phone was ringing.

And ringing.

Four rings. He didn't pick it up, the machine did—and I hung up softly.

■■■■■

To everyone's relief the day's shooting was uneventful.

Somehow Roberta had wrangled permission to shoot in the old graveyard outside Innisdale, and it actually made for a wonderfully eerie location—although I felt they were spoiling that ambiance by staging a shoot-out between Lady Ree, Gerry Salt, Faith, and David.

I watched Tracy and Todd darting from behind headstone to headstone exchanging shots with Mona and Norton—there was a great deal of running and jumping and shooting. I told myself that it was better than listening to the dialogue Walter had cooked up, but a morning of watching Tracy play *Charlie's Angels* was wearing on my nerves.

In fairness, though, she did run well—and she handled a gun like she meant business. Mona also displayed a casual and convincing familiarity with firearms. Todd, on the other hand, seemed uncomfortable brandishing weapons, and Norton dropped his pistol several times, resulting in Miles repeatedly having to yell, "Cut!"

"What the hell's the matter with you, Edam?" he bawled finally. "Do you think you could manage to run from point A to point B without your pants falling down?"

"*Not* a line of discussion I'd open if I were Miles," Roberta, sitting next to me on a folding chair, commented lightly.

"Is Miles really that bad?"

Roberta's smile was definitely strange. "Miles is really that *good*." Meeting my stare she said, "Very like your own Mr. Fox."

I considered this unemotionally. "But Miles was married at one time?"

"According to Mona. And I suppose she'd know. She and Miles were together a long time—considering Miles's record with relationships. And they've managed to stay friends, which is even more rare. Especially considering everything that happened between them."

Naturally, I wanted to ask about what that *everything* was, but I had a feeling Roberta would close up if I showed too much interest. I said instead—taking a shot in the dark, "You've stayed friends."

"For the most part. It hasn't always been easy." She glanced at me. "At least I never tried to kill him."

My jaw dropped. "Who tried to kill him? Not Mona?"

She laughed. "It was before she started on the path to spiritual enlightenment."

"What did she do?"

"She tried to shoot him. With one of his own hunting rifles." The lenses of Roberta's glasses were glinting; I couldn't read her eyes, but she was smiling.

■■■■■

Late morning, the rain began to fall. It was one of those fleeting Lake District showers. One minute the sun was shining; the next, low clouds seemed to catch on the tree branches and tear open. The daffodils around the lake bent and bobbed beneath the wet breeze while the water grew dark and choppy. Filming halted while we broke for an early lunch supplied by the Hound and Harrier.

We crowded into the trailers for sandwiches made of ham and pickle or cheddar and chutney, crisps, apples or grapes, and spice cake—all washed down with strong, hot tea. I'm not sure why, but the tea is better in England. The quality of the tea doesn't matter or how you prepare it, it just tastes different over here.

About forty-five minutes later the rain stopped and filming resumed, the moors and dales ringing with the sound of gunfire.

An hour later the rain started again.

"How the hell long is this going to keep up?" Miles asked me.

"All year," I said. And I wasn't completely joking. After all, the Lakes are the wettest part of England, with something like eighty inches of annual rainfall. March is one of the drier months, but even so, rarely a day passes without some precipitation.

Cast and crew grew restless waiting for this shower to pass, which it did—only to resume twenty minutes later. It began to feel like Mother Nature was giving us a gentle raspberry. Miles, Pammy, and Roberta held another of their conferences, and we were all finally excused for the day, packing into cars and vans and driving back to the village.

Not wanting to spend another afternoon in the bar of the Hound and Harrier, I walked down to the library, stopping in to say hello to Roy Blade, the librarian. I found him typing energetically away on a post to the popular Annoyed Librarian blog.

"Are you causing trouble again?" I said, poking my head in the door to his rabbit warren of an office.

Blade looked up, his piratical countenance lightening. "Librarians *are* trouble," he informed me. "Just ask any Conservative."

Despite the Oxford accent, Blade certainly looked like trouble—black leather, tattoos, and an eye patch. Most of the librarians I knew were more careful about their camouflage.

"So you're back then?" he remarked. "For good?"

"Or evil," I agreed. Nodding at the computer screen, I said, "Still rousing the rabble?"

"We wouldn't want them oversleeping," he said. "Well, Fox must be pleased. Are you staying at Craddock House?"

"The Hound and Harrier," I admitted. "Perhaps he's not as pleased as you might think."

His smile was twisted. "Now you're fishing, Ms. Hollister."

"I know, but they don't seem to be biting." I sighed. "Any gossip you'd care to share?"

He treated me to the news that the coppers had arrested some local hellions for drinking and vandalism, that my dear friend Sally Smithwick had soundly trounced all comers in the local flower show, and that MP Angela Hornsby—whom he strongly disapproved of for a number of reasons I got to hear in detail—was planning to marry. Same old, same old.

"And there were the two shoot-'em-ups at Craddock House," he added as an afterthought.

"Oh, yes. I'd heard."

"Once upon a time this was a quiet little village. Then you came along."

"Ah, memories. Speaking of which," I said, inexplicably cheered by this attack, "have you got Swaab's new collection of Sara Coleridge's poems?"

Blade assured me the library did indeed own the latest collection of her work. For many decades Sara Coleridge, Samuel Coleridge's daughter, was chiefly famous for her work as her father's editor and archivist. A sensitive and complex woman, Coleridge wrote and published fairy tales, essays, and poems for children. It was widely believed that her addiction to opium—and the legend of her father—prevented her from realizing her own potential as a poet. But when going through Sara Coleridge's papers, Dr. Peter Swaab, a professor at University College, London, discovered one hundred twenty previously unknown poems in a bound volume Coleridge had called "The Red Book." The poems dealt with everything from love to nature and religion, and elevated Coleridge's status to that of minor poet and an important link between the Romantics and the Victorians.

I left Blade typing to his Internet cronies and spent the rest of the quiet, rainy afternoon reading Coleridge's work. Especially fascinating were the poems to the young Irish poet Aubrey de Vere following the death of her husband, Henry. Sara's guilty struggle to reconcile her attraction and liking for the much younger de Vere made for fascinating reading, but I wondered what she'd have thought of her private reflections—poems she had chosen not to publish—being puzzled over by future academics and scholars.

It was after teatime and during one of the infrequent pauses in the rain that I started back to the inn, stopping off at the old vicarage where I had formerly rented the gardener's cottage, and spent a few pleasant minutes chatting with Sally Smithwick.

Naturally Sally wanted me to see the prize-winning roses, so we stepped out into the damp garden for a short time. I admired the roses—and they were truly lovely: old-fashioned cabbage roses in a pale, sugary pink—and I stared at the burnt ruins of the gardener's cottage.

Catching my gaze, Sally said, "Will you be moving in with Peter?"

"As soon as he feels things have settled down." I hoped that was true.

Sally was too polite to comment one way or the other. She reminded me that the battered Citroën that Lady Vee had loaned me the previous summer was still sitting in the stable. We walked down the long garden, with the primroses just coming into bloom, and ducked into the stable.

"I take it for a spin now and then," Sally said, "to keep the battery alive."

It took a few minutes—and I nearly asphyxiated Sally and myself, but I finally got the old car started and drove back to the inn.

The girl at the desk informed me that Detective Inspector Drummond had phoned while I was out. "Any other messages?" I asked hopefully.

She shook her head apologetically, reaching for the ringing telephone.

I told myself that it was silly to fret because Peter hadn't called me first thing—or left any messages—or appeared to have any burning desire to get together anytime soon. I reminded myself that I could always call him.

I went upstairs and called Brian instead.

He was reassuringly happy to hear from me, and invited me to dinner once again—and this time I accepted.

■ ■ ■ ■ ■

"We've got a lead on the gunmen," Brian informed me over carrot, courgette, and dill soup.

I reached for the salt shaker. "Do you know who they are?"

We had driven into Kendal for dinner at the Garden House. The hotel restaurant was in the conservatory of an old Georgian house set in two acres of a secluded garden. Though it was still far too chilly to eat on the restaurant patio, the long dining room with its lovely mural and view of the wooded garden was very pretty, very romantic—and not at all crowded at this time of year.

"They sound like a pair of local bad boys—twins by the names of Barry and Barney February. They were overheard talking at their local by a couple of neighbors."

"They actually admitted shooting up the movie set?"

"They were drunk, and our informant didn't hear the entire conversation, but what he did hear certainly seems promising. The Februarys have form—criminal records—as long as your arm."

I said reluctantly, "Do you know why they want Peter dead? What motive they might have? Is there some reason to believe they're connected to him?"

"Other than the obvious connection: they're all felons?"

I said, a little irritably, "You know, Peter was never convicted of anything in this country."

Before Brian could respond, the waiter appeared. I ordered the trout and Brian opted for the pork fillet. Our soup bowls were removed, our wineglasses replenished.

Privacy restored, I asked, "*Do* the Februarys have a motive that you know of?"

"That's why we want to talk to them."

"So you haven't arrested them yet?"

"Not yet. They weren't at home when we came calling this afternoon."

"Do you think someone tipped them off?"

Brian shook his head. "I doubt it. They're not popular people. No, they were probably busy going about their business."

"Their business? Do they keep regular hours? Or do they actually have day jobs?"

"Not as you or I would recognize them. They're the usual bad lot. Barney is just out of stir." His smile was wry. "I'll let you know when we have them in custody, shall I?"

"Yes, please."

The rest of the meal passed agreeably enough. I enjoyed Brian's company—other than when he was complaining about Peter. He laughed as I filled him in on my adventures in movie-making, he listened patiently as I enthused to him about Sara Coleridge and Laetitia Landon and Ann Radcliffe. The evening passed quickly, and before I knew it, it was nine o'clock and Brian was driving me back to the Hound and Harrier.

"Feel like a drink in the bar?" he asked as we walked into the lobby.

"Thanks, but I don't think so," I said. "We start shooting at the crack of dawn."

Which was certainly true, but I couldn't help but notice—after Brian kissed me good-night on the cheek and departed—the noise level in the bar as I passed on the way to my room. I poked my head in, and as usual, most of the tables seemed to be filled up with members of the Kismet Production Company.

Mona waved to me from where she sat with several members of the crew. I waved back, but continued on my way upstairs.

However, once I let myself into my room and stared at the stack of books waiting for me I was seized with a sudden restlessness. I touched up my makeup and hair and went back downstairs and outside, got in the battered Citroën, and headed off to Craddock House.

The way the Citroën smoked and sputtered, I imagine Peter heard me coming a mile off. I parked beneath the trees next to a silver rental car I didn't recognize, and went up the flagstone walk.

The shop was in darkness but the upstairs lights were shining amiably.

I rang the bell. The draperies twitched overhead, and then a few moments later the shop lights came on.

The front door opened, bells tinkling softly. Peter stood before me in faded jeans and a soft heather-hued tailored shirt. The collar of his shirt and a couple of buttons were undone; he looked very relaxed.

"Hello," I said. "Is this a bad time?"

"For what?" He sounded interested, moving aside for me to enter. I moved past him into the shop, glancing at a display of colorful vintage tins, a pair of barley twist candlesticks, my gaze lighting on a Victorian aneroid barometer. The barometer needle rested permanently between Rain and Change. I was glad that I wasn't a superstitious woman.

"I noticed the car out front."

"Tracy's here," he said. I couldn't read anything in his tone—I was too busy trying to process what I felt at that news.

"Great minds," Tracy said from the top of the stairs. I looked up. She was standing in the doorway to Peter's living quarters, leaning back against the frame, brandy snifter in hand. Her hair was tousled and she was scantily dressed, but since she was always scantily dressed, I didn't place too much importance on it.

"Hi!" I said brightly. I'm sure I looked as thrilled to see her as she looked to see me.

"Just happened to be in the neighborhood?" she inquired.

"Well, no," I said.

I heard something behind me that might have been the whisper of Peter's laugh, and I started up the stairs.

Tracy watched me every step of the way. I had to give her credit: she had nerves of steel.

"How was dinner?" Peter inquired. "I heard you dined out."

Indeed? No mystery where he'd heard that. But he knew Brian and I were friends, and I was sure he wasn't making any more of that than I was of Tracy lounging around his living room at ten o'clock in the evening.

"It was nice," I said. "We went to the Garden House in Kendal. Did you know, at one time Alfred Wainwright lived there?"

"Any relation to Wainewright the Poisoner?" Tracy inquired.

Now that brought me up short. If I'd thought Tracy could read at all, I'd have expected her literary taste to be confined to *Cosmo*. Thomas Griffiths Wainewright was a contemporary of Byron and a friend of Charles Lamb, William Blake, Henry Fuseli, and many notable others. A talented artist and an infamous murderer, he ended his days in Tasmania where he was transported after murdering his uncle, mother-in-law, sister-in-law, and a few other people who got in his way. There were three biographies of Wainewright that I knew of, but I couldn't imagine Tracy reading any of them.

"Not that I know of," I said. "Different spelling for one thing. This Wainwright was famous for his handwritten, hand-drawn pictorial travel guides of the fells."

As we reached the landing, Tracy outflanked me by moving back into the flat. She took a chair across from the red leather sofa and stared down at her brandy glass. I sat on the sofa. Peter closed the door to the flat behind us.

I said to him, "Brian thinks they have a lead on the gunmen."

He didn't seem particularly impressed. "A lead but no arrests?"

"Not yet. But he's sure they'll pick them up tomorrow." I didn't want to say more than that in front of Tracy. In fact, Brian would probably have considered even that much too much.

Tracy said, "I didn't think people in this country were even allowed to own guns." For the second time in five minutes it occurred to me that Tracy might be brighter than she appeared. I suspected that she was one of those women who felt she would get farther playing dumb and trading off her looks.

"All automatic, semi-automatic, and hand guns of .22 caliber and above were outlawed over a decade ago," Peter said. He met my eyes levelly. I didn't know much about guns but I was willing to bet that the pistol he'd been carrying yesterday was not legal issue.

"Brandy?" he asked.

"Yes please."

He looked inquiringly at Tracy. She shook her head. He poured a brandy, and brought it to me. There was a rather awkward silence as he sat down on the sofa next to me.

After a moment Tracy drained her own glass.

"Well, I guess I should be going. We've got an early start tomorrow." She gave me a long, cool look.

I met it equably. "See you tomorrow bright and early."

Her smile was a little tight, but she covered well. Peter rose to see her out, and I leaned back on the sofa staring around the familiar room. High ceilings, black wooden beams, glossy wooden floors. Even at night it felt bright and open. A beautiful old curio chest functioned as a coffee table. There was an enormous moon-faced grandfather clock against the far wall. A mounted telescope stood before white-framed Georgian windows.

I knew this room well, and maybe it didn't make sense, but I felt welcomed here. My tension drained away.

I heard the jingle of the bells, and the lights in the shop went down. I heard his footsteps on the stairs, and then he was inside the room, his back to me as he closed the door.

Peter turned slowly to face me. He was smiling.

I smiled back.

CHAPTER 12

"WHAT TIME is it?" I asked sleepily.

Peter's chest shifted beneath my head as he turned to read the clock. "Five-thirty."

"Mm. I should probably get up." But I made no move, and neither did he. It was lovely like this: warm and comfortable in bed together, listening to the soothing sound of the rain on the roof.

His fingers drifted lazily through my hair. His heart was beating in slow, steady thumps against my ear. I felt boneless, sated, drowsy. In fact, there was nothing I'd have loved better than to permit myself to fall back to sleep.

Instead, I asked, "Do you know Barney or Barry February?"

"No." There was no hesitation in his voice; his heart's rhythm was calm. "Who are they?"

"Brian thinks they're the two men gunning for you."

Just for an instant his fingers paused in that absent caress. "I see."

"The police are supposed to bring them in for questioning today. If they can find them."

"Drummond told you this?"

I nodded. We hadn't wasted the night in talking. Oddly enough Tracy might have done me a favor. Not only had her mention of my dinner with Brian bothered Peter just enough to get him past his chivalrous qualms about spending time with me, her presence had apparently reinforced his own weariness with his former lifestyle. Not that he'd exactly *said* so, but I felt I could safely draw a few deductions from his enthusiasm once we were alone.

"It sounds like they're career criminals," I said. "Ne'er-do-wells."

"What else did Drummond tell you?"

126

"That was basically it. That they had a lead on these two. But you don't know them?"

His head moved in slight negation.

"Why do you think they came after you?"

"Grace—" He bit it off, but I could hear the weariness in his tone. "I don't know. I've thought it over. There's nothing. No reason. Not now."

"Not now?" I raised my head and met his eyes—shadowy and blue like the distant mountains.

He acknowledged, "Once, maybe. I was in a line of work that…encouraged bad behavior. I fell out with people. Made a few enemies, I suppose. But not the kind of enemies who would wait years to come after me—and not for the kinds of things that we fell out over."

"What about Catriona?" I asked of his (I personally believed) mentally unbalanced former girlfriend.

Peter said wryly, "If Cat wanted me dead, she'd kill me herself."

"That's *so* sweet," I cooed. "That special bond the two of you still have."

He laughed.

"So you don't believe there's anyone in your mysterious past who might want you dead? What about someone from the Istanbul job?"

Peter's last job as a jewel thief had been to steal a fabulous Turkish artifact called the Serpent's Egg from the Topkapi Palace. Though he had succeeded, he and his team had been betrayed by the man who hired them, Gordon Roget. Peter's team had escaped but he had been taken prisoner and spent fourteen months in a Turkish hellhole of a prison before finally escaping with the help of a corrupt guard. Roget had disappeared with the stone, never to be heard from again.

But what of the other members of that betrayed team? What if someone who didn't know the full story blamed Peter? What if someone believed Peter had the stone, that Peter had double-crossed his partners?

"No," he said. And there was something in his tone that warned me he was not going to be open to discussing this angle. But when did I let a little thing like infuriating my lover get in the way of my sleuthing?

"You said there were six of you. Was that counting Roget?"

After a long moment, he said unwillingly, "Yes."

"So discounting you, Cat, and Roget, since he ended up with the stone, that leaves three people who might blame you for—"

"For what? I'm the one who went to prison." He sat up, dislodging me, pulled a pillow over and stuffed it behind his back. I sat up, too. We stared at each other. After a moment I slipped my hand into his. He squeezed it, instinctively, but I could feel the restless anger humming in his system. He hated talking about this. And right then he was probably regretting ever telling me anything about his past.

"Do those three people know that Roget ended up with the Serpent's Egg? Is it possible that someone believes you have the stone?"

He opened his mouth to refute this idea, then seemed to consider it. "I don't know. It's not like we held a reunion. I escaped, returned to England, and settled here. I never tried to make contact with any one of them again."

Not even Catriona—for which she would never forgive him. Ideally.

"So it's possible that someone believes you managed to hide the stone. Hayri Kayaci believed it." Kayaci was the corrupt prison guard who had helped Peter escape; Peter had tricked Kayaci into believing he had hidden the stone before his capture. "They might believe that you recovered it once you escaped. That all this—" I gestured with my free hand, indicating Craddock House and Rogue's Gallery, and by extension, the comfortable, gracious existence Peter lived "—was purchased with their share of the loot."

He frowned, elegant brows drawn together. "Why wait seven years to come after me?"

"Maybe they didn't know where you were. It took Catriona nearly that long to hunt you down."

"Cat wasn't in the U.K. for most of that time."

I really didn't want to talk about Catriona—or think about the fact that he knew what she'd been doing during those years. I said, "Is it possible to find out what's become of those three men?"

"It's possible." He said carefully, "I'm not convinced it would be wise."

I looked my inquiry.

"An ounce of prevention. I've taken pains to steer clear of most of my former associates. I have enough problems with the law without resuming my old criminal contacts."

"Well, unless you can think of anyone else who might want you out of the way—"

"Other than Brian Drummond?"

"Brian?"

He was smiling but I didn't have the impression that he was entirely joking. I glanced beyond him to the clock, and pulled my hand free. "I'm going to be late!"

I left him, his arms folded behind his head, listening reflectively to the rain brushing against the window.

■ ■ ■ ■

Miles Friedman was more of an optimist than I had imagined, which was why we were all standing in the graveyard at ten o'clock in the morning while rain poured down around us. So far we'd managed to get in all of one hour's filming before the skies opened up again.

Several of us had taken shelter beneath the high portico and classical columns of a crypt. Tracy stood behind me listening to Madonna on her iPod. At least, she seemed to be listening to music; I was pretty sure she was listening in on my conversation with Roberta.

"Did you ask Peter about filming in Rogue's Gallery?"

"He declined," I told her. "I knew he would."

"Couldn't you have pushed a little?"

"I felt it was pushy enough to ask at all," I said dryly.

Her mouth tightened, but she let it go. Instead she pulled her jacket up over her head and left the shelter of the crypt to trot across the grass and graves to where Miles, Pammy, and some of the others stood beneath a tarp awning.

I glanced at Norton Edam who was leaning against one of the marble columns. He smiled politely—the way people do when they feel like talking but can't really think of anything to say.

The tinny music behind me stopped. "So what is it you find so interesting about poetry?" Tracy asked.

I glanced around, surprised. She said, apparently serious, "You don't really look like the type. I mean, you look like a teacher, but you don't look like *that*."

That? What in the world could *that* be? Did Tracy imagine that female academics were by definition frumps and freaks?

I said, "Well...poetry wasn't regarded the way it is today. It wasn't a special thing that only a few academics and literary types were interested in. Poetry was one of the most common forms of expression in the Romantic period. It was how educated people amused themselves, informed themselves, and communicated with one another. There were dozens of literary journals and periodicals. Poetry was featured regularly in newspapers. Knowing how to write verse was considered a necessary skill. Literate people exchanged poems the way we exchange e-mails now."

Sounding bored, she said, "I'm not talking about your book or why people back in the old days wrote poetry. I mean, why are *you* so interested in it?"

And the weird thing is, for a moment I couldn't think of a way to explain it to her. I was pretty sure she didn't want a lecture on preservation of old culture versus fostering creation of new, and I knew I didn't want to get into a rant about the subsidized subculture of modern poetry. I said finally, "That's like asking why someone likes art or music. It's interesting to me for many reasons. It's beautiful. Language—just the words themselves. The richness and texture of them. We've lost that as a society. We communicate so...mechanically. So simplistically. The way we shy away from using adjectives or adverbs..."

I thought she was probably sorry she'd asked, but she didn't interrupt, and despite myself I warmed to my theme. "And it's not just words. It's how they're used. The craft of saying something subtle and clever within the framework of rhythm and meter. The skill and discipline required to effectively use devices like rhyme, alliteration, consonance and dissonance. Poetry communicates in a way that nothing else does. Well, with the possible exception of song lyrics."

She continued to stare at me as though she couldn't quite think what to file me under.

"Do you write your own poetry?" Norton asked.

"Yes, but it's very bad," I said.

"I understand what you're saying," he said—to my surprise. "Art is art. Whether it's painting or poetry or acting."

Guiltily, I reflected that I'd never really considered acting much of an art. I thought of it more like mimicry. Something a person might have a talent or aptitude for, but not really an art to be refined and polished. That was my own intellectual snobbery at work.

"How long have you been in the business?" I asked them both.

"I started out modeling," Tracy said vaguely.

"It's in my blood," Norton said. "My great-grandparents were in vaudeville. They were singers. Hope and Lester Springer. Their act was called Hope Springs Eternal."

Tracy laughed.

"My grandparents, my parents: I guess my sister and I caught the showbiz bug from them."

"Is your sister an actress, too?" I asked.

His face changed. "She was. She died years ago."

"Oh, I'm sorry."

He nodded.

"Now I know who you are," Tracy said. "You played that little kid on TV. That show about the witch who works as a housekeeper for the cop. And the oldest girl was your sister in real life."

"That's right."

I knew the show Tracy was talking about—although in theory my brothers and I hadn't been allowed to watch it. My mother had strong feelings about television sitcoms—let alone television sitcoms about women with magical powers and plastic breasts.

"I loved that show," I said, which was perfectly true. Norton smiled.

And now I knew the sad story of what had happened to his sister. It was one of those Hollywood child star tragedies. A hugely successful youngster who wasn't able to translate her preadolescent popularity into an adult career within the industry—and couldn't be happy outside of it. I vaguely recalled that she had died of a drug overdose.

Thinking of adolescents reminded me that I hadn't seen Cordelia since Monday. I made a mental note to give her a call and arrange some kind of outing.

"Looks like the rain is letting up," Tracy said, and sure enough, the rain had stopped once more and watery sunlight was shining off the puddles and sparkling on the dripping leaves and funeral statuary.

I spent the rest of Thursday afternoon watching Tracy, Norton, Mona, and Todd chase each other around the lake and the graveyard. White smoke drifted on the rainswept breeze, and the greenwood rang with the echo of fake gunshots.

CHAPTER 13

"I'VE LOST my flask *again*," Mona sighed.

"Subconscious, innit?" Todd inquired, setting an Irish coffee in front of her. "Your unconscious mind tellin' you not to drink that wheatgrass swill."

Thursday evening we were crowded into the bar at the Hound and Harrier. I hadn't spent so much time in a pub since college.

"Swill?" Mona repeated thoughtfully. Then she picked up the cup and took a cautious sip. "Mmm. Who needs sleep anyway?"

"Yummy. Though not as yummy as in the States," Roberta remarked. "They do something different to them at home. Add brown sugar instead of white maybe?" Inferior to home the Irish coffee might be, but she was already on her third and we'd only settled in the bar forty-five minutes earlier.

"You add a shot of Baileys," Norton said, joining us. He squeezed in between Mona and Roberta and glanced around the bar. "No Tracy?"

Mona shook her head.

"I'll tell you 'ow real Irish coffee is made," Todd said. "You add one shot of Bushmills and one teaspoon of brown sugar to a proper Irish coffee glass. Then you tilts the glass over a burner and roll it 'til the whisky starts to smoke. You straighten the glass and watch the whisky light, *then* you add the coffee and a dollop of heavy cream."

"And a shot of Baileys," Norton said.

Todd looked disgusted. "Nah, no Baileys, mate."

"And a sprinkle of cinnamon or chocolate on the whipped cream," Roberta said.

"No!" Todd shook his head. "None of that trash."

Todd and Norton began to argue about the merits of Baileys. I glanced at the doorway of the bar and spotted Cordelia. She caught sight of me waving, and wove her way through the tables.

"How old is that child?" Mona inquired.

"Old enough," Todd said, and I gave him a look. He laughed and put his hands up as though trying to block my X-ray vision. "Joking, luv. I'm 'armless, I promise."

"If only that were true," I remarked. "She's not quite eighteen," I said to Mona, still eyeing Todd. He grinned irrepressibly.

"Older than Helen of Troy," Mona remarked, which didn't exactly settle my nerves.

"Where've you been?" I asked as Cordelia dragged a chair over and dropped down in it. "I thought you were coming by the set yesterday?"

She shuddered. "I thought I'd never get away! Auntie's had me helping with preparations for the bloody church bazaar." She combed back her blond mane with black-tipped fingers. "Two bloody days of sorting junk. Before I forget: you're all invited to tea tomorrow."

The others expressed surprise and delight at the notion of formal tea at a genuine stately home with a real live Lady of the Realm. One would have thought the tour bus had just pulled up outside the Hound and Harrier.

True, there was a time when I would have felt just the same. Not these days. Not when it came to Lady Vee anyway. "You're kidding," I said to Cordelia.

She shook her head. "I think Auntie's hoping someone will decide to make a film out of one of her books." She looked across at Todd and winked.

He gave me the sort of look you generally see in a grammar-school setting—usually accompanied by pointing fingers. I ignored him.

Roberta graciously accepted the invitation of tea on behalf of the rest of us. Todd went to fetch Cordelia an Irish coffee minus the Irish, and the conversation flowed and eddied around us, as usual mostly centering on the day's filming.

Not looking at me, Cordelia said, "Grace, would you want to have lunch one day?"

"Of course! I'd love to. We haven't had a chance to talk since I got back."

She threw me a sideways look, and smiled. I smiled, too. Sometimes I forgot how young she really was. How it felt to be feeling your way through the rituals and routines of adulthood.

I watched her flirting with Todd, inwardly shaking my head. When she excused herself to use the loo, Roberta gestured to me. I followed her out into the lobby anteroom.

Roberta said, "That girl. Cordelia. She's a student at RADA?"

"She will be when she's old enough—assuming she stays interested in the idea of acting. Right now she's at the Arts Educational School."

"But that's an acting school, right? Can she act?"

"I have no idea."

Roberta bit her lip. "When you introduced her the other day you said she was the cousin of Jacinda?"

"Who?"

She looked a little impatient. "Jacinda Croydon. Your Allegra Brougham from the book."

Uneasily, I admitted Cordelia and Allegra were second cousins.

"Do you think she might be interested in playing the role of Jacinda?"

"I don't know," I said, although I did—only too well. "You could talk it over with Lady Vee tomorrow. She's sort of Cordelia's guardian." Not that Lady Vee would object to any project that kept Cordelia out from underfoot. My own reluctance toward the idea surprised me. In some ways it would be excellent hands-on experience for Cordelia, and we'd get to spend a little time together—and while she occasionally drove me nuts, I was very fond of her.

But there was something about the production of this film that made me uneasy. I couldn't put my finger on it. Nothing had happened, really, other than Walter Christie's death. Well, there had been the attack by gunmen, but that was apparently a case of mistaken identity. And I had every reason to believe that Walter's death had been an accident. An accident that had happened overseas, so there was small reason to think there was any danger to any of us.

And yet…with each day that passed I grew more certain that there was something…strange. Something bizarrely amateur and off-kilter about this whole setup. Just the fact that Roberta was suggesting on the spur of the moment that we replace a professional actress with an untrained, *unauditioned* student…

I said, "Please don't say anything to Cordelia until you've spoken to her great-aunt."

"Oh, no," Roberta said quickly. "I realize there are certain protocols here."

Here? As though getting the consent of a minor's legal guardian was the arcane custom of this tiny foreign land?

We went back inside the bar. Cordelia had returned to the table—and changed her seat for one beside Todd. She giggled at my expression. I shook my head. Roberta took her seat on the other side of the table next to Cordelia.

More Irish coffees were ordered. I'd never seen people put Irish coffee away like this crowd. Apparently they were under the impression that it was a traditional British pub beverage—or maybe it was just that they couldn't bear to be without coffee in some form for more than a few minutes at a time.

Miles arrived with Tracy, and Norton immediately took himself off. The bar grew noisier and more crowded. I thought about going upstairs and getting some work done. Peter had a dinner with his colleagues from the British Antique Dealers Association and didn't plan on being home 'til quite late, so I was on my own for the evening.

And then my thoughts were interrupted as Cordelia began to emit squeals of excitement. I looked across the table and Roberta gave me a sheepish smile. *"Sorry!"* she mouthed, the smoky lenses of her glasses winking in the mellow light. "It just…came up."

For a moment I was so angry with her I wasn't sure I could

conceal it. I only tried because Cordelia was absolutely thrilled, for once completely abandoning that blasé pose.

"Grace, did you hear that? I'm going to be in this film!"

"I heard," I said mildly.

"My first movie!"

And on and on. A round of celebratory Irish coffee was ordered and drunk. Pammy called it a night. Miles and Tracy disappeared. Mona excused herself and went upstairs.

There was no hope of my getting away to my room because I wasn't about to leave Cordelia on her own with the remaining piranha.

But finally Todd excused himself to make some transatlantic phone calls, and Cordelia glanced at her watch and exclaimed that she had to get home. She grabbed her purse—a cloth bag with a silk-screen photo of Humphrey Bogart and Lauren Bacall—and took off into the night leaving me alone at the table with Roberta.

Roberta smiled. "Now, Grace, before you say anything—"

She obviously didn't know me well if she thought such a thing was even a possibility. I said, "I can't for the life of me think why you would do something so irresponsible. You don't even know whether she can act her way out of a paper bag."

"What does it matter?"

That threw me for a second. "What do you mean, what does it matter? Even if her aunt gives her permission, you don't know whether Cordelia can act—" I stopped short. "Is this film actually going to be completed?"

Roberta's expression was difficult to read. "Of course it is."

I couldn't tell if she was telling the truth or not, but once the suspicion had occurred to me, I couldn't quite shake it.

"How many films have you produced?"

"What does that have to do with anything? How many scripts have you written? Who are you to question my qualifications?"

I didn't bother arguing with her. "How many films has Kismet produced?"

"Oh for—! Look it up," Roberta said. She rose. "I don't have time for this. We've both got to be up at the crack of dawn." She turned away from the table, then stopped and faced me. "Look, Grace. I apologize for telling the kid before I talked to her aunt. It just came up. She *asked* if we were hiring any extras. It seemed natural to mention it to her. There's no point talking to her aunt if she wasn't interested in the part, right?"

I suppose it made sense from Roberta's standpoint. Seeing my hesitation, she said, "For God's sake, let's not you and me argue. This project is tough enough without that. I made a mistake. It won't happen again. We'll treat the kid with—er—kid gloves, I promise."

"All right," I said. "I don't want to argue either."

"I think it's all this caffeine we're drinking," Roberta offered. Her smile was wry. "They put something different in it here."

I nodded politely. I couldn't shake the peculiar feeling, as I watched her on her way out of the bar, that beneath the anger—and then the sudden about-face and apology—Roberta was frightened.

■■■■■

I awoke to find the lights on. I was lying in bed, my copy of *Letty Landon* lying open on my chest. I blinked up at the dark beams, listening, trying to remember what woke me.

The muted bang of a closing door.

Not my own door. Not next door either. Not…close by. Perhaps the sound came from downstairs?

I glanced at the clock. Three-fifteen. I smothered a yawn. All was quiet—the heavy silence of late night. Not so much as a floorboard squeaked.

The last thing I remembered, I'd been reading about Landon's broken engagement to John Forster, the noted Dickens biographer. Landon's enormous popularity, combined with her casual friendships with men—she had several male mentors—made her a target for jealous and slanderous tongues. And not all of them female. Her engagement to the much younger Forster had been the first casualty.

I closed the book, set it on the night table, and turned out the lamp. Light from the lamppost in front of the inn cast a golden fan against the wall. I watched it quiver gently with the draft stirring the draperies.

As often happens, once jarred awake, I couldn't relax enough to fall back to sleep. I wondered how Peter's BADA dinner had gone, and whether he was home and in bed by now. I wondered again about that funny feeling I'd had about Roberta. And I wondered about the timing of that stolen car bearing down on Peter, Walter Christie, and me as we happened to be standing on Highland Avenue.

It had been so close. Even another second would have meant the difference between life and death.

I tossed around in the blankets, fluffed the pillows, then rose and went to pull the drapes closed all the way.

For a moment I lingered at the window gazing down at the cars in the car park below. Frost gilded the grass and the roofs of the vehicles. All except one. The silver rental car that Tracy had been driving the night before. There was no frost on its roof.

Interesting. Had the door I wasn't sure I'd heard closing actually been the car-park entrance to the inn?

Well, if Tracy had hoped to pay a surprise visit to Peter, tonight the surprise would have been on her.

CHAPTER 14

"CHOCOLATE CHIP SCONES," I said. "If I didn't love you before, I do now."

"I knew the secret lay somewhere near the top of the food pyramid." Peter handed me a cup of tea.

Friday morning found me sitting in the window seat of Craddock House watching the Kismet Productions cast and crew slowly assembling outside Rogue's Gallery.

"I'm supposed to ask you again whether you'll consider letting us film inside Rogue's Gallery," I said.

"You're not serious."

"I'm not. They are. I promised I'd ask."

He was shaking his head.

I said, "It's not necessarily a bad thing—look at the other day. The film crew's presence kept those goons from going after you—or at least, their mistaking Todd for you, did."

He smelled of aftershave and freshly laundered cotton as he stood there buttoning his shirt. His eyes were thoughtful. "Did your pet plod manage to bring in the Februarys?"

"I didn't hear from Brian yesterday, so I'm guessing no. And why do you both refer to each other as 'mine'? I'm not in the slave trade."

"Bit touchy this morning, are we?"

I sniffed. "I didn't get a lot of sleep last night."

"No?" He picked up my scone, took a bite, and put it back on my plate. "That's two of us."

I barely heard him. I was staring at my scone. It sounds ridiculous, but it was the first time I remembered him taking a bite from food on my plate. It was such a simple and ordinary moment of domesticity that I actually felt...moved.

Peter had already moved away in search of his wallet. He was getting ready to deliver two rosewood Rococo armchairs and some other items to Angela Hornsby's estate and would be out all day. Which was probably a good thing with the film crew back on the premises. It would save wear and tear on everyone's nerves if Peter were safely out of the way for most of the day.

"Is it all right if I use your computer this afternoon?" I called.

"What's mine is yours." I couldn't help noticing how unconsciously sexy he was in those jeans and the blue cambric workshirt that emphasized the worldly blue of his eyes. "I'll see you later tonight, will I?" He stooped and kissed me.

And then kissed me again.

"Oh, yes," I said.

■■■■■

The sunshiny promise of the morning held, and filming went smoothly that day—at least from what I understood. To be honest, I spent a good portion of the morning closed up in Rogue's Gallery trying to find out what I could about the Kismet Production Company.

The problem was, there were several Kismet film companies. There was a Kismet Media Group, which was a talent and brand management company; Kismet Entertainment Group, which was an indie film production company that seemed to handle everything from comic books to video games; and there was Kismet Films, based in New York, which was a feature film and commercial production company.

Kismet Films initially looked promising, but I had trouble believing that the company that had produced several critically acclaimed documentaries, shorts, and corporate image pieces was one and the same as the haphazard assembly I was part of.

There was a Kismet dance production company, a Kismet cleaning service, and several Kismet import companies.

None of them looked to be my Kismet Production Company, but I couldn't completely rule them all out at first glance. I was going to have to dig a little deeper and perhaps make a few phone calls while being careful not to give my suspicions away in case I truly was unduly paranoid.

I Googled and Yahoo'd "Miles Friedman"; and there was no question that he was the genuine article. The genuine article being a second-string director with many more romantic conquests than film credits. But he did have film credits—and some of them were quite good.

I had less luck tracking Roberta down. Twelve pages into a search for "Roberta Lom," and nothing relevant was coming up. I tried the Internet Movie Database and there were one or two mentions of an actress named Roberta Lom. No pictures. It was possible that Roberta had started out as an actress. She was known to Miles and Mona, so she couldn't entirely be a fake—and maybe movie producers, unlike movie directors, didn't get a lot of press.

I decided to try to find out what I could from Mona and some of the other cast members and then try searching again.

And I could always ask Brian for some help. Not that he ordinarily approved of my sleuthing, but being in law enforcement he probably endorsed paranoia on general principles.

When I had done about all the online detecting I could accomplish in one sitting—and eaten all the chocolate chip scones—I went downstairs to observe Cordelia's theatrical debut.

Her first scene basically consisted of crawling around the outside of Rogue's Gallery, peering in windows, and then getting knocked out by Norton using what looked like a lethal lead (but was actually rubber) pipe. No dialogue was required, unless Cordelia's quite realistic yowl of pain counted.

Of course I could have told her from having been knocked out myself on one memorable occasion that there's no time for yelling when you've been struck unconscious, but it did make for a nice dramatic moment.

Undeterred by the camera pointed her way, and the number of people watching her, Cordelia, in character as Jacinda, did a convincing job of slinking along the wall of the building, scowling ferociously into the unlit windows. I suppose I found her performance especially amusing since she was pretending to be her cousin Allegra. Al and I had initially got off on the wrong foot, and diplomatic relations hadn't improved over the years.

Collapsing dramatically into the flowerbed, Cordelia, cushioned by daffodils and crocuses, won a round of applause from the crew. Miles pronounced himself happy with this take, and because of the cast members taking tea with Lady Venetia Brougham later that afternoon, we were all excused.

I found myself being driven back to Innisdale by Cordelia in a sporty little black Jag convertible, which she informed me had been a present from her parents upon her acceptance into drama school.

"My reward for keeping out of their hair," she told me with that coolly adult cynicism that always took me aback.

"But you're still staying with your great-aunt on weekends?"

"Off and on," she said cryptically, punching the accelerator so that we might zip around yet another long, dawdling tour bus on the wide country lane.

I felt my hands bunching into fists, and deliberately smoothed them out. Cordelia, hair whipping around her head, threw me a quick grin as though reading my mind.

She was actually not a bad driver, though she was definitely a bit of a speed demon. We flew down the road, the countryside passing in a green-gold flash of grass and sunlight and daffodils.

"How do you like drama school?"

"It's all right." She shot me a quick sidewise glance. "They all take themselves far too seriously." She combed strands of hair out of her mouth. "I suppose it's all about the slow and painful decay of the middle class, isn't it?"

"Isn't what?" I asked carefully over the howl of wind in my ears.

"Oh, you know. Other people imposing their values. What it's really all about is art and passion and being true to yourself. Or it should be."

Ah. I called upon the experience of years spent teaching adolescent girls. "Are you seeing someone?" I asked.

She blushed. And she was not a girl given to blushing. Flushing a painful and awkward red when she tripped or dropped something or said something she didn't mean to say...yes. Not this delicate flush of color in her thin face. "His name is Douglas," she told me, and I could see the struggle it was for her not to smile when she spoke his name. "I call him Dougie."

I smiled, too. "And he's planning to be an actor as well?"

"Oh no," she said blithely. "He's done with all that. He's an instructor at the school. And a playwright. He's writing a play for me. It's called *Wild Cherries*."

I swallowed hard and managed not to say the first thing that occurred to me. "Is he?" I got out weakly. "Have your parents or... your aunt met him yet?"

"Auntie Vee?" She burst out laughing at the idea, and I chuckled feebly with her, wondering what the hell I should do about this—if anything. Cordelia was nearly eighteen; she was my friend, not my student or daughter or little sister. And maybe cherry-flavored Dougie was a perfectly decent, not very old, unmarried instructor.

Right. And maybe Peter and Brian would one day be the best of pals—and Catriona would act as my maid of honor when I married her former lover.

We were nearing the environs of Innisdale, and Cordelia slowed from suicidal to merely reckless speed. As we wound through the narrow village streets, she continued to chatter about what Douglas thought about this and that—he was certainly an opinionated man—but while I ended our drive knowing how Douglas felt on such vital topics as Oprah's book club, architecture and urbanism, and sexual politics, I still had no idea of how old he was or whether he was married.

I knew better than to ask outright. In fact, as I had surmised, the less curiosity I revealed about Douglas, the more I heard. None of it reassuring.

Cordelia followed me into the inn and upstairs, sitting on my bed while I did my makeup and then changed into a skirt and sweater.

"Is your aunt really hoping someone is going to make a movie out of one of her books?" I asked, checking copper earrings against my Ralph Lauren cable-knit cardigan.

"Partly. Partly I think it's just an excuse to see you," Cordelia said, rising to try on a pair of my earrings.

"Why would she want to see *me*?" I questioned suspiciously. Not that I didn't believe her. I'd been caught up in several of Lady Vee's schemes, and I suspected she viewed me in the light of a never-failing patsy. In fact, my friendship with Cordelia began when her great-aunt coerced me into acting as a sort of companion–chaperone the previous summer.

"No idea," Cordelia said cheerfully. "Could I borrow these?"

"Not until you return the amethyst ones you borrowed."

"Oh, I'd forgotten about those!"

"I hadn't."

She giggled, untroubled, and watching her face in the mirror I felt a twinge of something uncomfortably maternal. I knew I was eventually going to have to find out more about this new man in her life—which probably wouldn't be a problem since I seemed to spend a lot of my time snooping.

We went downstairs and found most of the cast getting ready to leave for the tea party, the usual debate ranging about who would drive with whom. Mona, delighted to have finally located her missing flask on the mantelpiece in the anteroom next to the lobby, hitched a ride with us in Cordelia's black Jaguar.

"I've always wanted to have a real English high tea," she said, not blinking an eye as Cordelia roared away from the inn. "Do you suppose there will be crumpets and cucumber sandwiches?"

I don't think I've ever had a decent cucumber sandwich in my life, but I murmured noncommittally. Being vegetarian, Mona probably approved of cucumber sandwiches in all their soggy glory.

"High tea is dinner," Cordelia informed her, throwing a wind-blown look over her shoulder. "We're having afternoon tea. Low tea."

Mona raised her eyebrows, exchanging a look with me, and I explained, "You and I, well, most Americans, think of high tea as a fancy, full tea, but it's actually the evening meal. Usually with meat. We're going to be treated to an afternoon or a cream tea, I'm guessing. Savories and sweets, scones—crumpets, probably." I didn't tell her that Lady Vee would be serving crumpets as a concession to the Americans.

"Desserts," Cordelia said. "Auntie has a new pastry chef."

Mona licked her lips. "Lovely."

The subject of tea and crumpets exhausted, I asked casually, "Mona, how long have you known Roberta?"

She shrugged a bony shoulder. "We both worked on a TV special a few years back. I hadn't seen her for ages. Not until I got the call for this project."

"You've never done a film for Kismet Productions before?"

She gave me an odd look. "I don't believe they've done many films. They're fairly new from what I picked up."

"But you knew Miles?"

She laughed. "Oh, yes. Miles and I go *way* back."

"When I first talked to Walter Christie he said some things about Roberta and Miles not really being in control of the production."

"Poor little Walter," she said regretfully. "Well, Miles and Roberta have to answer to their corporate overlords like all the rest of us minions."

I'd have liked to ask her more questions, but she leaned back in her seat, lifting her face to the pallid sun and enjoying the wind through her hair.

■■■■■

"Grace, my *deah*," drawled Lady Venetia Brougham in welcome, vaguely waving her guests to the invitingly placed chairs and settees littering the elegant drawing room. "You decided to return after all. I admit I feared we would never see you again. Dear *Petah* must be utterly...flummoxed."

"Oh, but I always enjoy our little visits," I retorted. "Peter knows that."

She snickered, eyeing me with her lizard-dark eyes. In an unexpected concession to her age—which was eighty-something—

Lady Vee had finally given up the raven-haired Cleopatra bob. Her pale silver hair had been cut pixie-style. And, in fact, being tiny, wizened, and more than a little malicious, the cut suited her rather well.

"And how did you find your family and friends?" she inquired politely, meanwhile directing servants and guests alike with her long ivory cigarette holder. Uniformed maids placed heavily laden silver trays on several low tables in front of my fellow guests.

I resisted the urge to say something uncharacteristically smart-aleck, like I'd found them without any problem since they weren't trying to lose me. "I'm happy to say everyone was quite well."

"We did wonder when you kept coming up with exc—reasons for postponing your return. I think *Petah* had given you up as a lost cause, my *deah*. I know Allegra had the impression you were not expected to return anytime soon."

I happened to notice Cordelia open her mouth and then close it. She gave me a funny, guilty look. What did *that* mean? Oh, I knew what Lady Vee was implying, but that didn't worry me unduly. She liked needling me with the idea that her niece, one of Peter's former lady friends, was still—to use one of her own sporting metaphors—in the running.

"Well, I'm back now," I said brightly.

"And you've brought such *enthrahlling* friends and colleagues with you this time." She made it sound like I'd arrived with elephants and trapeze artists in tow, but before I could respond—had I a suitable response—Lady Vee turned on her party manners and began to wow the colonials with her lemon curd and Earl Grey.

Pammy's plate was piled BBQ-fashion with pastries and sweets. I could see Mona observing our hostess quietly and taking mental notes, but she was too shrewd to make the fatal mistake of mentioning that she was playing a Lady Vee clone in *Dangerous to Know*. Although one never knew: Lady Vee might actually have got a perverse kick out of her cinematic reincarnation.

Miles and Tracy sat on one of the velvet love seats next to the ancient harpsichord, whispering and eating. At one point Tracy was actually feeding Miles cake, so I really couldn't blame Norton for the glowering looks he was sending their way, although I didn't think he was glowering for the same reason Roberta was.

Everyone else seemed suitably impressed and enthusiastic, although Todd was overplaying the forelock-tugging a tad.

But then tea at Lady Venetia's—any meal, really—was always a sumptuous affair, and that afternoon was no different. The quantities of jam-filled scones, blue-frosted fairy cakes, chocolate sponge cake, and blackberry tarts were provided in keeping with North American notions of portions. The tea itself was exquisite, delicate and flavorful, and I could see the old beldame watching with glinting amusement as her guests puzzled over whether the milk went into the cups before the tea, whether they were supposed to balance fragile cups on dainty saucers or hold them separately, whether the paper-thin slice of lemon went in the cup or not, and what to do with those gleaming sterling teaspoons.

Something about Lady Vee and her centuries-old surroundings made even the most confident person suddenly want to reach for the latest edition of Emily Post.

When we had finally finished gorging ourselves on sweets, and Lady Vee had grown bored with torturing the savages with small talk, we were invited to view the justly famous rose gardens.

It was growing late in the afternoon as we filed out to explore the series of garden rooms boxed by green hedges and bordered by huge, ancient rosebushes. The scent of herbs and musky roses perfumed the neatly trimmed walkways. As expected in a classic English garden, there were numerous whimsical structures and topiaries pruned into imaginative shapes, as well as several lovely marble statues positioned amidst the harmoniously laid-out flowerbeds. Everyone oohed and ahhed appropriately.

"Has Cordelia mentioned to you that she's been hired to act in this film?" I asked Lady Vee as we happened to find ourselves standing by the goldfish pond while everyone else wandered along the paths and out of immediate earshot.

"The *deah* child may have said something about it," Lady Vee replied vaguely. She had brought a basket and a pair of secateurs with her, and was ruthlessly clipping withered blooms. I suspected at first it was just part of her Lady of the Manor act, but she was getting too much pleasure out of the snipping.

"And you're all right with that?"

The gimlet eyes met mine. "Shouldn't I be?"

I had no desire to sabotage the film production of my own work, but honesty compelled me to say, "I don't know. There's something I can't quite put my finger on. Don't you think they're all a little…strange?"

She said sweetly, "They're Americans, my *deah*."

"I realize that. But besides being born on the wrong side of the Atlantic—"

A shrill scream split the rose-scented tranquility. Lady Vee went rigid, her eyes meeting mine.

Turning, I ran down the path following the hysterical babble of voices—there were more screams and then they cut off sharply.

I rounded the corner of a wall of yew trees. Several people formed a horseshoe around a body sprawled on the ground. I stared at the horrified faces: Tracy clung to Miles—and so did Roberta. Norton knelt on the ground beside the body, staring down at the twisted face.

"She's dead," he said in a sleepwalker's voice.

"Jesus Christ almighty," Miles said.

Someone gave a sob, and I looked at Cordelia. She was in Todd's arms. Her face was white and streaked with tears; but seeing her, I relaxed a fraction: it had been her scream that sent me racing through the garden.

Cordelia quavered, "S-she took a drink and then she…started gasping for breath…and then she fell down and began to…went into…c-convulsions."

"And then she died," Roberta said dazedly. "Just like that. It was so fast. She was…*dead*."

In silence we all stared down at Mona. Her hair lay in long strands across her face, not quite concealing her staring eyes. A few inches from her outstretched fingers lay her small silver flask.

CHAPTER 15

"POISON. THAT'S clear enough," Chief Constable Heron said. "Though it'll be a few days before we know what kind of poison."

"It was something that acted almost instantly, from what Cordelia said," I told him.

"Yes, we've got the young lady's statement."

With the privilege of being—literally—to the manor born, Cordelia had been questioned first and was now tucked up in bed upstairs with a hot water bottle, a cup of cocoa, and a couple of nice sedatives.

I, on the other hand, was still sitting in Lady Vee's elegant study several hours after the tragedy. A fire had been laid in the grate, and a tea tray—much less sumptuous than the one provided earlier—sat on the table where Chief Constable Heron and DI Brian Drummond, both my friends very much in their official capacities, were making notes.

Naturally the police had to question each of us before allowing anyone to leave the estate. Not everyone was taking this in civic-minded spirit. I was lucky. I'd been brought in to the study almost immediately. Not that I ever looked forward to being interviewed by the police, but it was even more nerve-racking with all of us crowded in the drawing room under the watchful eye of a young constable—forbidden to talk about the thing on every mind.

Having numbly answered most of Brian's and the chief constable's questions, there wasn't a lot I could add to whatever they had already learned. I had only known Mona a few days; my relationship with her had been friendly but not close, although I'd liked her very much. As far as I knew, everyone did. I'd seen nothing to indicate she hadn't got on well with the entire cast.

"She found her flask right before we left the inn. It had been missing for a day or so—but it wasn't the first time. She was always losing it. And it was always turning up."

"Where did it turn up this time?" Brian asked, topping off Heron's teacup and then his own.

"On the fireplace mantel in the little room next to the lobby of the Hound and Harrier. But that's exactly where someone might leave it if they found it and there was no one at the desk. Or Mona could have set it there herself."

"Was this Ms. Hotchkiss especially forgetful?" Heron asked. He was a large man with a waxed mustache and shrewd, black-cherry eyes. He could easily have played the master detective in any number of *Mystery!* productions. Through the years we had forged a cordial if occasionally adversarial relationship.

"I didn't have that impression. Maybe a little absentminded about where she'd left her jacket or set her purse."

"Did she keep the flask in her purse?"

"No, she didn't. She usually carried it in one of her pockets. She had an enormous suitcase of a purse, but she rarely bothered bringing it with her—partly because it was so big and unwieldy. I think that's why she tended to forget it when she did lug it somewhere."

"And this silver flask that she was always drinking from: what was in it?"

"Some kind of special homemade energy juice—she was very health-conscious." My throat closed unexpectedly. It took a moment before I was able to say, "She called it her 'magic elixir.' I can't remember everything that she said went into it. White ginseng, juniper berries, that kind of thing."

Brian glanced at Heron. "I've heard of juniper berries making someone ill. Never killing them. Still, it wouldn't be the first time someone accidentally poisoned herself with a herbal home remedy."

I have to admit, the idea that Mona might have accidentally poisoned herself had simply never occurred to me. And what a sad state of affairs that was: that every death appeared to me to be suspicious.

I said, "She seemed very knowledgeable about homeopathic remedies and herbal medicine, but I suppose those are the very people who are most vulnerable to that kind of accident."

Heron, studying me, said, "What's really bothering you, Grace?"

"One too many accidents," I admitted, and told him about Walter Christie dying in an unsolved hit-and-run on Highland Avenue.

"Two violent and unexplained deaths," Brian commented. His tone was neutral, but I could see him thinking it over.

"There's something strange about this whole production," I told them, warming to my subject. "I spent hours this morning researching on the Web, but I couldn't find any history on the production company, and this film is apparently their first."

"That's not conclusive," Brian said. "Just because this is their first project doesn't mean they're not legitimate."

"But there are all kinds of weird things. Almost no one really seems to know what they're doing. Granted, I don't know a lot about making movies, but they seem to be making this up as they go along. I mean, frankly, hiring me as a script doctor was strange."

Brian said, "I don't see anything strange about it. The script was based on your book. Who better to doctor it?"

"That's not how it works," I said. "They should have—ordinarily would have—hired someone with scriptwriting experience. Writing a book is a very different thing, especially since my book was nonfiction. But they practically insisted that I take on this project."

"They?"

"Roberta Lom, the producer. And possibly the director, Miles Friedman, is in on it, too."

Brian exchanged a glance with the Chief Constable who was watching me in that quiet, thoughtful way of his. "*In* on it?"

"They're paying me an exorbitant amount of money to work on this script."

"And you see that as sinister?"

"I see it as unusual. Improbable. Strange. And even more

strange is moving the production over here after starting in California. It must be costing a fortune, and this is not the kind of movie that gets a large budget. There isn't any possibility of Kismet making its investment back, I don't think."

"Perhaps it's a tax deduction," Heron said. "Perhaps they expect to lose money on it. Perhaps they need to lose money on it."

As in the classic film *The Producers?* I considered the idea, but dismissed it. "There's something not right," I said. "I don't know that it ties into two accidental deaths—maybe Walter and Mona really did die accidental deaths—but something is…off."

Heron pulled his pipe out, took time to light it. "You've given us something to consider, Grace," he said politely at last. "You can safely leave it in our hands."

■ ■ ■ ■ ■

Don't you worry your pretty little head about it!

I was surprised Chief Constable Heron had refrained from just saying it out loud. Clearly he and Brian both thought I was paranoid. Or, at the least, borderline hysterical. And I hadn't even admitted the worst of my suspicions: that the only reason the production of *Dangerous to Know* had been moved to the Lakes was so that I'd have no excuse for not taking part, so that I would remain part of the project.

Which, even I had to admit, made no sense at all. Not that I agreed with Peter; I happened to think my first book made a terrific subject for a film. A documentary would have been preferable, but as fiction, it wasn't any worse a subject for a feature film than A.S. Byatt's *Possessed.*

Still, as little as I wanted to concede the point, there did seem to be something very wrong with this film production. And as much as I'd have liked to think that perhaps Mona had tragically mixed up her herbs, I just couldn't quite make myself believe it. Not that I was thinking clearly; I still felt cold with shock. I'd liked Mona. In fact, she was about the only cast member I really had liked.

"What did the police ask you?" Roberta's voice jarred me out of my reflections. We were packed into the back seat of Tracy's rental car. We had all given our statements to the police, and Miles was driving the four of us back to the inn. He and Tracy had spent most of the drive speaking in low voices in the front seat. This was the first comment Roberta had made since we left the estate.

I answered, "Probably the same questions they asked everyone. Did Mona have any enemies, did she argue with anyone, did she seem afraid or nervous."

"That's odd," Tracy said, turning in the front seat to stare. "They hinted to me that they thought her death might have been accidental."

"Same here," Miles said.

"I think I gave them that idea when I told them what Mona kept in her flask."

"But you don't think it was an accident?" Roberta asked.

"I have no idea," I answered, equally terse.

They continued to discuss it amongst themselves, and by the time we reached the Hound and Harrier they all seemed convinced that Mona's death was a tragic mistake. I left them to reinforce their relief in the taproom, and went upstairs to call Peter.

The answering machine picked up. I checked the clock on the night table. It was nearly nine-thirty, but Peter rarely went to bed before midnight. His sleep patterns were erratic at best, and he hadn't mentioned going out for the night.

In fact, he had mentioned he would see me that evening.

Which could be construed as an invitation. Did I really need an invitation? Weren't we going to be "making a go of it" any minute? Whatever that meant to him.

I washed up, tidied my hair, changed my clothes, and tried phoning again. Again it went straight to the machine.

I began to get irritated. I didn't want to be on my own that night—not after the trauma of the day. And I wanted to talk my suspicions over with Peter. I wanted him to either reassure me that I was imagining things or convince me that I was justified in fearing the worst.

Could he have been held up at the Honourable Angela's this late? It seemed unlikely, even given his masculine charms and the susceptibility of middle-aged ladies.

Had he made other plans for the evening? It was possible, but one thing about Peter: he was scrupulous about keeping his bookings straight. No doubt a skill developed in order to make his life of crime more manageable. No, he might have been held up, but he wouldn't forget our plans for the evening, and he wouldn't cancel them without a word.

Not that I really needed to wait for Peter to reiterate that I was welcome in his home. After all, I had a key. Both to Rogue's Gallery and Craddock House. And he'd said he would see me that evening....

I recalled Cordelia's guilty, uncomfortable look at tea—it seemed a lifetime ago—when Lady Vee hinted that Peter hadn't really expected me to return to the Lake District. That he had resumed his old ways.

I never thought of myself as particularly insecure, but something about Peter and his history of relationships—which always struck me as more on the lines of a romantic epic—made me uncharacteristically hesitant to assert my...rights. "Rights" didn't even seem like the proper word for my position in Peter's life. It was all so undefined, and I hated things to be left undefined.

Rising from the bed, I began tossing clothes and makeup into my overnight bag. After I'd tossed in my books on Laetitia Landon, I tried phoning one last time.

And again it went straight to the machine. I didn't leave a message. At this point I was liable to sound desperate.

Instead I carried my bag downstairs, sneaking past the taproom where the mood, even from the doorway, seemed grim. I realized I would never be able to think of Irish coffee again without being reminded of Mona.

Letting myself out of the inn, I walked across the grass, a light frost crunching beneath my shoes, my breath smoking in the wintery night air. The car park was filled, moisture beading windshields and the tops of cars. I'd parked down at the end near the little copse that separated the car park from the footpath leading to the river.

It was very quiet. I could hear the street lamps buzzing through the rustle of the trees, and the distant trumpeting of the swans on the river—and someone groaning.

It was an eerie sound, freezing me in my tracks.

"Is someone there?" I called.

Silence.

Of course, in books and films it's always so annoying if the protagonist doesn't instantly run for help at the first sign of something out of the ordinary, but in real life none of us do that. No one wants to appear foolish or cowardly. It's one thing if there's a tangible threat, but just a little groan? Especially when the groan sounds like someone or something in pain?

After an undecided heartbeat, I started down the long line of cars, keys clutched between my fingers weapon-like, checking to see if someone had hit a dog or if an elderly person had fallen.

I saw the cowboy hat lying just beyond the front fender of Tracy's rental car—and I knew immediately.

Hurrying down the aisle of fenders, I leaned over the silver hood, and there lay Miles Friedman face down in the gravel. Even in the stuttering lamp light I could see the dark, wet patch on the back of his head.

I knelt down, putting my hand to his throat, feeling for the carotid artery, and I could feel a faint pulse tripping away beneath my fingertips.

He moaned again, and I nearly overbalanced in my surprise.

"Miles, can you hear me?"

There was no answer, and I rose, staring at the shadowy corners of the car park, the rows of unmoving vehicles. One thing for certain, *this* was not an accident, and I was afraid that if I left Miles even for the time it would take to run back to the inn, whoever had attacked him might take the opportunity to finish the job.

Of course Miles's assailant might be long gone—was hopefully long gone—but what if not? I gave it a moment's thought, then I stepped over Miles and tried jamming my key in the rental car door lock. As I'd hoped, it triggered the car alarm, electronic wailing shattering the peaceful night.

Before long one of the waiters from the inn's restaurant strode outside. I waved to him, and as he approached, holding his ears, I shouted and pointed down at Miles.

In a matter of minutes the parking lot was full of people, and an ambulance had been summoned.

The police were also called, and as Miles was carted off, still unconscious, to the nearest hospital, I found myself once again facing Brian across a table.

He looked tired and very grim.

"Do you still think my imagination is running away with me?" I asked before he had a chance to do more than jot down a couple of notes on the little blue pad he was never without.

He sighed and put his pen down. "Explain to me once more what you were doing in a car park at ten o'clock at night."

"I was on my way to Craddock House."

His mouth tightened. "I see. And you heard Friedman groaning, so instead of going for help—"

I also sighed—not very patiently. "I heard the sound of something in pain. It could have been an animal for all I knew. There wasn't any reason to suspect foul play."

"No? Yet you're the one who this very afternoon was suggesting that Kismet Production Company is the front for some nefarious activity."

Was that what I had been suggesting? I suppose it was, although I hadn't thought of it in exactly those terms.

"But I didn't make that connection at that moment. I just heard what sounded like a groan or a moan, and then I noticed Miles's hat lying out in the open. And a moment later I spotted Miles."

He knew all the rest of it. "You didn't see anyone when you first walked outside? Did you pass anyone? Was anyone coming inside the inn as you were going out?"

"No." I thought about it. "I glanced inside the bar as I was walking past, and I saw Roberta and Todd sitting at a table."

"Did you notice anyone else?"

"It was just a split-second look. I barely stopped. Everyone could have been in there; I just happened to see Roberta and Todd."

"And once you left the inn?"

"I didn't notice anyone. I think I would have because it went through my mind how quiet it was."

Apparently that should have been my tip-off that evil was afoot, because Brian gave me another of those disapproving looks. I have to admit, however, his next words caught me off guard.

"Where's Peter Fox?"

I stared at him, trying to decipher what those words meant. They couldn't possibly mean what it sounded like.

"I don't understand," I said finally.

"It's a simple question. Where's Fox? Were you supposed to meet him somewhere?"

I said slowly and carefully, "I was on my way to Craddock House. I—tried phoning him earlier and he didn't answer. Are you saying he's—what *are* you saying?"

Brian's eyes held an expression I'd never seen before. He said bluntly, "We found the February brothers. They were in the barn behind their house. They'd been there for several days—how many we're not sure yet."

"They're dead?" I said. I knew it was a silly question even as I got the words out of my very dry mouth.

"Oh," Brian said with a cold smile, "very dead."

CHAPTER 16

ONE THING I've learned—learned the hard way—is that while people sometimes disappoint, good poetry never does.

When I finally separated from Brian on that long, horrible night, I went up to my room and tried one last time to phone Peter. The phone rang and rang and then the machine picked up.

I replaced the receiver quietly.

For a long time I sat on the edge of the bed, trying to make sense of this latest news bulletin from hell. One thing I had no doubt about: I didn't believe for one second that Peter had killed the February brothers. I didn't even think that Brian really believed it. He just wanted to convince himself of Peter's guilt on general principles—sort of like when the U.S. government goes after mob bosses for tax fraud. Although, assuming Peter was a killer because of his larcenous past seemed to me a stretch.

Certainly, I didn't believe him capable of cold-blooded murder, and it couldn't have been self-defense because he was far too pragmatic to have tried to tackle the Februarys on his own. Which didn't explain where he was or why he'd disappeared.

Assuming he had disappeared voluntarily. Brian refused to entertain any other possibility, but the Februarys had allegedly tried to kill Peter. Twice.

Twice…

Yes, surely two sets of masked gunmen were not after Peter? So it had to be the February brothers both times. Which didn't say much for their success rate. But putting that aside for a moment, since Peter had been convinced he didn't know the Februarys, and they had no reason to want him dead, one obvious possibility was that someone had hired them to eliminate Peter.

And even Peter had admitted that three other people who might conceivably think they had a legitimate grudge were his three former criminal associates from the fateful Istanbul job.

I could see Peter deciding to lie low for a while, but I couldn't believe that he'd disappear without a word to me. Not when he'd followed me all the way to the States. So what did that mean?

I had no idea what it meant. And it was late, and I was tired, and I already been through one of the worst days of my life. One thing I did firmly believe: Peter was well able to look after himself. So there was nothing to be gained working myself into a state. A bigger state than I was already in.

Resolutely, I told myself I would wait to hear from Peter, and until then I would refuse to give into nerves and dread. I took a long, long hot shower, and crawled into the large, very comfortable bed. I picked up my copy of *Letty Landon* and determinedly began to read. I turned pages for some time, but my gaze kept straying from the yellowed paper to rest unseeingly on the cabbage-rose drapes closing out the world from my literary cocoon. I stared at the flowers and the box of chocolates on my dresser.

Peter loved me. I knew that. We had been through enough over the past couple of years that I did know—believe—that he loved me. But I was also experienced enough to know that love doesn't necessarily conquer all.

Letty Landon, case in point. Following the abrupt end of her engagement to John Forster, who apparently couldn't resist telling his side of the scandalous story—such as it was—to everyone who would listen, Letty, at the height of her writing powers and popularity abruptly made the decision to marry the governor of Cape Coast Castle in West Africa and leave behind everything and everyone she knew, for a foreign and dangerous land. All for a man who had likely concealed the fact that he was already unofficially married to a local native woman—a man who might have ultimately murdered his troublesome English bride.

Despite my research, I didn't really feel that I'd come to know Laetitia Landon. It was difficult getting a real handle on her motivations from reading the Enfield and Ashton biographies.

Both writers took such an unsympathetic and deprecating view of the poetess—both her work and her character.

In fact, both biographers claimed Letty was creatively burned out and personally disgraced by the time she retreated to what was then called the "Dark Continent." I was surprised by my own defensive reaction to their conclusions. At thirty-five Letty had certainly reached an age when an unmarried woman was officially considered "on the shelf"; but despite the rumors that surrounded her, she was still welcomed in polite and literary society, she was still a notable celebrity, and she was still continuing to produce commercially successful prose and poetry.

Clearly something beyond her childhood fascination with the place must have motivated her choice to depart for Africa, especially since Governor George MacLean was such an unprepossessing specimen. Did she really flee because she couldn't stand to be gossiped about or to bear the indignity of spinsterhood? Surely somewhere in all of Great Britain there was a quiet corner where she was unknown—and a man willing to marry a still attractive and gifted woman?

Laetitia Landon remained an enigma to me—and to her biographers, I suspected.

Once again, I studied the portrait of her in *L.E.L.: A Mystery of the Thirties*. Letty smiled vaguely across the decades.

■■■■■

I think I'd half hoped that my sleep would be disturbed by a phone call from Peter, but no call came.

The next time I opened my eyes it was morning, and wan, rainy daylight spilled through the parting of the draperies. It was after ten o'clock in the morning, but the lateness of the hour didn't matter. Even if it had not been the weekend there would be no filming today. In fact, I suspected that the production of *Dangerous to Know* might now be halted once and for all.

I dressed and went downstairs. As I walked past the lobby heading for the dining room, Roberta was hanging up the pay phone—the only long distance line available to the guests of the inn.

"How's Miles?" I asked.

She shoved her dark curls back with an impatient hand. "*Apparently* that stupid cowboy hat saved his life. *Apparently* God looks after fools, drunks, and men with no clothes sense!" She seemed more frazzled than relieved. "He's got a mild concussion. They're keeping him for observation until this afternoon."

"That's good news," I said.

She looked at me like she didn't understand the words. Then she blinked. "Yes. Of course it is. It's wonderful." She stared at the phone again.

"Is something wrong?" I added, "I mean, besides all the obvious things that are wrong."

She gave me another of those deer-in-the-headlights looks, then she said, "I have no idea what to do. When they release her body—Mona's, I mean—we've got to get her back to the States. Her daughter is asking when that's going to happen. I have no idea!"

I had no idea either, but I knew the place to start. "I can talk to DI Drummond for you."

She nodded. I had the feeling she wasn't really listening to me. I asked, "Was Mona married?"

"Divorced. She has two daughters, I think."

I waited to see if she wanted to add anything, but she turned away and began dialing the phone again.

Making my way to the dining room, I found the mood there as dismal as the weather on display out the wet-streaked windows. Todd and Tracy were sharing a rasher of bacon between them. A few members of the crew and production team sat quietly talking and eating at other tables.

Todd waved me over. "'eard anything, luv?"

"Miles is going to be all right."

"We already know that," Tracy said. "You're friends with the police. What do they have to say about Mona?"

I said, surprising myself with my own testiness, "I just woke up. I haven't talked to the police this morning. Sometimes I go entire days without talking to the police."

She gave me a long, narrow look. Todd laughed. "All on edge, that's our trouble!" He pushed the plate of bacon my way. "'ave some breakfast, luv."

I shook my head, nauseated by the greasy pile of meat. British bacon is more like ham or Canadian bacon. I prefer my bacon in crisp paper-thin strips. The way God intended.

"I'll have some tea in a minute."

Todd said confidentially, "What everyone really wants to know is—"

"Are we canceling the production?" finished Tracy.

"I haven't heard."

"Not if I have anything to say about it," Roberta said from behind me.

We all jumped guiltily, although our doubt was reasonable enough, given the number of catastrophes.

Todd and Tracy were, of course, relieved and happy—in an appropriately subdued fashion. I studied Roberta curiously. "*Do* you have anything to say about it?"

"What's that supposed to mean?"

"Don't the investors or the board of directors at Kismet have the final word about this string of bad luck and tragic deaths?"

"There hasn't been any bad luck—other than the deaths."

"I think Miles might disagree with your idea of bad luck."

"You think people don't get mugged in California?"

So that was the theory of choice for the attack on Miles? That he had been mugged? In a village that hadn't had a mugging in five years? I didn't particularly want to argue with Roberta, but I simply couldn't believe she was still intending to proceed with the production. I said, "Just from a practical standpoint, you're now talking about replacing two of the original cast members. Or were you hoping to hire Lady Vee to play herself in the film?"

"Believe me, it won't be difficult to find an elderly out-of-work British actress in this country," Roberta replied. "We'll just have to reshoot Mona's scenes."

Tracy put in flatly, "What do you care? You're picking up a paycheck. Your book is being filmed. I would think you'd be glad that Kismet is committed to this project." Her gaze was blue and gelid.

All three of them stared at me with various degrees of distrust.

I said, "The contents of Mona's flask haven't been analyzed yet. You're all assuming that she overdosed on—on alfalfa sprouts or something, but what if she didn't?"

"You think someone would kill Mona?" Roberta looked at me with incredulity. "Did you *know* Mona? Why would anyone want to kill her? What would the reason be?"

"Maybe someone with a grudge against the production?" Todd offered doubtfully. The other two rounded on him in exasperation. He shrugged. "Saw a film like that once."

"Don't you think it's a bit of a coincidence that Mona finds her missing flask in the lobby and the next time she drinks from it she conveniently falls dead?"

"Nobody knows for sure she died from drinking what was in the flask!" Roberta said. "The police are assuming that. She might have had a stroke or some kind of seizure. She might have had an allergic reaction to something at the tea party."

Either Roberta had a gift for self-deception like no one I'd ever met before, or I really was becoming paranoid.

Tracy was watching me with narrowed eyes. "Mona was always losing that flask. Why should yesterday have been any different?"

Since this was the very thing I'd brought up to the police, I was surprised that I had apparently come up with an answer. "Maybe that's why someone chose to poison her that way. Mona was the oldest member of this production. She knew everyone, knew everyone's history, everyone's back-story. Maybe she knew or had learned something about someone here."

"What?" asked Todd.

"Who?" asked Tracy.

Now *that* I didn't have an answer for, so I was surprised to hear myself say, "Maybe she knew who killed Walter."

The silence was deafening. I had the impression that everyone in the dining room stopped eating to stare at me. Not so much as a clink of glass or scrape of fork on china penetrated that hush.

But of course that was my imagination. No one actually stopped eating or talking except my three companions. The listening stillness emanated from them. From one of them in particular, but I couldn't quite figure out who. In fact, I wasn't sure a moment later whether I had imagined that strange, quiet moment.

Roberta had gone so white, I wondered whether she was about to faint. "What are you saying?"

I said slowly, feeling my way to the truth of it, "It's possible, isn't it? Walter was killed in an unsolved hit-and-run. Everyone assumes it was just an accident or that—" I glanced at Roberta "—someone else, such as Peter, was the intended victim. But what if Walter *was* the target? What if he was murdered?"

Tracy sighed and pushed her chair back. "I don't know what you're smoking, Grace, but I hope it's usually more fun than this. I'm going to go get my nails done. Will someone let me know later on if we're canceling the production? I'll need to let my agent know."

She walked away, passing Norton on his way into the dining room. He looked ghastly as he took a seat at our table. Pale, blue-jawed, eyes rimmed in red. He looked like the expendable cast member hiding A Guilty Secret in a schlocky thriller.

Roberta said furiously, keeping her voice low with an effort, "Why would anyone kill *Walter*? What would the motive be for killing Walter?"

Todd watched us in fascination, Norton in horror.

"I don't know. I'm saying, isn't it a possibility? Couldn't one thing be connected to the other?"

"No, they couldn't. Because there's nothing to connect." Roberta also pushed back from the table. "If you'll excuse me, I have some phone calls to make. I'm trying to save all of our jobs for us."

In the wake of her departure, I turned back to Todd and Norton. They stared back at me. After a moment, Todd said cheerfully, "Sure you won't have some bacon, luv?"

■■■■■

Driving out to Craddock House an hour later I was forced to concede that Mona had not seemed like someone who knew another person's potentially fatal secret. True, she seemed to know every member of the cast's life history, but she seemed neither like the kind of person who made moral judgments nor went around blabbing. Nor had she appeared to be the possessor of dangerous knowledge. In fact, it would be harder to find anyone more relaxed and comfortable than Mona on the last afternoon of her life.

I pulled up outside Craddock House and sat watching while the rain ticked down on the Citroën—leaking in the poorly sealed windows.

The shop was dark. There was no sign of anyone at home upstairs. No lights, no smoke from the chimney. I told myself I hadn't expected it, that I would have been dismayed if Peter had been there and hadn't contacted me, but it was still somehow daunting.

I saw no indication that the police were watching the house waiting for Peter's return, but I supposed they could be hiding in the woods with binoculars. And if Brian was out there I hoped rain was trickling down the back of his neck.

At length I got out of the car, opened my umbrella, and ran up the flagstones to the door of Rogue's Gallery. I unlocked the door and let myself into the shop, my eyes adjusting to the gloom. I could see a platoon of little tin soldiers, an old ship's wheel, and a gentleman's top hat sitting on a hatbox marked B. BASILE, BRUSSELS. For some reason these items struck me as terribly poignant as I stood there in the silent, empty shop listening to the rain.

Why had I come here? I wasn't even sure. I suppose I wanted to see if I could find some hint of where Peter might have gone—as unlikely as it was that he'd carelessly leave a copy of his escape itinerary—or an extra airline ticket.

If Peter wanted me to know where he was, he'd have told me. If he were able. And if he weren't...

But I refused to believe that. Peter was the most self-sufficient person I'd ever met.

After a moment I shook off my apathy and went upstairs. Using my key to let myself into Peter's living quarters, I closed the door behind me—and instantly realized there was someone in the flat.

Floorboards squeaked. In Peter's bedroom, a drawer slid open and a moment later, closed.

Heart pounding, I stood there—caught between fear and hope. In the end, hope won. I started softly across the floor. I hadn't taken more than a step or two when the outline of a man filled the bedroom doorway.

For a moment Peter and I stared at each other. His eyes were blue as the heart of a flame. I'd never seen that look on his face. He looked…terrifying somehow: his face hard with tension, his mouth thin and unsmiling—and those blazing eyes.

"I…" For once I ran out of things to say.

He didn't exactly relax, but the fierce lines of his face eased. "I was coming to see you."

Was he? He was carrying his black Gladstone bag. He was going away.

I said, "Then you know the Februarys are dead?"

He looked blank for a moment. Then, if possible, his face grew more implacable. He said, "I want you to go home, Grace. I want you to go back to the States."

Whatever I'd expected to hear, it wasn't that. "You're serious?"

"Never more so." He certainly looked serious. Grim as death.

"Do I get an explanation?"

"Not just yet."

"Really?" I began to get angry. "But someday? Maybe in a decade or so when you make another trip to the States?"

He said curtly—and his tone was as foreign to me as his expression, "Don't be ridiculous."

"Well, I'll try not to be." I added, "But you have me at a disadvantage here. I thought we were going to—"

"Oh, for Christ's sake!" he interrupted. "This has nothing to do with us! Surely I don't have to explain that to you?"

"You sure as hell need to explain *something* to me!" I yelled. "You just disappear for a day and then you calmly show up and tell me to go back to California, and that you'll explain it to me the next time you're in town. Do you realize the police think you killed the Februarys?"

"I didn't even know they were dead," he said, all at once sounding perfectly calm. "Look, I know I'm being...rather mysterious. Can you not just this once trust me?"

I gaped at him—there's probably no other word to describe my open-mouthed and indignant stare. "*This once?* When have I not trusted you? Maybe it would be easier to trust you if you'd let me know what's going on. Something has obviously happened."

"Yes, something has happened. And no, you don't trust me." He smiled, but it was a peculiar smile. "You love me, but that's not quite the same thing, is it? I can't keep proving myself to you, Grace. Sooner or later you have to take me on faith—or admit that this isn't what you really want."

I felt like something had rushed out of the darkness and thrown me to the ground. Where had this come from? What were we really talking about? Suddenly everything I cared about seemed to be at stake, and I hadn't even realized my dreams were on the table.

My mouth felt dry, my heart tripping against my breastbone as I choked out, "Maybe what you mean is, this isn't what *you* really want."

He shook his head. "You were gone *six months*." And then his gaze met mine. "Would you have come back if I hadn't followed you?"

"I was booking my flight that week."

That strange smile again. "But you didn't. Even after I arrived it took you a few days to actually buy the airline ticket."

I opened my mouth to argue this, to explain why...but I couldn't seem to find the words. I knew he wouldn't believe me.

Peter said quite gently, "I think this is the truth. The romantic in you would like to believe you can be happy here away from your home and friends and family. But I think the pragmatic Miss Hollister who lives deep down inside knows that you can't be happy without trust, and you can't trust someone you don't know—and I don't think that even now you feel that you know me well enough to trust me. And I don't believe that you ever will."

This was not the conversation I had anticipated having with

Peter—not that I had anticipated having a conversation, but if I had thought about it, I'd have pictured him on the defense trying to explain to me why he hadn't gone to the police with whatever had happened to make him stand me up the night before. It hadn't occurred to me that he might simply pull the plug because...

It was getting to be too much work? Because he didn't love me? Because this was a smoke screen to keep me from pursuing why he was trying to pack me off to the States?

Anyone of those—or even a combination—might be the real answer.

I said quietly, "So if I'm not willing to take on faith your assertion that I need to go home and not pester you with questions about attempted and actual murder...then, what? Our relationship is over?"

"If you're not willing to take me on faith," he said equally calm, "our relationship *is* over."

I felt as if I were staring at a stranger—and I supposed that confirmed at least part of the point he was trying to make. "I take it you're not planning to stop off and talk to Brian before you head out to wherever you're going." I nodded at his Gladstone.

"I'm not, no."

"I see. Well, good luck, then," I said. "If you change your mind, you know where to find me."

Something changed in his face. There was an emotion in his eyes I couldn't quite pinpoint. He said, "I'll see you out."

But I was already moving to the door. "That's all right," I replied. "I believe you already did."

CHAPTER 17

"ARE YOU all right?" Cordelia asked.

I turned from watching the rain running in silver rivulets down the window overlooking the wet and glistening gardens of Rothay Manor. "Yes. Why?"

"Because you've been scowling at that soup since it arrived."

I made an effort to shake off my preoccupation. When I had returned to the Hound and Harrier this morning I'd found a message from Cordelia asking me to lunch. And because I thought it would be good for her to get out after the trauma of seeing Mona die—and because I thought it would be good for me as well, the awful scene with Peter coming on top of my sorrow over Mona—I'd suggested a nice long drive and lunch at Rothay Manor in Coniston by Ambleside.

Ambleside is one of the loveliest and most popular destinations within the Lake District. Centrally located, and only about six hours from London, it offers everything from charming shops to rambling lakeside walks—or even a challenging mountain climb. The town predates the Roman occupation, and of course Ambleside was the home of William Wordsworth in the later years of his life. He's buried beneath a yew tree in the churchyard at St. Oswald's where the River Rothay flows.

It was a not a day for sightseeing, though, even if either of us had been in the mood. The drive had been longer than usual due to the dreadful weather, but that, too, had given me something to think of besides Peter—and murder. Not that the two things were inextricably linked in my mind, although I wasn't feeling terribly friendly to Peter at the moment.

Cordelia had been unusually quiet on the drive, whether

because she believed I needed all my concentration to keep us from floating off the road into the nearest lake, or because she was still feeling overwhelmed at the previous day's tragedy.

I said, "The soup is excellent. I'm just…"

"I know," she said, and she shivered. "I've never seen anyone dead before. Let alone…die."

"I'm sorry," I said. "Do you want to talk about it?"

She shook her head, but then her fawn-like gaze met mine. "She looked at me like she wanted me to help her. She put her hand out." She stopped, swallowing hard.

I said, "It must have been very quick. She probably didn't…" I stumbled a little "…suffer very long."

Cordelia nodded, unconvinced. After a moment, she asked, "Why would anyone kill her?"

"It's not certain that anyone did," I said. "It could have been an accident, I suppose."

"Is that what you really think?"

"No," I admitted. "But my view has become warped living here."

She giggled shakily, and returned to spooning up her passion-fruit sorbet, which served as palate-cleanser between courses. Then her hand stilled. "They found those men. Did you see in *The Clarion* that their bodies were discovered—the men who shot at us the other day, I mean." She shivered. "They'd been killed 'execution-style' according to the paper."

To my astonishment I heard myself say, "The police think Peter might have been involved."

Cordelia scoffed loudly at this notion. "Oh, pshaw!" Despite the tone of teenage cynicism, she sounded so much like her great-aunt, I blinked. "You mean *Brian* thinks," she said. Her instant and total repudiation of the idea of Peter's guilt reassured me. Illogical as that might have been.

I finished my soup—cream of mushroom with a hint of dill—and my glass of wine.

Cordelia said, "Why do you think someone would have killed her? She didn't seem like the kind of person to be murdered."

Was there a particular kind of person who got murdered? I didn't know.

I said, "Supposedly the basic reasons people kill are greed—maybe that includes jealousy and lust—revenge and fear. Well, and insanity, but I guess you could argue that anyone who resorts to murder is partly insane."

"Or accidents," Cordelia said. "People who are killed by mistake."

"You don't poison someone by mistake."

"Well, if you mixed ingredients up. If you were making salad for someone and you mixed up mushrooms and toadstools or something like that. Or if you used some kind of corrosive cleaning fluid and didn't get it all washed away."

I gazed at her in mild horror. "But that would just be an accident."

She frowned thoughtfully. "Well, but what if you knew about the toadstools, but meant for someone else to eat the salad, only your friend dropped by and ate it instead."

I said, "Who are you and what have you done with my dear little friend Cordelia?"

She giggled. "*Little.* I wish I was little." She was in fact very nearly six feet tall, and model-thin—and had not figured out how to use this to her advantage yet. "It's possible, though, isn't it? Because Mona really didn't seem like the sort of person who gets herself done in. Do you suppose they'll cancel the film now?"

"Roberta doesn't want to, but I don't see how they can help it." Or perhaps I didn't want to see how they could help it. I was still trying to decide whether there was any point in staying on in the Lake District if Peter and I were no longer lovers. Surprisingly, it wasn't a straightforward yes or no.

Cordelia said, "That's a pity. I could have used the experience."

I didn't respond to that and she chattered on about acting and school and—eventually—Douglas, the married-but-separated playwright. I listened with half an ear, running through my last conversation with Peter while I poked at my savory crêpes with spinach and bacon filling, and watched the windows of the restaurant fog with rain and mist.

"I think he missed you a lot."

It was the silence that followed Cordelia's words that jerked me out of my reflections. It took me a moment to rewind the last few seconds of her conversation. "Who?"

"Peter. He didn't say much, but it was obvious."

I couldn't imagine him saying *anything* about it, let alone "much." I hated myself for asking, but I couldn't help it. "How was it obvious?"

She shrugged a bony shoulder. "He was just…different. Quiet. Preoccupied. He used to go out walking a lot."

"Walking?" I couldn't picture that.

She nodded. "Well, until it got to be winter. Then I think he just stayed home and read." She added neutrally, "I think he expected you to come back sooner. We all did."

She was frowning at me from beneath her dark brows, and something in that look of hers made me feel guilty. I said briskly, "Somehow I can't picture him moping around."

"He wasn't moping. He was just…quieter." Yes, her tone was definitely critical.

"I meant to," I admitted. "Things just kept…coming up." I remembered something. "Yesterday at tea your great-aunt mentioned Allegra and Peter. You made a face…"

Cordelia grimaced. "Oh. Al was over there all the time. They all were. All the ladies of the county. I think Roy Blade finally told her off. That's why she left, you know. Mr. Blade told her she was making a nuisance of herself, and she got offended and went on a holiday cruise."

"I see." Which was a sweeping overstatement. I was floundering, trying to picture our biker librarian telling one of our favorite aristos—a woman he was rather sweet on himself—to stop pestering the local ex-jewel thief with her attentions.

Cordelia laughed. "I expect that's why Peter really wanted you back, so you'd scare the femme fatales off again."

"Just a poor helpless rabbit hypnotized by all those snakes,"

I said dryly, but I admit I was feeling more uneasy by the moment.

"He missed you, Grace. We all did. He just missed you more."

The candor of that left me with nothing say.

■■■■■

When I returned to the Hound and Harrier that afternoon, I learned from the girl at the desk that Miles had been discharged from the hospital that afternoon. Roberta and the others were in the bar, and the mood seemed much more cheerful than that morning's. Roberta waved and called out to me as I was trying to slink past the doorway. As I didn't want to continue the hostilities, I went to join them.

Norton nodded in greeting. He still looked very under the weather. Pammy didn't look particularly well either.

"What are you drinkin', luv?" Todd inquired, getting to his feet.

"Gin and tonic," I said. I didn't think I would ever drink Irish coffee again.

As Todd moved off, my thoughts returned to the Februarys trying to kill him in mistake for Peter—unless the Februarys had been hired to further disrupt the production? But no, that couldn't be, because they had first attempted to kill Peter before *Dangerous to Know* had even moved to the Lake District.

And yet it was one more strange connection between Peter and this film.

Twice the Februarys had tried to kill Peter and failed. Was that because they weren't very good at killing people? Or were they not really supposed to succeed in their attempts on Peter's life? In which case, what purpose was served by these attacks? Attacks that could have injured or killed many people. Surely this spoke to a uniquely ruthless mentality?

"The police were looking for you, Grace," Tracy said maliciously, interrupting my reflections.

"Not very hard, apparently." The others laughed, though I was quite serious. "Any word on Mona's death?"

"No." That was Pammy. She looked very grim.

"Not that they're saying," Roberta said. "But it's the weekend. I suppose the crime lab or whatever they call it here is closed 'til Monday."

"Were you able to get through to your home office?"

Her face tightened. "No. But it's the weekend."

Norton, who I now realized was not under the weather so much as quietly smashed, looked up from his glass and said, "I'm leaving as soon as the cops give us permission."

Pammy groaned and put her face in her hands.

"You have a contract," Roberta reminded him.

"I don't care. I'm flying home as soon as they say we're free to go."

"Look. We're all still upset. Let's not make any rash decisions until we've had time to consider."

He stared at her in disgust, shook his head, and returned to brooding over his glass.

"Well, I'm in for the duration," Tracy said. "I need this film."

"I'll say. You need *any* film," Norton retorted, surfacing briefly.

Tracy opened her mouth and then closed it. If looks could kill, Norton would have been groping for the knife in his back.

Todd brought me my drink and took his seat again. "Where's Peter? The coppers were asking about him, and Tracy said the shop's closed."

"I don't know where he is," I answered. "He's frequently away on buying trips." I stared at Tracy, who gave me a sweet smile in return.

"Always was a bit of a scallywag, old Peter." Todd seemed amused at the idea. "You should have seen him in the old days."

I tried to imagine meeting Peter in his criminous old days. I couldn't imagine that we'd have had a lot to say to each other.

"How's Miles?" I asked the table in general.

"You can ask him yourself," Roberta said, looking past me. "Miles, what the hell are you doing down here?"

Miles, one hand steadying himself on the table edge, sat carefully down in the chair next to me. There was a white square of gauze on the back of his head. He smelled rather strongly of antiseptic and hospital. "I can't relax up there," he said. "I can't take naps. I'm not a nap-taking kind of guy."

He answered the questions about his health brusquely.

I asked, "Do you have any idea of who attacked you?"

He started to shake his head, stopped, and said carefully, "No. I didn't see a thing. I went out to the car to grab my jacket. Next thing I knew I was in an ambulance and some limey bastard was asking me how many fingers he was holding up." He glanced at Todd. "No offense."

"None taken," said Todd. He made a rude gesture. "How many fingers am *I* holding up?"

"Two," said Miles, clearly not getting it.

Pammy frowned at Todd. Norton nearly spilled his drink laughing.

Tracy said, "Miles, are we going ahead with the production?"

I thought that was an interesting question coming from her. I'd got the impression that they were a couple, but that sounded like they hadn't spoken since Miles was bashed over the head. So either the romance wasn't proceeding smoothly or Miles could have given Peter lessons in not communicating well with significant others.

"Why wouldn't we?" he answered Tracy shortly.

He looked to Pammy. She shrugged. He looked to Roberta who said, "I don't know. I haven't been able to reach anyone in New York."

New York? I'd been thinking they were based in Hollywood. But I suppose that made sense. The money, the power brokers would be in New York.

"The answer is yes," Miles told Tracy. "We're going ahead."

"You don't know that." That was Norton, surfacing once again from his alcohol-induced stupor. He held Miles's gaze challengingly.

Miles retorted, "Let's put it this way, if I have anything to say about it, we're not pulling the plug."

"The show must go on!" Norton said with sarcasm.

"That's right, Edam, the show must go on. We've all got to eat.

We've all got mortgages to pay. What happened yesterday was a tragedy, but canceling the production isn't going to bring Mona back—Mona was a trooper. She'd want us to carry on."

Norton sneered, "What the hell do you know or care about what Mona ever wanted?"

There was an uncomfortable silence.

"What do *you*?" Miles returned finally. "I knew Mona for twenty years. How long did you know her?" He reached into his shirt pocket and withdrew a small flask.

"I knew her well enough to—"

"Are you out of your mind?" Roberta demanded, cutting right across Norton's low voice. "You can't drink alcohol with a head injury!"

"I'm past the point of danger," Miles said, unscrewing the top to his silver flask. We all watched as he took a swig.

And as Miles indulged in his teatime cocktail I knew why Mona had died. Or, rather, in whose place she had died.

CHAPTER 18

WHAT I DIDN'T know was why anyone wanted Miles dead.

I'd heard plenty about Miles's womanizing ways, but did people really kill each other over that kind of thing? My knowledge of such matters was strictly relegated to reading *People* magazine in the dentist's office. True, Mona had apparently tried to kill Miles during—or was it after?—their affair, but since Mona was the one who had died, I didn't think that was relevant.

Tracy's affair with Miles seemed to have cooled considerably, but Tracy didn't seem like the sort of woman who killed for passion. She didn't seem to have a passionate bone in her body. She was sexy, yes. Very. Men found her very sexy, anyway. But it seemed to me that passionate and sexy were not necessarily the same thing.

Besides, the day of Lady Vee's tea party, Tracy and Miles were still cooing like lovebirds and feeding each other cake like newlyweds. True, she would have ample opportunity to spike his flask, but by the same token she'd have been unlikely to get the flask mixed up with Mona's.

"What an expression you have, Grace," Roberta commented, her gaze screened by those cat's-eye glasses.

"I just remembered what a lot of work I have to do this evening," I said. "I should go up to my room."

"We won't be shooting tomorrow. It's Sunday. Stay and have another drink."

I smiled, rising. "I don't think I'd better. I still have to work on my book this evening."

Todd said, "Stay, and I'll tell you about the time Pierce—er, Peter—had a skinful of French champagne and decided to borrow a houseboat on the Seine."

"I'm sure Grace has heard all Peter's stories about the good old days," Tracy drawled.

"Oh, I doubt that!" Todd said with a little smirk.

■■■■■

"Cyanide probably," Brian told me over cheese toasties and pints at the Cock's Crow later that evening. "We can't be sure 'til we've had a look at the coroner's findings, but...every indication is of cyanide. The flask even smelled like bitter almonds."

I said, "I think I know who the intended victim was. What I don't know is why anyone wants Miles Friedman dead." I explained why I believed Mona's flask had been laced with poison when the intended victim had probably been Miles, finishing, "I think there may have been earlier attempts on his life, as well. The brakes went out on his car a couple of times before he left the States. Everyone assumed it was shoddy work on the part of his garage, but looking back...I think those failed brakes may have been someone's first try."

"If these attempts began in the States..."

"Yes. It would have to be someone in the cast or crew."

"You don't have any idea of whom?"

"I do, actually. I think Roberta Lom might have a grudge against him. They were lovers at one time, and they share responsibility for this film. There might be some kind of insurance policy or clause in case the film fails or is cancelled. Something along those lines. I was thinking you might be able to check into that."

"I suppose I could." He made some notes. "That's it?"

"Well, the problem with Roberta as a suspect is, I don't believe she would have mistakenly murdered Mona. She knew that Mona had a flask, and she knew Mona kept misplacing it. I really think whoever killed Mona killed her by mistake, but that means the murderer has to be sort of...oblivious."

"Oblivious?"

"Well, either that, or so focused on killing Miles that nothing else really impinged on her—or his—consciousness."

"And does someone in this motley crew strike you as particularly oblivious?"

"Well, of course I don't know all the crew members, but Tracy Burke seems fairly self-preoccupied. Then again, I don't like her so maybe I'm not the best judge. Norton Edam is pretty much oblivious. He drinks a lot and he seems to really dislike Miles—so much that I'm surprised he agreed to work on this project. Although I don't suppose his career is at a point where he could turn work down. I don't know what his motive would be, though. The only thing anyone seems to have accused Miles of is womanizing. There hasn't been any suggestion that he ever sabotaged someone's career—or is even a particularly bad director."

"Norton Edam." Brian made another note.

"And I already mentioned Tracy. One of the actresses. Miles has been seeing her."

"The one playing you," Brian said, grinning.

"You had to say that, didn't you?"

"You have to admit—"

"No, I don't. In fact, I refuse to admit any such thing."

He laughed. "So the lovely Tracy and Miles are lovers?"

"Well, they were. There seems to be a chill in the air between them—and suddenly there's *a lot* of air between them."

I glanced at the fire crackling in the stone fireplace a few feet from our table. It was very warm in the pub, but a shiver rippled down my spine as I said, "I think the attack on Miles was motivated by sheer rage. Rage at having failed again to kill him. Or maybe rage at having killed the wrong person. Whoever struck Miles unconscious took a terrible chance. It was luck he didn't see his attacker, or that someone else didn't see them in the parking lot. I think someone willing to take that kind of a chance must have a powerful motive, and it seems to me that such a motive would show up with very little investigating."

He snorted. "I'll try not to take offense at that. Is that your entire list of suspects?"

"Well, everyone bears looking into, naturally."

"Naturally."

"But those are the people who seem the most likely to me. Although…none of them really seem *that* likely. None of them seem like the kind of people who commit murders."

"If there's one thing you should know by now," Brian said, "it's that no particular type of person commits murders."

"Speaking of which," I said, "what's happening with the investigation into the deaths of the February brothers?"

His expression changed. Closed. "You know I can't discuss the case with you."

I didn't think it would be wise to point out that he was willing to discuss the *other* part of the case with me.

"But you *are* making headway?"

"Yes."

"Can you at least tell me when they died? That will be a matter of public record shortly."

He sighed. "The coroner is setting the time of death sometime after eleven o'clock on Wednesday night. And before you say anything, I'm already aware that you were with Peter Fox at least part of Wednesday evening because Tracy Burke was able to confirm it."

Now there was irony: having to be grateful to Tracy for corroborating the alibi I was going to supply Peter.

I said, "Peter and I were together the entire night—until seven o'clock the following morning."

He sighed. "Grace—"

"It's true, Brian. Surely you know me well enough by now to know that I wouldn't lie to protect Peter if I believed he was guilty of murder?"

"I suppose not," he said grudgingly. "But just because you don't believe it doesn't mean it's not true."

"I would know if Peter were capable of killing someone in cold blood. If Peter were the kind of man capable of cold-blooded murder he wouldn't be who he is."

"Don't push it," Brian said dryly. "I believe you if you say you were with him the night of the twenty-fourth. I'm not buying the plaster-saint makeover."

"Fine. Don't. But isn't Peter entitled to the same protections and freedoms as anyone else in this country?"

He was silent.

"I believe your original suspicion was correct. I believe these attacks on Peter were made by—or, rather, hired by—criminal associates. But not like you think. Not current associates. I think these are past acquaintances. I think this has to do with the jewel robbery that went wrong in Istanbul."

"Not the Curse of the Serpent's Egg again," Brian said, shaking his head.

"I think so. Because nothing else makes sense. According to Peter, they broke into Topkapi with a six-man team. Well, technically a five-man—person—team including him. After they stole the jewel, Peter and Catriona Ruthven were cornered. He gave her the jewel and a few moments' head start. He was taken prisoner. She escaped and eventually handed the jewel off to their fence, the man who had brokered the heist. His name was Gordon Roget and he disappeared with the jewel. The problem is, the only people who knew Peter didn't have the Serpent's Egg for longer than a minute or two were Catriona and Roget. And neither of them apparently bothered to tell the remaining three thieves."

"And you think these remaining criminal confederates are now out to get Peter?"

"I think it's a possibility. I know Peter thinks it's a possibility, whether he's willing to admit it or not. Until that possibility arose, I think he was truly bewildered as to why anyone would want him dead."

Brian's eyes looked almost dark in the firelight. "Do you know the names of these men?"

I shook my head.

"That's why you're telling me this," he said slowly.

"Yes," I admitted. "You have the resources to find out who these men were. Or at least you have a better chance of finding out than I would since I would have no idea even where to start."

"Do you know where Fox is?"

"No."

"Is he looking for these men?"

I tried to consider this objectively. "I don't think so. At least… he didn't seem to have any interest in pursuing it. He may have thought better of it." I remembered that awful morning…in fact, it had been *this* very morning, although it felt like days ago. Peter had been...angry. Shocked, I thought. I hadn't registered it at the time. I had been too angry and shocked myself.

Now it occurred to me that something had happened to him. Something had changed his attitude. What? He had been fine the day before. We had talked and laughed, and he had not seemed to take my suspicions about his former cronies in crime all that seriously.

That evening he had stood me up without a word, and when I saw him the following morning he had been packing to leave—and he had told me to go home to the States.

So what had happened in the interim?

A little wearily, Brian said, "All right, Grace. I'll look into it. I'm not making any promises, mind. But I will look into it."

■■■■■

What had happened to change Peter between Friday morning and Saturday? The question still haunted me after I had undressed and climbed into bed that night with my Laetitia Landon book.

Though my eyes moved down the faded pages describing L.E.L.'s strange engagement to Governor MacLean, little registered on my consciousness. This was not a part of her story I enjoyed or understood. It seemed clear from the exchange of letters that MacLean had serious doubts about marrying Landon—in one letter to Letty's brother he had even denied the engagement existed. He had done everything but flat-out refuse to marry her, citing—mostly—that the Cape was no place for a gently bred white woman. Why he hadn't simply and finally cried off was a mystery to me—second only to the mystery of Landon's determination to marry *him* and leave England.

She had been deserted once; perhaps that was part of it. She bore the burden for supporting her family, financing them through her prolific literary output, and perhaps she sought stability and security of her own—if so, it seemed to be the stability and security of a reed buffeted by the wind.

At first her friends tried to talk her out of it. Later they rallied and—for the most part—supported her decision. Her enemies seemed mostly amused by her odd choice. No one seemed to believe the marriage would last. No one except Laetitia Landon.

As the date of her wedding drew nearer she settled all family business, completed all her works in progress, sold her home, and gave away the possessions she could not take with her. She made her farewells. MacLean would not consider a formal wedding, so they married in a parish church with only their witnesses in attendance.

A short time later they sailed for Africa on the *Governor MacLean.*

In "The Polar Star," written on that long, horrible voyage that Landon spent mostly sick in her cabin, she wrote:

Fresh from the pain it was to part—
How could I bear the pain?
Yet strong the omen in my heart
That says—we meet again.

I laid aside my book, took my spectacles off, and frowned into the distance of memory. One thing that I knew for sure that had happened to Peter yesterday was that he had gone to deliver a pair of chairs to the Honourable Angela Hornsby.

And what in the world could have happened to rock him so at the estate of a middle-aged Member of Parliament? Probably nothing. It was very unlikely, but what else did I have to go on?

Brian had said he would check into Peter's unknown accomplices in Istanbul, and I knew he would. He had given his word. But I had no idea how long that might take—and there was no guarantee that the answer to the attempts on Peter's life lay in Istanbul. Perhaps the solution was closer to home than I'd dreamed.

Perhaps the solution lay on the other side of the sleeping village: yet another secret concealed within the walls of the old Monkton Estate.

CHAPTER 19

I SPENT SUNDAY morning making phone calls from Sally Smithwick's house. I couldn't take the risk of being overheard phoning from the downstairs lobby at the Hound and Harrier; so I called my sister-in-law, Laurel, from Sally's kitchen while Sally fed me cocoa and gingerbread cake, and her enormous black cat—formerly belonging to Miss Webb of the Innisdale Historical Society—watched me balefully from the sunny window seat.

"Am I going to help you solve a mystery?" Laurel asked. "Not that I'm unhappy to sit and read *People* magazines all day, but is there a higher purpose?"

"I hope so," I said. "It's a long shot. But Miles seems pretty predictable in his habits—and his tastes."

"Okay. I'm on it," Laurel assured me. "I meant to ask: how are things going with Peter?"

"Ah," I said. "Interesting."

"Good interesting or bad interesting?"

"Oh, you know."

"Or…you-can't-talk-right-now interesting?"

"That would be it," I said.

"Gotcha. Do I call you back at this number or wait to hear from you?"

"If you find something, leave a message at the Hound and Harrier, and I'll run over here and call you back."

Laurel agreed, I rang off, and Sally, who was cleaning up the morning dishes, said, "The papers are full of that poor actress lady. I didn't realize she was the one from that police show. *Blue Angel.* It ran over here for a few years."

"What do the papers say?" I asked.

"Oh, you know. Mostly they go on about the time she tried to shoot that director, Mr. Friedman. And they talk about her marriage to that actor. The one who died in that car wreck. And then her second marriage to that other actor. The one she divorced. Her daughters are both actresses, did you know?"

"No. I don't know much about her."

"She was very active in a number of political causes: animal rights and clearing mine fields and vegetarianism."

Was being a vegetarian a political cause? I said, "Did it sound like the police were making any headway in the investigation?"

"Oh, they never say much, do they? The police, I mean. Not 'til they're ready to make an arrest. There were reporters prowling through the village this morning."

"I know. They're camped outside the Hound and Harrier." I glanced over the headlines of *The Clarion*, which was spread out over the opposite side of the large kitchen table. It looked very like Innisdale was once more being tagged as the Murder Capital of the Lake District. "Has there been any news on the investigation into the death of the February brothers?"

Sally finished loading the dishwasher and turned it on. "It didn't sound that way to me. They've connected those two louts to the shootings at Rogue's Gallery through some shell casings."

"Well, that was only a matter of time." I gazed at the cat, which was now dozing lightly in the patch of sunlight. "Did you know them?"

"The February boys? I knew of them. Between them they didn't have the brain of a dizzy weasel. If someone really hired them to murder Mr. Fox it was someone not from these parts. No one here would be that foolish."

I thought that over as I called Brougham Manor and asked for Cordelia.

We chatted briefly, then I asked, "Can you think of a way you might be able to use your family connections to get in to see Angela Hornsby?"

"The MP?"

"Yes."

"Are we sleuthing again?"

"Maybe."

She laughed merrily. "Leave it to me!"

We made arrangements to meet later that afternoon, I thanked Sally for the use of her phone and kitchen—which she waved off, and I walked back to the Hound and Harrier.

■■■■■

Partly to distract myself, and partly because I had a deadline looming, I spent most of the time before lunch working on my book.

After glancing through my notes, I reread the final pages of both fictionalized biographies of L.E.L. Whatever dramatic and possibly erroneous conclusions Enfield and Ashton might have drawn, Landon's letters spoke for themselves. She did her utmost to make the best of a bad situation. Her husband, whatever kind of government official he was—and he was apparently a competent and conscientious one—was an indifferent and selfish spouse. In one of her final letters she wrote:

He is the most unlivable-with person you can imagine...He says he will never leave off correcting me 'til he has broken me of my temper, which you know was never bad.

With the exception of Mrs. Bailey, her serving woman, Landon was the only white woman on the coast. As well as being the seat of the Gold Coast colonial government, the fort was a bastion of the transatlantic slave trade. The legendary Gates of No Return was the exit through which slaves passed as they were herded onto the waiting ships. The company of slavers, bachelor officers, and merchants was a far cry from the literary salons of London. Landon was untrained and mostly unprepared for her new life, for days filled with cooking, cleaning, and housekeeping.

There was little time to write, but she did manage to keep in touch with her family and friends, though her connection to her old life grew more and more tenuous as the months passed. As she was no longer producing stories and poems in feverish quantities, the fickle public began to forget her. Yet she apparently resisted returning to England, and was not entirely unhappy. Though she seemed to spend most of her life in a state of near-exhaustion, Landon appeared to view herself as someone living a great adventure in a new, exotic life.

As for MacLean, he seemed essentially to have lived his life in a parallel but separate existence to Landon. Undoubtedly, his was a position of great pressure and responsibility. He could hardly have chosen a less suitable wife, but Landon clearly did her best. Perhaps MacLean had loved her in his own inexpressive and self-occupied way. Or it may have been that he was pressured into the marriage by guilt and chivalry, and felt he did not owe Landon much beyond giving her his name and a home. He probably did not expect her to last long—and she didn't. Though whether he expected their marriage to end in her death remained shrouded in mystery.

■■■■■

"Ouch!" Cordelia complained as I tightly plaited her long, blond hair. "I don't understand why I have to go collecting for charity while looking like I've escaped from a nunnery."

"You're an actress. You should understand about preparing for a role."

"What role am I preparing for? The lead in *The Song of Bernadette?*"

"Well-bred young nob collecting junk for the local church bazaar."

Cordelia muttered under her breath as I finished her hair.

"I think you look sweet." I fished in my traveler's jewelry case, and removed a pair of delicate pearl earrings. "Here. Take out those—what are they supposed to be?"

"Handcuffs," she said smugly.

"Planning on a career behind bars when you graduate from school?"

"Ha ha." She was grinning, and I shook my head.

■■■■■

I had to give her credit though, she played her part beautifully.

We drove through the gates of the old Monkton Estate just before teatime, parked the Jag, and went up to the front door.

Cordelia looked every inch a Sloane Ranger in her own jeans and my pastel beaded blouse. Hair and makeup were just right, if I did say so myself, and her manner was perfect. Maybe it was genetic or maybe it was simply years of mimicking her cousin Allegra. She had that perfect blend of well-bred arrogance and slight ditziness down cold. All I had to do was try to look equally well bred and smile politely.

We got past the housekeeper with the mere mention of the Brougham name. Then we had to face the slim young male assistant I remembered from that morning at Rogue's Gallery, but Cordelia's spiel about the church bazaar and her Auntie Vee's regrets about some mislaid garden party invitations made short work of him. Finally we were shown into a lovely, long room hung with gray silk wallpaper. The furnishings were all white and black—muted and elegant. There was a grand piano near French windows looking over a velvet-green lawn. A cadre of sterling-framed photographs crowded the top of the piano. There were some exquisite watercolors on the walls and a few choice pieces of antique furniture that reminded me painfully of Peter. In fact, I recognized a small Chinese side table from Rogue's Gallery.

A carved ivory-and-sterling chess set was on the table. It, too, looked antique, but I didn't recognize it. Not that I was now familiar with every item in Rogue's Gallery.

While we waited for the Honourable Angela I wandered over to the piano and studied the photos. There were several posed pictures of a plain-featured woman with an excellent haircut and intimidating eyebrows—whom I took to be the MP. In the latest (judging by the age of the subject) of the photographs she was accompanied by a tall, sandy-haired man with a bland, very English face.

And there was a very large, framed photographic portrait of the same man on his own looking stolidly into the camera.

"What are we looking for?" Cordelia asked softly from behind me.

"I have no idea," I whispered back.

"Is that her husband?"

"She's not married. At least…I think someone said that she was newly engaged."

A door opened behind us and a rich, sonorous voice announced, "My dear Miss Dumas. How delightful of you to come in person. I'm a great admirer of Venetia Brougham's work."

Angela Hornsby was a very well-preserved sixty-something. Her hair, nails, and makeup were all flawless. She was not pretty, but she clearly made the most of what she had, and the result was a poised and well-groomed woman, one whose success was based on much more than looks or charm.

Cordelia responded engagingly, apologized on behalf of her great-aunt who, if I'd understood her correctly on the drive over, would die a martyr's death before she fed a member of the Labour Party her prawn canapés, and blithely invited Ms Hornsby for the following weekend's festivities.

"This is my *deah* little friend Grace Hollister." Cordelia was hamming it up shamefully as she introduced me to the MP. We shook hands briefly. Angela studied me with her cool gray eyes, and smiled.

"The author?"

"Why, yes." Now *that*, I admit, surprised me. It's not as though my work was on a best-seller list anywhere.

Angela Hornsby inclined her head toward the large photo. "George, my fiancé, mentioned your book and that you were living locally. He's a great fan of history and adventure stories."

"Does your fiancé live nearby?"

The man in the photograph was not familiar to me, but that didn't prove anything. A lot had happened in six months. I realized belatedly that perhaps my question might be a little personal, but Angela answered composedly, "No. George lives in London. We'll be using this house mostly as our weekend retreat until we retire."

Cordelia's eyes met mine. "You must bring George…er… Mr.…?"

"Robinson," Angela supplied.

"You must bring Mr. Robinson next Saturday as well," Cordelia said. "I know Auntie would insist."

"That would be delightful. He was supposed to come down this weekend, but he was delayed on business. We hope to see him tomorrow or Tuesday."

We. I wondered if that was the royal "we" or if she was referring to herself and her slim, elegant young aide.

I said, "I suppose we've come to the wrong house to collect for the church bazaar. You're bringing lovely things in, not chucking them out." I nodded to the little Chinese table. "I recognize that from Rogue's Gallery."

She raised her eyebrows. "That's correct. Mr. Fox did deliver that table and two magnificent Rococo chairs just a day or two ago. An exquisite piece, isn't it? Such a personable young man." She smiled at me in a way that indicated she was aware of my relationship to Peter. Now why would that be? I suppose Peter might have mentioned something in passing, but it didn't really seem like him. He was not much given to casual discussion of his personal life.

I indicated the chess set. "Do you play?"

"George is a chess fanatic. I'm afraid I'm a rather indifferent player. It's a lovely set, isn't it? George gave it to me as an engagement gift. The board is marble. The pieces are hand-carved ivory and sterling. It's Turkish. Early nineteen-hundreds, I understand."

"When is the wedding?" Cordelia asked, as Angela beckoned us toward a pewter gray brocade sofa.

"May. I'm determined to have the house ready by the end of April." Angela waited till we'd seated ourselves on the long sofa, and then tucked herself neatly into a matching armchair. "Shall I ring for tea?"

We assented—trying not to seem too eager about it—and a tea tray arrived shortly after. Angela poured and discussed several political issues that "meant a good deal to her," and then chatted about her bird-watching hobby. I watched and listened to her, and wondered if I was totally on the wrong track.

I simply couldn't imagine anyone less nefarious than Angela Hornsby. She seemed a little dull, a little stuffy, but well-informed and purposeful. She reminded me of Margaret Thatcher. And I had no reason to believe she would make any less redoubtable a foe. Not that I could see why we should be foes. But unfortunately, the only clue I had to Peter's mysterious behavior was that the day before he changed so drastically he had come to this house. Perhaps to this very room, if the little Chinese table indicated anything.

Sipping my tea, listening to Cordelia make small talk with our hostess, I tried to recall Peter as he had been that last morning. He had been tired. I hadn't recognized it at the time, but looking back he had looked desperately tired, as though he hadn't slept in days. And he had been angry. But more than angry, it had seemed as if he'd received a bad shock. And he was not easily shocked—or angered, really.

Of course his anger and shock might have nothing to do with this house, this room, this woman. For all I knew he had gone straight back to Rogue's Gallery and received whatever shocking or angering news there. Or he might have gone someplace entirely different that I knew nothing about.

I gazed around the pleasing, newly furnished room again. There seemed nothing here to indicate anything but gracious and genteel living. I studied Angela Hornsby as she nibbled on a biscuit and listened politely to Cordelia's blithe chatter about how theater reflected our understanding of the individual groomed to cope with the stifling pressures of modern society.

"I'm afraid I don't really know what that means, my dear," she said as Cordelia paused for breath.

Could anyone seem less like the possessor of a guilty secret than Angela Hornsby?

After forty-five minutes of tea and small talk, Cordelia and I escaped with a small petit-point footstool for the church bazaar.

"Is it my imagination or was that a total waste of time?" Cordelia asked as she slipped behind the wheel of the Jag.

"I don't know," I admitted. "Did anything about her strike you as strange?"

"No," Cordelia replied promptly. "Except that anyone *that* normal has to be off her nut."

■ ■ ■ ■ ■

When we reached the inn I found there was one message from my sister-in-law, Laurel, and another from Brian.

"Nothing else?" I asked the girl at the desk.

She shook her head.

I started up the stairs to my room, struggling not to give in to the wave of disappointment. Now past my initial hurt and anger, I couldn't believe that things between Peter and me would end on such a strange note. I couldn't believe he wanted this separation any more than I did.

Did he really feel my refusal to instantly abandon the country and our plans merely on his say-so showed lack of faith in him? Or had he forced this estrangement in an attempt to protect me?

I thought of his unfair interpretation of my delayed return to Innisdale. Six months did sound like a long time, but there had been so many legitimate reasons to postpone the trip. So many things to arrange. Or was I telling myself comfortable fibs? I had missed Peter horribly, that was true. Surely he knew that was true? But...I had enjoyed the time with friends and my family. It had been two years since my impulsive decision to stay in Britain. Two years since I had seen my loved ones. Was it so amazing that I'd put off leaving them again?

Maybe it *had* appeared like I wasn't in a hurry to come home to Peter. Maybe I *had* seemed hesitant, uncommitted.

And the truth was...maybe...I *did* have a few doubts. Not about Peter. Not really. Maybe about myself. Maybe about whether we could ultimately make each other happy. I didn't take commitment lightly. He knew that. And for me this was a huge step. A huge decision.

As it was for him.

I misstepped on the stairs, and reached for the banister as that thought struck home. Funny how until that very moment it simply had not occurred to me that if commitment seemed a big step for *me*, how unfamiliar and treacherous the territory must have appeared to Peter. Like walking out onto an ice floe.

Norton Edam, on his way down the staircase, glanced at me as

I stood there having my untimely epiphany.

"Forget something?" he asked.

I blinked at him. He looked better than he had at breakfast. He'd shaved anyway, which was a start.

"Yes," I answered. "I think I did."

He smiled politely, edging past me.

"Any word on the production?" I asked.

"Not that I've heard."

"Are you still planning to leave?"

"As soon as we get permission. Yes." He kept moving, clearly not in the mood to stay and chat. I continued upstairs to my room.

Brian didn't answer when I called on my cell phone. I left a message on his machine, changed out of my skirt and blouse into leggings and a sweatshirt, and seated myself at the little table before the window with a pen and paper—and the hitherto-unopened box of chocolates.

I began to chart who had been present each time Mona had mentioned losing her flask. Granted, it was a long shot, but I remained convinced that Mona had been killed in mistake for Miles—especially having remembered that her flask had an "M" engraved in the front of it. Not that someone might not have wanted Mona dead for her own sake, but I felt the attack on Miles, and prior problems with the brakes on his car, were pretty good indications he had been the true target.

Aided in my reflections by a chocolate-raspberry truffle, I tried to remember the first time Mona had mentioned misplacing her flask. Had it been just after we arrived at the Hound and Harrier? I remembered for sure that she'd mentioned that it was missing at breakfast the morning before we'd been shooting the big lakeside gun battle. Roberta had made some joke about it. Who else had been there? Pammy. Tracy. Tracy had made some smart-ass comment that I couldn't remember.

Miles had been in the restaurant, but I had an impression that he'd walked out before Mona mentioned her flask—yes, because a few minutes later I'd heard him and Todd arguing in the little room off the lobby.

Not that I thought Miles was trying to kill himself. Of course he could always make it look like the attempt had been made on his life when the real target was Mona. But...no. While Miles could conceivably have faked the brakes going out on his car, he didn't fake knocking himself out. And I felt certain the two things were connected.

So that left Todd.

No. Because I remembered passing Norton walking into breakfast as I was walking out. He'd said something about grabbing a bite before we left for location.

Todd and Norton. Both of whom had run-ins with Miles. I jotted my notes down, and popped another truffle into my mouth. Creamy hazelnut: divine. All I needed now was a glass of fine Merlot. And someone to share my sleuthing with. Someone like Peter.

I shook the thought off.

There had been another time I recalled Mona mentioning losing her flask. When had that been? I couldn't remember, but I was pretty sure it had been in the taproom here at the inn. And someone...Todd, I thought...had made a joke that Mona must subconsciously be deliberately misplacing her flask.

Had Norton been there, too? I couldn't remember.

Certainly both he and Todd were aware that Mona *had* a flask. A number of cast and crew carried flasks. It all came down to whether it had occurred to someone that Mona's flask was frequently out of her possession. That the discovery of a small flask marked "M" might be Mona's and not Miles's. I had no idea if Miles's flask was monogrammed or not. I had never seen it out of his possession.

It was such a horrible risk to take with other people's lives, reinforcing my belief that whoever had committed this terrible crime was either totally oblivious to those around him—or her—or so obsessed with seeing Miles dead, that they simply didn't care who got in the way. Which in itself was just another form of obliviousness.

Who had that kind of motive? Butting heads over creative differences just didn't seem to cut it. You'd have to hate someone an awful lot to kill. Not just that…to risk being caught and imprisoned.

I glanced at the clock beside the bed. It was supper time. Just out of courtesy I knew I should really wait to walk down to Sally's, as eager as I was to learn whether my sister-in-law had discovered any useful information.

Picking up another piece of chocolate, I eyed it thoughtfully. Poison was supposedly a woman's weapon, but tampering with brakes suggested the masculine touch to me—sexist though that sounded.

The phone rang, jarring me out of my sinister reflections.

CHAPTER 20

"I HAVE NEWS on Peter Fox," Brian said.

We were having dinner again at the Cock's Crow. Plaice and chips in a pub—about as casual as one could get, but I still felt that I was having far too many meals with Brian—for both our sakes.

"Tell me," I said.

"He was spotted on a Gatwick security cam—returning from a flight to Bergerac."

Bergerac. The home of Cyrano. The Dordogne—where British ex-pats flocked. *Catriona.*

All right. There could easily be other inducements for Peter to travel to France, especially such a beautiful part of France, besides wanting to see his psycho former sweetheart and partner in crime, Catriona Ruthven.

Offhand I couldn't think of one, but maybe I wasn't really trying.

"Was he alone?" I asked.

"Yes. That is, as far as I know. Officially he was traveling alone. Why?"

Although Brian was obsessed with Peter's criminal past, apparently he didn't know that Catriona was now living in that part of France. Maybe he didn't care. Maybe he was only concerned with Peter and not Peter's favorite former accomplice. We'd never really discussed it—Catriona Ruthven being one of my least favorite topics of conversation.

"I just wondered," I said. "Why are you tracking Peter's movements since he's not a suspect in the murders of the February brothers?"

"He has an alibi," Brian said. "That's not the same thing as not being suspect. Any move Peter Fox makes, I want to know about."

I ignored yet another implication that I would lie for Peter. After all, Tracy was helping provide that alibi as well. "Have you made any progress investigating their deaths?"

Whatever Brian might have answered, I missed it because I was mulling over the abrupt realization that if Peter had gone to Catriona, I must be correct in my deduction: whoever was trying to kill him was tied into the ill-fated Istanbul job. Catriona was the other person most affected—most injured, if I wanted to be fair—by Gordon Roget's betrayal.

Besides Roget, Catriona was the only other person who knew Peter had not double-crossed his mates. She was probably the only person who could intercede on Peter's behalf with his former colleagues. And I was now convinced that the Februarys had been hired by one of the three remaining crooks.

Except…why didn't Peter's former criminal pals just take care of him themselves? Why hire two apparently boneheaded local assassins? Why had both attempts on Peter's life taken place in broad daylight with lots of witnesses? Were the Februarys really that dumb or had there been some point to these attempts at public execution?

Granted, Peter's felonious friends might not have all been as potentially murderous as Catriona, but surely they had the contacts to hire real professionals?

Whoever had hired the Februarys apparently didn't know any better—or hadn't been in a position to pick and choose.

I said, interrupting Brian's discussion of forensics, "Were you able to find out anything about the other members of Peter's team in Istanbul?"

He gave me a long, level look. "Yes. Davey Donnelly was the driver. He died last year in a car smash-up on the M42. The other two men were Lew Shaw and Martin Collins. Collins is currently serving time at Franklin Prison near Durham."

"Are you positive—?"

He said with great patience, "I checked, yes. Collins is still a guest of Her Majesty's Prison Service. Shaw—you'll like this—entered the St. Mina Monastery in Mariut, Egypt, five years ago."

It took me a moment to process what this meant, because if Brian's facts were correct—and Brian's facts were *always* correct—Peter's former partners in crime were *not* trying to kill him. And how could that be?

As though reading my thoughts, Brian added, "Catriona Ruthven's whereabouts are unknown."

I opened my mouth to correct him, but then bit the words back. Instinctively I knew Peter would not forgive my betrayal of Catriona. It wasn't logical or fair, but I knew it in my heart. He might not still love her, but a strong bond remained between them—which was why he had gone to Dordogne.

Though not, apparently, to ask her to intercede with their former co-workers.

Why then? Because I knew Peter was right: if Catriona wanted him dead, she'd handle it personally. The only other time I could remember him trying to contact her was when Hayri Kayaci, one of the guards at the Turkish prison where Peter had been held, had turned up trying to blackmail him. Peter had gone to France to warn Catriona that, in his own words, "the vermin is gnawing its way out of the woodwork."

What had he gone to tell her this time?

"So you see," Brian said, "Nobody in Fox's past is out to get him. I think he unwisely used the February brothers in some deal that went sour. And when they tried to get payback, he had to eliminate them."

I raised my gaze from my confused thoughts to Brian's intense expression. He genuinely believed what he was saying. He disliked Peter too heartily, believed too firmly in his guilt, to see how unlikely that scenario was.

He said softly, "He's a villain, Grace. An attractive, charming villain. Why can't you see it?"

That one may smile, and smile, and be a villain....

I said, "There's no point saying this to me, Brian." I remembered Peter's words at Craddock House that awful morning. *I can't keep proving myself to you, Grace. Sooner or later you have to take me on faith—or admit that this isn't what you really want.* I felt the curious sensation of prickling behind my eyes. Was that how it had seemed to Peter? That he was forever having to prove himself, and never quite reaching some invisible yardstick? Why had he kept trying? He was the man who said that commitment, steady relationships, routine had never been his thing, but he had kept attempting to build those things with me.

Brian reached across the table, covering my hand with his. "Grace, you know how I feel about you. I can't stand to see you tear yourself up over that worthless swine."

"Stop." I tried to say it gently, sliding my hand out from under his. "You can't say these things to me and expect us to continue being friends. I love Peter. I trust him. I have faith in him." I said it firmly, as though these were my wedding vows, and I thought that if I ever got to the point of marrying Peter, these *would* be my wedding vows because these were the things I expected of him as well.

"I have to say them," Brian said, "because I can't go on just being your friend. I feel too much for you."

We stared at each other across the crowded tabletop. The half-eaten fish and chips, the vinegar bottle and salt shaker, the red-and-white-checked tablecloth: what a place for friends to part.

"If it wasn't for Peter Fox…" he said.

"I don't know that that's even true," I said, although I suppose it was. If it hadn't been for Peter I probably would have fallen in love with Brian. But it was too late now, and "love" was a pale word for what I felt for Peter.

So maybe I did understand a little about why Laetitia Landon had been willing to risk everything, and even when things didn't work out the way she planned, she had continued to see the grand adventure in her choices.

"You're a smart woman in everything but this."

It was painful because I liked Brian; I hated to lose his friendship, especially now when I felt more than a little cast adrift between my old life and my new.

I said, "Whom we love isn't a logical choice, Brian, or you'd have picked someone other than a woman already in love with another man. It's not as though I led you on or ever pretended to feel more than I do."

He stared at me for a long moment. "I don't know who I feel worse for: you or me. There doesn't appear to be a happy ending in either of our futures."

I was afraid he was right about that. After a moment, he said, "I'll drive you back to the inn."

■ ■ ■ ■ ■

Todd was by himself in the bar at the Hound and Harrier. The television in the corner was on, a news program playing softly in the background. Todd sipped what looked like whisky and watched the TV. He glanced up with something like relief when I sat down across from him.

"Where is everyone?" I asked.

He shrugged. "Dunno. Sunday night. Maybe they're all catchin' up on their beauty sleep."

"Are we filming tomorrow?"

"Far as I know."

"Doesn't that seem a little odd to you?"

He studied me. It was strange because superficially he looked so much like Peter—and yet he was so different once I started analyzing him feature by feature. "Whole gig is queer if you ask me."

"I do want to ask you, as a matter of fact," I said. "It's not my imagination, is it? This is a very strange production?"

"Yeah. Strange hardly cuts it, luv." He sipped his drink. "Never seen anything like it. No location manager, no stand-ins, no second unit. And 'alf the crew doubling for the other 'alf." He shook his head disbelievingly. "'s mad, thass what it is."

"The screenwriter isn't usually on the set once the filming begins, right?"

"Right."

"Have you ever worked with Miles or Roberta or anyone in this production before?"

"Nah. Never met any of 'em before this. 'eard about Miles, naturally. *Virtual Ninja.* Great film, that."

"Because I heard the two of you arguing one morning."

He looked blank.

"You said something like you both knew who was calling the shots or who wasn't."

"Oh." He repressed a cheeky grin, and took another sip. "Yeah. Didn't like the way he was filming the scenes, did I?" He raised a dismissive shoulder. "Deliberately kept shooting my bad side just to get *her* good side."

I had to stop and work that out. "I didn't realize you *had* a bad side," I said finally.

He turned his left profile to me, waited—apparently giving me time to analyze the disaster area—then turned back with an inquiring expression.

I said apologetically, "I can't really see a difference."

"The camera sees a difference," he assured me, reaching for his drink again. "Anyway, know it's your book and all, luv, but the story is really about Pierce, innit? David, I mean. Peter."

"Ah…" I decided to let that go. "So you were just discussing the way Miles was choosing to shoot you and Tracy?"

"Pretty much."

"And what did you mean about Miles ultimately not being in charge?"

The blue eyes were quizzical. "'eard quite a bit, didn't you, for someone who just 'appened along?"

"Your conversation caught my attention because Walter, the original screenwriter, said something very similar about Miles and Roberta not having final say on anything."

Todd considered this. "Yeah, well. Wasn't hired by either of 'em, was I? The call came direct to my agent. Didn't have to audition or anything. Got the impression someone else was pulling the strings behind the scenes. Someone who wished to remain anonymous. You talk to Roberta? Never produced a film in her life. She's an actress."

Silently, I absorbed this. Mona had mentioned that she had

met Roberta when they were both still acting, so I wasn't totally shocked to hear it. "Do you know that for a fact?"

He nodded. "Mona told me. Mona knew everyone, didn't she? Said Roberta admitted it to her when she hired her. They'd known each other donkey's years, see?"

"So Mona was hired by Roberta. Do you know if there were other actors who were handpicked the way you were?"

"Dunno."

My attention was caught by the television. There was local news footage of Angela Hornsby making some kind of speech to a group of people in Wellies and plaid jackets. Todd and I watched for a few moments while the MP on the screen graciously did the honors and officially opened a local gardening center.

■ ■ ■ ■ ■

Roberta didn't answer my knock right away. When she did come to the door, she wore a pale blue bathrobe, her hair wrapped in a towel, her face greasy with a facial treatment.

"May I talk to you for a minute?" I asked.

Warily, she backed up, letting me inside the room. As she closed the door after me, I looked around curiously. The room looked as if it had been ransacked. The bed was unmade, closet open, drawers open, suitcases turned upside down, clothes strewn everywhere. But apparently it was supposed to look that way because she simply scooped up the clothes piled on the only chair and threw them on the bed, gesturing for me to sit.

"Unfortunately, unlike you, I don't have one of the royal suites," she remarked, jerking the coverlet over the sheets, and curling up on the bed with her tumbled clothing.

"Home team advantage," I said, quoting Peter. "You've got a nice view of the mountains though."

She snorted.

So much for the small talk. I said, "I wanted to ask if we were shooting tomorrow?"

Roberta just stared at me for a long, long moment.

"Is there something wrong?" I asked.

"You know damn well there's something wrong," she said.

"You've been saying since practically day one there's something wrong." Her eyes glittered behind the too-cute glasses.

I made sure I kept my tone nonconfrontational. "I've been talking to Todd. He said this is your first film."

"And you already know that, too." She reached over to the side table and picked up a pack of cigarettes. I hadn't seen her smoke before, but then I'd never seen her look quite so nervous and haggard, either. "Just get to the point, Grace." She lit up, and took a defiant drag.

I said, "I knew you didn't have a lot of experience as a producer, but Todd says you're actually an actress."

"That's right. Why, is there some law that an actress can't move on to producing or directing?"

"Don't get mad at me. I'm not the one who got you into this," I said.

To my astonishment, her face twisted up and she began to cry. She cried soundlessly, but it was painful to watch for all that. I didn't know what to do. I rose, moved over beside her on the bed, and put my arm around her shaking shoulders.

"What is it? Roberta?"

"Mona," she said. "Maybe she would still be alive…"

"If what?"

She shook her head, pulled away from me, going over to the window and staring out at shadow mountains and the starry night beyond. After a couple of deep, shuddering drags on her cigarette, she got control of herself.

"I tried to reach our office in New York. I've been trying for days. Even before Mona…" She stopped, struggled for control. "The number is disconnected. I thought it was a mistake at first. I called a friend in New York and asked her to drop by the building—the address I had. She went there, and it's a giant empty warehouse. There is no Kismet Production Company."

It took a little effort to absorb that. Although I'd been convinced there was something screwy with this project, I hadn't really considered the possibility that, from beginning to end, the entire production of *Dangerous to Know* might be one gigantic fraud.

"But all the money," I said. "Where did that come from? I've even received a paycheck. A nice one."

"There was a company checking account," Roberta said. She wiped her eyes. "But it's been closed. Our company credit cards have been cancelled as well."

"Maybe you better start at the beginning," I said.

She nodded, struggled for control. "There was an ad in *Variety*," she began.

Gradually, in between my interrupting with questions, Roberta got the story out. It was like something out of Sherlock Holmes. Roberta had auditioned for the part of "Producer" in the screen adaptation of an obscure nonfiction book by an equally obscure American schoolteacher living in the English Lake District.

"So there was never any real film production," I said. I wasn't surprised by then, but it was still disappointing.

"But that's the thing," Roberta said. "We really *were* making a film."

"There was film in the cameras?"

"What part of *really making a film* do you not get? We had the authority, and the money, and *the film*—to go ahead and begin producing the movie."

"We?"

"I suggested Miles for the project—we'd known each other, worked together—I knew he needed a project right away, and I knew I could...trust him. Mr. Green interviewed him, and then hired him as the director."

Mr. *Green*? Why had they bothered? Why not just leave it at Mr. Smith and be done with it? "This Mr. Green—" I began.

"I'm sure he was an actor like me. In fact, I know he was, because I'd seen the ad he responded to in *Variety* the week before the ad ran that I answered. I just never put two and two together. Maybe I didn't want to."

"So did Miles know this was all make-believe from the start?"

"But it wasn't," Roberta told me. "That's what you're not understanding. We were supposed to go ahead and make the film. I told Miles the situation, and he was even more determined than I was to really make this film happen. We both needed it to be real, and there was no reason why it couldn't be real. We had the money and the resources. We had the green light."

No pun intended.

"But the project had been chosen for you already, and it was my book."

"Yes. There was no negotiating on that."

I tried not to be offended that she had apparently tried. The realization that my work—and I—had been deliberately targeted was a creepy one. "Who hired Walter Christie?"

"Mr. Green."

Which explained how Walter knew that Roberta and Miles weren't really in control of the production. Inexperienced as he was, either he knew enough about the way the business ran or something must have triggered his suspicions. Which made me wonder if Walter had not suffered an accident because he knew too much?

But then why not eliminate Roberta and Miles as well?

Too many bodies? Or because the film had to be made. Why? That was the real question. Why did someone go to the trouble of pretending to film my book?

"You, Miles, Walter, and Todd were all hired directly by Kismet Production Company. Was there anyone else who was hired directly by the mysterious Mr. Green?"

She shook her head. "Miles and I hired everyone else. We had a limited budget, but we were able to get a small crew together. We held auditions for most of the remaining roles." She got choked up again. "I called Mona's agent. We'd worked together before and I knew she'd be perfect."

The implications were overwhelming. For a few moments I just sat there trying to take it all in.

"So…when you originally asked me to take part in the production…?"

She wiped her eyes again. "We were told to try to get you on board one way or the other. To offer you any amount of money."

"Why?"

"I don't know!" She met my eyes. "Honestly. I don't know. If I had to take a guess…I'd have thought it was all some ruse to meet you."

"To *meet* me?" I was thinking about Walter's accident. Surely that hadn't been to ensure that I would join the cast? But no. There was no guarantee that I would join after Walter's death. And in fact, I hadn't any intention of signing on. Not until the production had moved to the Lake District.

Roberta said, "At first, yes. I thought it had to be some big romantic scheme to meet you. I've seen a lot of movies like that. I honestly expected Mr. Green to show up that first day you visited the set. But then later…I began to wonder."

"After Walter died, you mean?"

She shook her head. "No. When the decision was made to film on location over here."

"But that decision was made after Walter's accident, wasn't it?"

"No." Her expression was wry. "That decision was made within a few hours of my telling Mr. Green that you couldn't take part in the project because you were moving back to the Lake District. I was supposed to offer you the consulting job again, but then Walter died, so we just turned it into a script doctor position."

"I *really* don't understand," I said.

I was thinking aloud, but Roberta said, "Join the club."

"When did you find out the phone to Kismet Productions had been disconnected?"

"Yesterday morning. I hadn't been able to get through all week. I kept getting an answering machine, and then I kept getting the message that the machine was full. Yesterday I learned the phone had been disconnected."

"And you found out the company bank account had closed… when?"

"This afternoon. Pammy and I went out to pick up a few things. My card was declined. So was hers. I called my bank—of course they weren't open, but according to the computer system—our account is closed." She struggled against another flood of tears, and I didn't blame her. The entire production crew was essentially stranded overseas. Never mind the destruction of the dreams of all these people who believed they had jobs but really didn't, the "company" probably owed hundreds of thousands of dollars in equipment rentals, salaries, hotel, catering, and the like.

It was unbelievably cruel. Unbelievably cold.

"What does Miles say?" I asked.

Roberta stubbed her cigarette out. "He doesn't believe it. His credit card doesn't work either, but he's convinced it's all just a big mistake, and everything will be ironed out on Monday. Tomorrow." She smiled bitterly. "Miles has always been good at seeing what he wanted to see."

"What are you going to do?" I asked.

She shook her head. "I have no idea. We can't keep filming. We can't keep running up bills." She rubbed her forehead wearily. "Maybe Miles is right. Maybe everything will be back to normal tomorrow."

"Maybe so," I said, and I sounded as unconvinced as she did. Rising from the bed I went to the door. "Thank you for telling me."

"You don't have to say it. I know I should have told you the minute weird things started happening." Her eyes met mine briefly.

"That would have been the day you first auditioned with Mr. Green."

"True," she admitted. "I'm sorry anyway. Not that it's done you any particular harm."

That remained to be seen. I opened the door, and she said suddenly, "Oh, I just remembered. I don't know why it would matter, but Tracy was hired by Mr. Green as well."

CHAPTER 21

TRACY WAS NOT in her room.

Or if she was, she was sleeping very deeply. I checked my watch. It was now nearly midnight. Too late to pay Sally a visit. Actually, too late to pay anyone a visit—if I wanted to hear anything beyond a lot of understandable cursing. I returned to my room and sat down at the table with all my notes and books. In addition to my scribbles on Laetitia Landon and her contemporaries, there were my efforts at charting everyone's movements regarding Mona's missing flask.

I stared at them but my brain felt too worn out to process anything more that night. I had a chocolate from the open box, chewing slowly.

On one point Roberta had clearly been wrong. It seemed certain that all this chicanery had not been in aid of meeting me. Not for romantic purposes, not for any purpose. In fact, I didn't believe it was about me at all. I was pretty sure this entire murderous farce was entirely about Peter.

After all, the book was as much about him as me. And there were just too many strange coincidences. The two bumbling attempts on his life by the February brothers. His odd, angry behavior—and his demand that I return to the States at once. His refusal to explain anything. And then his trip to France—surely to see Catriona. Even Walter's fatal accident might have been an attempt on Peter's life. Maybe someone had followed him to the States.

True, that seemed a little farfetched; but one thing for sure, whoever had set up this elaborate film production hoax had money to burn—or believed any amount was worth it to…to what? Eliminate Peter? Apparently so. But why?

Because this person hated Peter?

Well, that seemed a given. But these events showed more than simple hatred. Because how hard would it have been really to kill Peter? A sniper with a rifle could have taken care of it within minutes. Clearly that was too simple. This was a cruel, cold personality who deliberately manipulated and ultimately cheated an entire group of people, completely innocent bystanders, leaving them stranded and legally liable on foreign shores.

Cold, cruel, but imaginative. Very imaginative. The whole idea of this fake film was so weirdly involved and risky. It was almost like a game.

A game. I thought of the beautiful antique chess set in Angela Hornsby's living room. The engagement present from her fiancé, the man who loved to play chess. An antique Turkish chess set belonging to a man named George Robinson.

If those photographs on the piano were of this George Robinson…and Peter happened to recognize Robinson…

I tried to remember the man in the photographs, but there had been nothing memorable about him. Just another bland, innocuous-looking man in late middle age.

A gray little man. The kind of chap you never took notice of. That was how Peter had described Gordon Roget, the fence who had double-crossed them in Turkey. The man who had stolen the Serpent's Egg, and left Peter to rot in a Turkish prison.

Gordon Roget. *G.R.* George Robinson.

The initials were right, I thought with mounting excitement. And if he were Roget, that would certainly help explain Peter's shocked fury—and why he had gone straight to Catriona. The other person in the world with reason to hate Roget as much as Peter did.

Not a reassuring thought, however. Catriona was hardly a stabilizing influence, and the fact that Peter didn't want to talk to me about Gordon Roget's reappearance in his life—assuming I wasn't completely wrong in my speculations—was not reassuring either.

But it did make sense. In fact, I grew more excited as I considered my theory. If Robinson was Roget, and he was soon to marry Angela Hornsby and move to Innisdale, his need to remove Peter once and for all became obvious.

What was also obvious was that he had been aware of Peter's and my whereabouts for some time.

■■■■■

"You have bloody well got to be joking," Roy Blade, Innisdale's biker librarian, remarked in less than civil tones when I finally succeeded in ripping him from his slumber some time later that night. "Why the hell don't you ask your other boyfriend the copper to go with you?"

"Because he *is* a copper," I said, trying hard not to stare at the ornate tattoos covering his hairy chest and back. Blade was wearing jeans and an eye patch—and neither was properly in place, testament to how fast he'd rolled out of bed—once he'd finally heard the doorbell buzzing. "And don't call him my other boyfriend. He's just a friend."

"Keep your hair on, Miss Marple. Put the kettle on while I get dressed."

The tea water was boiling when he walked into the kitchen a short while later. "You do know the time, eh?"

"I do, yes." I was afraid to look at the clock, to tell the truth.

"Explain to me what you want again?"

"I want you to come with me to the old Monkton estate."

"That's what I thought you said. I'd hoped I dreamed that part. Now explain to me why?"

"I have a feeling—"

"Christ on a crutch," he moaned. "Tell me I *am* dreaming. Tell me you didn't say you had 'a feeling.' You're supposed to be a bird of reasonable intellect. You're never dragging me out in the middle of the night on a bloody *hunch*?"

"It's a good hunch," I told him earnestly. "It's based on instinct, yes, but it's also based on my knowledge of the personalities involved, and—" I broke off as he was slurping his tea far too loudly to hear me.

I sipped my own tea and waited. I was pretty sure he wouldn't refuse. Roy Blade had a soft heart and an adventurous streak—the perfect combination for co-conspirator.

"Go on then," he said.

And go on I did. I told him all. Or nearly all. Blade listened and drank his tea. Then I finished and awaited his verdict. And sure enough, when he was done drinking his tea and giving me all the reasons this was such a bad idea, he handed me a helmet and escorted me out to his motorbike.

"We could always take my car," I suggested feebly as he threw a leg over the giant silver bike.

"Get on and hold tight," he ordered.

I obeyed gingerly, climbing in back of him, slipping my arms around his leather-clad back and waist. The bike rumbled into life with a metallic tiger's roar, and we shot off into the night. I closed my eyes and held on for dear life.

It took us less than five minutes to cross the village, winding through the lamplit, narrow streets, across the little bridge and down the wide lane to the Monkton Estate. We stopped briefly outside the tall iron gates, the bike grumbling exhaust into the frosty night air.

The house slept peacefully on its manicured lawns. No single light burned in a distant window. Nor was there any sign of life on the grounds.

Blade squeezed the handlebar throttle, and we veered away, prowling quietly down the lane, turning off to bump our way over the small stone bridge, then cutting through the woods. At last we came to the iron fence guarding the back of the house. I was disappointed to see there was no car parked here beneath the trees. I had been fairly certain....

Blade turned off the engine, lifted his helmet. I did the same.

"Enjoy that, did you?"

"Oh, the song of the road!" I enthused. "The wind in my hair, the bugs in my teeth!"

He chuckled, his smile very white in the darkness. "The helmet keeps the wind out of your hair," he assured me. "Right. Still set on doing this?"

"I don't know. I kind of thought we'd see some sign that Peter was here, watching the house."

He made a sound somewhere between a groan and a growl. "One of us needs to be sure about what we're doing tonight, and I happen to think this is a bloody awful idea, which leaves *you*."

"Well, okay. I'm pretty sure he's here somewhere. I'm sure he's watching the house waiting for Robinson to show up."

"If Robinson isn't inside already, he sure as hell isn't going to come pulling up at two o'clock in the morning." Blade stared at me as I slid off the bike and walked over to the tall iron fence, peering through the bars at the acre or so of trimmed trees and hedges. The last time I'd been here, the garden had been an overgrown wilderness. The careful landscaping had eliminated much of the possible concealment.

"Grace?"

I looked back at him.

"Fox's a decent bloke. Intelligent. Knowing. I reckon if he thinks this Robinson needs killing, he's right."

The cold I felt had nothing to do with the nippy March night. "I don't think he's planning to kill him. That's not why we're here—to stop him committing murder."

"Of course it is," Blade said calmly. "You're afraid you won't be able to marry him if he's nicked for murder. But so far you're the only one who's put the pieces together."

I hissed, "I don't think any such thing! He wouldn't kill someone in cold blood."

"'Course he would. This Robinson tried to kill him, didn't he? Best way to put a stop to the problem. Can't arrest him. What proof is there he ever paid to have Fox killed now that the February brothers are dead? Fox can put an end to this marriage to the Honourable Angela all right, but Roget will still be out there—more determined than ever to get rid of Peter Fox."

I turned back to the fence. Through the trees I could just glimpse the distant dark windows, the tall chimneys.

"There could be a security system now," Blade said. "There probably *is* a security system now."

Perhaps it had been a crazy idea. I had been so sure I would find Peter out here intent on…intent on what? I didn't believe he would kill Gordon Roget, but Blade was right. There were not many options open to Peter other than telling Angela Hornsby that her fiancé was a crook. At best an ex-crook.

But not every woman found that an insurmountable obstacle.

I put my helmet back on and walked to the bike, climbing on behind Blade.

"Let's go," I said.

And we did, speeding through the dark and slumbering streets of Innisdale.

■■■■■

Tracy's rental car was parked in the parking lot behind the inn when I pulled up. I rested my hand on the hood, and felt that it was still faintly warm. She had returned not long before me.

Letting myself in the side door, I quietly made my way through the hushed dining room with chairs stacked on tables, up the stairs, and down the hall to my room.

I felt half-dead with weariness as I unlocked the door and let myself into my room. I felt for the wall switch, and mellow light flooded the room, picking out the box of chocolates on the table, my notes and books, and Peter Fox comfortably sprawled in the chair by the window.

"Way past your bedtime isn't it, Miss Hollister?" he inquired.

CHAPTER 22

I OPENED MY mouth but strangely no words came. In fact, I felt a little lightheaded, but that was probably mostly due to exhaustion. I did have the presence of mind to close the door behind me—and lock it.

"Yes," Peter said calmly. "I rather feel the same."

"What are you doing here?"

"I was under the impression that you were looking for me."

I sat down on the foot of the bed. It was that or collapse on the floor. "So you *were* there? You were at the Monkton Estate?"

"The question is, why were *you* there? And why in God's name would Roy Blade encourage you in your derangement?"

"Because he knows me well enough to know I'd have gone without him."

"Well, you're nothing if not stubborn," Peter said. "I'll give you that."

"The real question," I said, getting my wind back, "is why are you *here*? I thought we…ended things."

"I never said I wanted to….end things." His black brows drew together. "I asked you to for once trust me and go home and wait till I could explain things to you properly."

"There seemed to be an ultimatum in there somewhere."

His mouth quirked in a smile that was unexpectedly rueful. "Yes, I suppose there was. Well, it was easier said than done."

"Two things you should understand," I said. I held up one finger. "I do trust you." I held up another finger. "*This* is my home."

"Someone ought to tell Mrs. Zinn," he replied. "I believe she's counting on having the room back."

"Now you're doing it. I used to have to make a stupid joke every time you said something sweet or romantic to me. I'm trying to tell you how I feel, and you're the one making stupid jokes."

To my surprise, he rose, came over, and sat down next to me on the bed, putting his arm around me. I leaned against him—grateful for anything keeping me propped upright—and he rested his cheek against the top of my head.

"Six months is a long time, Esmerelda."

"I know. I guess I was a little afraid to take that final step."

"I'm not actually asking you to walk into thin air."

"Maybe that was a little part of the problem, too. I'm not exactly sure what you *are* asking?"

I felt his cheek crease, heard the faint smile in his voice. "Your father asked me what my intentions were."

"Oh my God," I murmured.

"I think he felt very much the same." And now the smile was a hint of a laugh. "He poured us two very stiff drinks before he could bring himself to inquire."

"That was totally my mother. Dad would never dream of it." I closed my eyes. "What did you tell him?"

"I told him I wanted to marry you, if you'd have me." He said it so simply that it literally robbed me of my breath. "Will you?"

"Yes."

He raised his head, our eyes met. "It's not exactly how I planned this."

"Did you plan it?" I found myself smiling. "That's nice to know."

"I planned it for six months."

I winced.

He chuckled. "It's all right. You can make it up to me later on."

Which reminded me abruptly of how I'd spent the last few hours. I said, "I can't make it up to you if you're in prison. Roy Blade thinks you plan to kill Gordon Roget."

He raised one eyebrow in that maddening way of his. "You *have* figured it out, haven't you? I should have known. Once you get your teeth into a puzzle, you don't let go. Regular academic pit bull terrier."

"You saw Roget's picture in Angela's drawing room, was that what happened?"

"Oh, yes. There was no mistake. It was him." The soft venom of that was so unlike him.

I admitted, "I made a huge miscalculation in originally discounting Roget as a suspect. I thought that because he ended up with the jewel, he had no motive to get rid of you. I was forgetting that motives are unique to personalities. He has an excellent motive in that he wishes to settle down into marriage and respectability with a woman who spends much of her time in the public eye."

Not to mention a woman who resided almost literally in Peter's backyard.

Peter said, "It gets old living life on the run, having to keep looking over your shoulder. He's not young—and he always did have a taste for respectability."

"You haven't answered my question," I said slowly.

His eyes were very blue. "Catriona wants to kill him," he admitted. "I'm not sure it's in our best interests."

The night began to take on a surreal feel. Were we really sitting up discussing whether Peter was going to murder someone? Then I sat up straight. "Is Catriona in England?"

"She's at Craddock House," he admitted.

"She's *staying* at your house? With you?"

"I'm actually *here*, if you'll notice."

"But…you know what I mean. She's staying with you at your house? That murdering, thieving, psychopathic bitch—"

"She didn't murder anyone," he said quite reasonably. And then, "Look, Grace, I know you two have had your differences—"

"Differences? That's an interesting way of putting it. She tried to kill me. She tried to kill *you*. I can't understand—"

What I really couldn't understand was how he could sit there shaking his head, rejecting the idea that Catriona Ruthven was dangerous to the health and well-being of both of us.

He said, still cool and reasonable, "I needed her help. Cat and I are taking turns watching the Monkton Estate, waiting for Roget to show up."

"And then what do you plan on doing with him?"

He was no longer meeting my eyes. "We'll decide when the moment comes."

"I can't believe you're even considering—"

He shut me up in the most pleasantly effective way possible, his mouth covering mine in a warm, gently insistent kiss. I gave into it; I let him silence me because I missed him, and because it was too late at night to begin trying to untangle this Gordian knot.

We fell back onto the soft comforter, and Peter reached up to snap off the light.

■■■■■

When I opened my eyes the next morning, he was gone.

It was not a surprise, but I still felt cast down when I reached out to touch the cool empty sheets next to me. Even the memory of Peter's proposal—finally—couldn't nullify my fear for the future. Gordon Roget, aka George Robinson, was a much more danger-ous enemy than I had imagined, but the real threat to our hap-piness—our future—was the apparently real possibility that Peter might decide the only long-term solution to the threat posed by Roget was extermination.

I blamed that on Catriona. Just the thought of her had my stomach churning with nerves and distress—but I knew that wasn't entirely fair. Beneath his charming and occasionally sensi-tive exterior, Peter possessed a core of cold steel. He was capable of ruthlessness—that was how he had managed to survive imprison-ment in Istanbul.

But despite racking my brains while I showered, I couldn't see a way both to neutralize the menace of Roget and to keep Peter from taking a morally irrevocable step. If there were some means of connecting Peter's archenemy to the *Dangerous to Know* pro-duction—but I couldn't see Roget being careless or foolish enough to have left any loose ends.

It was strange about the Februarys, though. Who had killed them? Roget? If he were up to committing murder personally, why hadn't he killed Peter himself? And why kill the Februarys at all? For goofing up twice? Or for coming to the attention of the police? But how would Roget have learned the police were zeroing in on the Februarys?

I wondered if there was a way I could find out whether Gordon Roget, aka George Robinson, had an alibi for the night the Februarys had been killed?

I wished I could go to Brian with what I now knew, but unfortunately he would probably immediately arrest Peter for conspiracy to commit murder or whatever they called it over here. Assuming that Brian even believed me. The story was a bit convoluted, and I didn't have much in the way of proof. Mostly it was speculation and hearsay—since Brian was unlikely to take anything Peter said at face value.

Still preoccupied, I went down to breakfast, only remembering when I stepped into the buzzing dining room the disaster that had befallen the Kismet Production Company.

Apparently Miles and Roberta had officially broken the news to everyone, because the room was humming like a hive with talk and whispers. There were more than a few pairs of red eyes and some angry voices.

There was no sign of Roberta or Miles, but Pammy was doing a brave job of fielding questions. "The one thing I can tell you is, as soon as the police give us permission, we'll be packing everyone up and getting you all back home as quickly as possible."

"Unbelievable," Tracy commented, buttering a slice of freshly baked bread. What she found unbelievable was unclear. She seemed pretty cool compared to everyone else, I thought, watching her.

Todd nodded a greeting to me as I sat down across from him. "They've pulled the plug."

"I heard."

"Nice while it lasted." He smiled in commiseration. "Too bad, luv. It would have made a great film."

"Yes," I agreed, although a part of me was relieved that monstrosity would never make it to anyone's television screen. The thought of not having to listen to my family shrieking with laughter at another one of Faith Bolton's "Why is this *happening* to me!" exclamations even cheered me up a little.

The thought of my family reminded me that I needed to get over to Sally Smithwick's to hear what Laurel had discovered on her end. I poured coffee and served myself a plate of truffled scrambled eggs from the buffet.

Tracy was finishing her meal as I sat back down at the table.

I said, "Roberta mentioned that you and Todd were the only other cast members hired directly by Mr. Green."

"Mr. Green?" She frowned. Then her expression cleared. "Oh, right. Mr. Green. Yes, my agent contacted me about the part."

"Didn't have to audition, did you," Todd said. "Same as me."

Tracy's eyes slid his way. She said easily, "That's right. No audition. It was a done deal." A moment later she excused herself and left the dining room.

"What do you think of her?" I asked Todd.

He raised his blond brows—and similar though their faces were, that simple gesture was so different from Peter's. "Nice legs."

"No, I mean—" The problem was, I didn't know exactly what I meant. "Is she a very good actress?"

He laughed.

"Is she a very bad actress?"

"Not the worst I've ever seen," he said generously.

I thought this over. One thing I was pretty sure of: I didn't believe Todd played a knowing part in any conspiracy. Yet he had been hand-picked to be part of this production, which meant he had a role to play—and I didn't think it was that of "David Wolf." I said slowly, "How well did you know Peter? Back in the old days, I mean?"

Todd shrugged. "We rubbed along all right. Did a lot of shoots together where they wanted brothers or lookalikes." He reached for his cup. "Don't think anyone really knew Pierce—was really close to him, other than Chantal."

Chantal? Right. Catriona's youthful alias. "How did you get on with Chantal?"

He grinned that cheeky grin. "Now *there* was a bit of all right!"

I said, "Would you have any reason to want Peter dead?"

"What?" The tea sloshed out of his cup onto the table. He gaped at me.

I put a hand up quickly. "I mean, could someone conceivably

make it look like there was an old grudge between you and Peter? Did you ever have a run-in—?"

"'ad lots of run-ins, luv." Todd looked uncomfortable for a moment. "Nothing serious, mind. Butted 'eads a few times, 's all. It was mostly the drink. I drank a fair bit in those days."

As opposed to now? Oh Lord.

"Did you know a man by the name of Gordon Roget?"

He frowned into some faded distance. "Dunno. Maybe. A friend of Chantal and Pierce's, was 'e?"

"Yes. Very likely."

He smiled. "Are you playing Sherlock 'olmes, luv? Recognize the signs." He tapped his forehead. "Seen a lot of detective films."

The theory that had come to me was so labyrinthine I could hardly credit it, but if it were true that Gordon Roget had financed a fake film production in order to camouflage murdering Peter, then hand-picking Todd to provide the handy scapegoat wasn't so far out.

I remembered Peter talking about Roget's originally coming up with the idea for stealing the Serpent's Egg from Topkapi Palace. Initially Peter had thought the idea absurd and outrageous, but ultimately they had been successful—maybe because it *was* such an outrageous idea. Equally outrageous had been Roget's double-cross of his criminal partners, yet he had been successful in that as well. And this murder plot had that same byzantine handprint all over it.

But how did I prove any of it?

The only immediate thing I could think of was going straight to Angela Hornsby and telling her what I knew. If she believed me, that would probably send Roget back into flight. Unless she already knew of her lover's unsavory past…but that seemed unlikely. The Honourable Angela just didn't seem like the type to condone murder.

I said, belatedly answering Todd, "Not really sleuthing, no. But if I were you, I'd be careful to have someone with me all the time."

His face lit up—apparently this wasn't nearly the bad news I'd thought it might be. In fact, Todd seemed flattered. "You think someone will try and snuff me?"

I replied, "No, I think someone will try to frame you for murder."

■■■■■

Sally was in her garden when I arrived at the old vicarage to phone Laurel back. She sent me inside, and I left her dividing forsythia.

I'd forgotten the time difference, and my brother Clark was none too thrilled to be awoken at three o'clock in the morning.

"For God's sake, Grace. You scared the hell out of us," my mild-mannered brother said for the third time. "We thought something had happened to you."

"Sorry, I just forgot the time difference," I apologized yet again—this time to static. Then Laurel got on the phone sounding equally groggy, but less annoyed about it.

"No, really," I assured her. "Everything is fine on this end. Did you find something out?"

"Yes, but it's not what you thought. Miles Friedman was married to a TV actress named Elise Andrews. The marriage lasted just over two years. They divorced and she moved back to Minnesota. And she's still there. She owns a gourmet cookie company. She's apparently hugely successful—and she's definitely still alive."

"You're kidding." Not that I begrudged Elise Andrews her wealth, health, and happiness, but I had been convinced that the answer to who wanted Miles dead had to do with his romantic past, and for some reason—I wasn't even sure why now—I'd been certain his single stab at matrimony was a factor in it.

"Well, you weren't totally wrong," my sister-in-law said. "The reason Elise and Miles got divorced was because he apparently had a fling with a barely legal teen actress by the name of Jonnie Alison. She starred on a show called *Dusted*. It was about a witch who worked as a housekeeper for a cop with three adorable children."

"I *loved* that show," I said.

"Me, too. Clark said you weren't allowed to watch it." Laurel smothered a yawn unsuccessfully. "Anyway, it sounds to me like

Jonnie Alison was a fragile kid to begin with, but from everything I read, and Callie and I read *a lot*—believe me, you owe us big time—Jonnie had a problem with pills and alcohol. And getting in the emotional deep end with Friedman was probably the worst mistake she could have made."

"She committed suicide, didn't she?"

"Probably. It was ruled accidental death, but the tabloids never let go of the suicide theory, and in all honesty, they were probably right. She washed down a bottle of Valium with half a bottle of Dom Perignon."

"Oh, God."

"Anyway, Jonnie Alison was her stage name. Her real name was Noreen Edam."

CHAPTER 23

"HOW CAN I help you, Grace?" Brian asked formally, when I was shown into his office. After leaving Sally's I'd headed straight for the police station. I'd asked for Chief Constable Heron, but he was not in, and I braced myself to face Brian.

I could see by his expression that it was going to be as uncomfortable as I'd feared. He was as cool and distant as he'd been when we first met just over six months earlier. He had been writing when the door opened, and he gestured with his pen to the chair in front of his desk.

Of course I understood that some of this was hurt on his part—and an injured ego—but he did care for me. I knew...because I cared for him as well.

I sat down in the chair. "I think I know who killed Mona, and I believe it really was a mistake."

He looked singularly unimpressed. "Go on."

And go on I did. Brian listened politely to my information about Jonnie Alison and her ill-fated affair with Miles Friedman, about her overdose death, and the fact that Jonnie Alison and Noreen Edam were one and the same.

"That's all very interesting," Brian said when I'd finished. "But it's hardly enough for an arrest. We need more than a motive."

"But you *have* more. Norton hates Miles. He makes no attempt to conceal it, and he's obviously guilt-stricken over Mona's death."

Brian inquired, "And was it obvious to you that he was guilt-stricken before you heard about his sister's overdose? Or did you merely believe he was upset about Ms Hotchkiss's death like everyone else?"

Ms Hotchkiss? It seemed strange to think of Mona so formally. I bit my lip. He did have a point. I hadn't placed any sinister significance on Norton's obvious upset until I had deduced that he killed Mona. I was reinterpreting his behavior now—which didn't change the fact that I was convinced I was right.

"I don't think he's just upset, I think he's borderline distraught."

"Maybe he's afraid for his life," Brian said evenly. "After all, there's a killer loose on your set. The Hotchkiss woman was definitely poisoned. Her flask contained enough potassium cyanide to wipe out the entire cast and crew."

"It's more than that. I know it is, Brian."

He appeared unmoved. So I told him about the brakes on Miles's car failing twice before we had left the States.

"Have the brakes on Friedman's rental car been tampered with here?" he asked.

"No. But they wouldn't be. We all drive together to and from location. There would be no way of knowing who might be in the car with Miles. Norton's not a homicidal maniac. I think he's suffering horribly over killing Mona."

"Before you go around stating that as fact, were the brakes on Friedman's car examined?"

"I don't know."

He sighed—and not patiently. "So again, this is speculation. There's no evidence that Friedman's brakes were tampered with, and there's no evidence that he was the intended victim of the poison the Hotchkiss woman ingested. You're assuming that this is the case."

"I'm not assuming that Miles was hit over the head. Someone attacked him after Mona died."

"He wasn't killed though, was he?"

"Only because there wasn't time. I walked outside and interrupted Miles's attacker." Despite my good intentions, my voice was rising slightly.

And Brian's voice rose in answer. "He could have been the victim of a mugging."

"Then why wasn't he mugged? His wallet was still there, his car keys—his car—"

He threw down the pen. "Because there wasn't time! Because you walked outside and interrupted the attack!" His face was flushed with an anger that I knew had nothing to do with what we were discussing.

"Fine, Brian," I snapped, rising. "Apparently you've got it all worked out. I suppose you think *Peter* knocked Miles out and poisoned Mona as well."

His face tightened.

I walked toward the door. He said curtly, "I'll talk to Edam of course. We're going to be speaking to everyone, naturally. It's a murder inquiry." He managed to add, as though the words choked him, "Thank you for this information."

■■■■■

After that encounter it was clear to me that there was no point talking to Brian about my suspicions regarding George Robinson. Which left me…totally at a loss. I couldn't stand by and let Peter be persuaded into killing someone, but equally I couldn't contemplate giving information to the police that might result in his arrest. Because if anyone deserved to meet up with Nemesis, it was Gordon Roget. And in this case I believed Nemesis was a red-haired Scottish woman with a very long memory.

Debating my limited options, I returned to the inn, and ran into Roberta and Tracy in the lobby.

Roberta hailed me immediately. "Do you know anything about this? We've been asked by the police not to arrange any flights home—"

"Mona was murdered," I said, and Roberta swayed as though I'd punched her. Apparently I was the only one who went around seeing sinister figures behind every suspicious death.

Tracy just stared at me with those arctic blue eyes. "Why aren't the cops questioning us if that's the case?"

"I think they'd only just received the autopsy report," I told her. "I wouldn't be surprised if they were on their way over now."

"Wow," she said, flipping her long blond hair behind her shoulder. "This has certainly been one interesting gig." She sauntered off to the taproom.

"Oh my God," Roberta moaned. "How does this work? We cannot stay here for weeks while the police investigate a murder. We've got to get these people out of here. Miles and I have spent the entire morning trying to explain to SAG and the IATSE and every other union and the equipment rental companies and the hotel and the airlines what's going on. We're going to be ruined. Personally and professionally—"

"Where's Norton?" I interrupted.

She broke off what she was saying, giving me a strange look. "Upstairs packing. I saw him a little while ago. He's insisting that he's leaving, that the police can't force us to stay."

"Where's Miles?"

She gestured to the bar. "In there. We may as well join him. I could use a drink after the morning I've had. And you look like you could, too."

I let myself be led into the bar, and ordered a round for everyone while I tried to think what to do. Now that Mona's death had been ruled homicide, I knew the police would be arriving on the scene momentarily. I also knew Brian was too conscientious to ignore everything I'd told him, no matter how angry he was with me, and Norton did not look to me like he could withstand serious police questioning for long; so perhaps all I had to do was keep Norton away from Miles for the next few hours.

The barmaid delivered the drinks to our table, and Miles lifted his glass and said, "When the going gets tough, the tough get going." He had clearly been delivering toasts for a while. So there went Plan B—which was to tell Miles I thought Norton might want to kill him. Even with Miles sober, I wasn't sure it was such a great idea. I could tell Todd perhaps, and ask for his help. I could even tell Roberta, but I had no way of knowing how any of them might react. if or when I revealed that I believed Norton was a murderer.

"John Huston you are not," Roberta told Miles.

"You can do better? Be my guest," Miles told her with a sweep of his hand.

Roberta took her glass and considered. "This is an Irish toast taught to me by my old granny," she said finally. "'May we all be alive at this time next year.'"

There was a silence.

"At the rate things are going," Todd said, "I'd be happy with next week."

We all laughed—with varying degrees of shakiness—and Norton said clearly and coldly from the doorway, "Well, if you want to blame someone, blame Friedman."

Miles stiffened, his face reddening. We all turned. Norton was framed in the doorway, holding the old hunting rifle that hung over the fireplace in the anteroom off the lobby.

Roberta squeaked out something, Tracy said something very unladylike, and Todd called, "Not funny, mate."

"Not meant to be, mate," Norton said shortly, and despite the crisp delivery, he was weaving as he stepped into the room.

Guests at the other tables were jumping out of their chairs, some knocking them over in their haste, moving over to the side of the room or under tables. Todd's hand fastened on my arm, pressing me to get down.

"What's your problem, Norton?" Miles demanded. "I'm in the same boat you are. I'm losing my shirt on this deal."

"Is that gun loaded?" Todd asked the stricken barmaid.

"I don't know," she quavered.

I couldn't believe it was, but what a way to find out.

"And it couldn't happen to a nicer guy! After everything you've done. It's your fault Mona's dead—" But Norton's words were cut short as several of the men who had maneuvered to the side of the room managed to get behind him. They rushed him together, and knocked him down on the floor. He kicked and wriggled furiously, convulsively squeezing the trigger, but nothing happened, and the rifle was wrested from his hand.

Tracy was swearing quietly to my left under the table where Todd had shoved me down when the men jumped Norton. I glanced back at her quickly; her eyes met mine, then her expression changed.

I looked back in time to see Norton being roughly hauled to his feet. Brian and two uniformed police officers appeared in the doorway.

"What's going on here?" Brian demanded in his best official tone. A number of the bar patrons began talking at once while Norton yelled and wrestled with his captors.

"Typical," Todd observed. "Never one when you need 'em."

I barely heard him as I pushed a chair out of my way, crawling out from under the table. I felt strangely shaky, but it wasn't due to Norton so much as what I thought I'd seen in Tracy's hand before she quickly turned away. I was almost positive she had been holding a gun.

I got to my feet and said to her, "Do you have a gun?"

She jerked around. "Who? Me?" She held up a small silver cell phone—laughing. "I was trying to call for help!"

■■■■■

It was some time before I got back to my room. After Norton had been arrested, and we had all given our statements to the police, the remaining members of the Kismet Production Company had spent the next couple of hours getting sloshed and reliving our greatest moments in the bar downstairs.

I could feel Tracy's eyes on me, but each time I looked at her, she was smiling at Miles or talking to someone else.

"When are you flying out?" I asked her.

"Tomorrow. Tuesday." She shrugged. "Maybe the next day. I haven't quite decided."

That started another discussion as to whether everyone would have to come back for Norton's trial—assuming he was brought to trial. I had spent a good forty-five minutes telling why I believed he had accidentally poisoned Mona. Inevitably, everyone began remembering instances of sinister behavior on Norton's part, little things he'd said, odd expressions, generally suspicious behavior.

"The police found a bottle of something that they're speculating contained cyanide in the trash bin behind the inn," Roberta said. "They're going to dust for fingerprints. It's hard to believe he could be that careless."

"Forget about love. It's hate makes you do the wacky," Tracy said. She smiled at Miles, who smiled twitchily back. He had been very quiet during my explanation of what I believed to be Norton's motives.

Finally, I escaped to my room to debate my next move. I considered going to Craddock House and talking to Peter again, but the conversation I envisioned was not one I wanted to have in front of Catriona. Of course, she might be off watching the Monkton Estate. Peter had said they were switching off, but if it were his turn to watch for Roget, all the more reason for me to steer clear of Craddock House.

According to Angela Hornsby, her fiancé was arriving Monday or Tuesday, which I felt certain meant Peter and Catriona would make whatever move they intended tonight or tomorrow night. I sat down at the little table with all my books and notes, and tried to weigh the pros and cons of doing nothing. Even if I had believed that was the best alternative, it simply wasn't in my nature.

I was glad I had been careful not to drink much, as I believed I had a long night ahead of me. I phoned the library.

After speaking at length—and as persuasively as I knew how— to Roy Blade, I called downstairs for a pot of coffee.

Replacing the receiver, I picked up one of my books, settled back against the stack of pillows on the bed, and began to read the final chapter of L.E.L.'s life. And despite the night I had planned, before I knew it I was engrossed in my study.

It seemed impossible to believe that a sensitive romantic like Landon, sheltered and sophisticated, the darling of the British reading public, could at the height of her fame and popularity happily resign herself to life in the wilds of Africa. Her letters home were full of little complaints and apologies, but always there was a certain reserve, an impenetrable façade of charm and wit and good humor that made light of what must have been exhausting and at times terrifying.

Had she been truly happy in her marriage, it would no doubt have been different, but it seemed likely from the accounts of those around her, the journals and letters of the gentlemen observers on the Gold Coast, that she was married to a cold and distant man who viewed her attempts at housewifery and playing Governor's lady with increasingly critical dissatisfaction.

Though she had recently formed a friendship with young Bodie Cruickshank, the governor of the fort of Anamaboe, Landon was essentially on her own in the wilderness. Neglected by her husband, with months between communications from home, her only feminine companionship provided by Mrs. Bailey, the steward's wife who had accompanied her to the Cape, she must certainly have been lonely and lost. Even if she loved MacLean, which seemed hard to believe, it must have occurred to her more than once to return home to England.

But according to her two biographers, there was no turning back for Landon. Both took the view that her literary popularity had been on the wane, that she had worn out her welcome with London society, that her only choice was exile. The assumption there—and I personally felt it was a faulty one—was that popularity, both literary and personal—once lost could never be regained.

Whether they were right or not, the brutal facts remained. On the morning following a small dinner party for Bodie Cruickshank, who was to sail that day for England—along with Mrs. Bailey, whose position as maid had been a temporary one— Laetitia Landon was found dying on the floor of her bedchamber, a bottle of prussic acid in her hand.

Attempts made to revive her were in vain. She died without regaining consciousness and was buried that same evening following the most cursory of inquests. Enfield's book offered the opinion that Landon had committed suicide; Ashton proposed that she had taken the poison by mistake—her doctor had apparently prescribed a few drops of hydrocyanic acid for heart spasms. All London—and her friends and family in particular—believed she had been murdered by MacLean.

The truth could never be known; Laetitia Landon remained

as enigmatic in death as she had been in life. Perhaps the greatest tragedy was that her work became overshadowed with her colorful life and mysterious death.

I closed Ashton's *Letty Landon*. Choices and consequences: That was life. Roberta and Miles had made choices; Mona, Walter Christie, and to some extent, Norton Edam suffered the consequences. Gordon Roget, Todd, Tracy, Angela Hornsby, the February brothers, Cordelia, Catriona, Brian…Peter—we had all made choices and were facing the consequences. Landon's life, my life…and the lives of those we loved and who loved us. Decisions and destiny. It seemed ironic that we had all been brought to this time and place by an unseen hand running something called Kismet Production Company.

CHAPTER 24

"NOT THAT I'm not flattered," Roy Blade said, staring through binoculars at the silent house across the vast greensward, "but why me?"

"It was you or Cordelia," I informed him, "and it's a school night for her."

"Nice to see you've retained your priorities, Ms Hollister."

I leaned forward, pushing aside branches of the tree we perched in. "Did you see something move? Over by the terrace..."

Blade trained the binoculars on the end of the long brick terrace. "Hmm. Yes."

"Hmm, yes *what?*"

"It looks like someone is skulking behind that tall urn."

My heart sank. Peter and Catriona were apparently going ahead with whatever their plan was...and whatever their plan was, I was quite sure it was neither safe nor legal. "Can you see who it is?"

He made a dismissive sound. "All cat burglars are gray in the dark."

"There will be two of them," I said. "They always worked as a team." There was a certain pain in facing it: that in this, Peter had turned to Catriona, that in this they were still one. And somehow reminding myself that both of them had slightly askew—or in her case, totally polarized—moral compasses, didn't really make me feel better.

Blade said, "I don't see anyone else. They picked a good night for it. It's black as pitch out there."

"Let's get down," I said, cautiously shifting position on the sturdy branch where I was sitting.

"And do what?" he inquired, still peering through the field glasses.

"I don't know. Get a closer look?"

"Are you sure you really want to see this?"

Was I? I opened my mouth, but he said suddenly, "Hang about." He leaned forward, refocusing the binoculars. "Someone's coming out."

"What do you mean 'coming out'?"

"Someone just opened the French doors onto the terrace."

"You mean one of them is already inside the house?"

In answer he pushed the binoculars my way. I brought them up to my eyes, staring at the terrace brought suddenly into giant and crystalline view. A tall man with fair hair stood outside the glass doors talking to another tall, slim figure in black. For a confused moment I thought it must be Peter and Catriona, but then I realized the man was older than Peter, his hair silver, not blond, and his face bland and lined in place of Peter's clever, elegant features.

I watched the man's mouth moving as he spoke briefly to the shadowed figure in black. I couldn't tell who that tall, thin outline—hair and face concealed by a black cap—belonged to, but the figure nodded and slipped away down the terrace. I followed him—or her—until it vanished into the shadows.

Robinson/Roget disappeared inside the house, closing the door and drawing the draperies across.

"What was that about?" I murmured.

"She's heading for the carriage house."

"*She?*"

Blade raised a burly shoulder. "Maybe not. Very slight build, very fast."

"Catriona," I said.

Blade reached out and I handed back the binoculars. "Yeah. She's going inside the carriage house."

"They're up to something," I muttered, and Blade began spluttering.

"I mean, I know they're up to *something*," I said. "But I'm guessing they've set up some kind of trap." And suddenly it made sense to me. Of course Catriona hadn't forgiven Peter. She was merely pretending to be helping him against Roget, but in fact she was working with Roget, and now the trap was about to be sprung.

"We need to get down there," I said.

To my relief Blade seemed to feel my urgency. He dropped from the tree, landing with a heavy thud and reaching up a hand to me as I clambered down more cautiously.

Quietly, carefully we made our way past the mounds of fountain grasses, skirting ornamental ponds, then cutting through the woods to the edge of the lawn.

Blade caught my arm. "Wait. There—"

Kneeling in the wet grass, we watched as the front door of the house opened, and a lone figure, Roget surely, in a parka came down the stairs and started across the lawn towards the carriage house. He strode briskly, casually without any effort at concealment.

"We can go round the back," Blade said.

I nodded.

We turned and started back, keeping to the edge of the prettified copse of trees, holding to the deep shadows. The carriage house was lost to view as we crossed behind the main house. I felt a frantic need to hurry. I felt certain Peter was being set up, that any minute he was going to walk into an ambush. Horrifying images came to mind as I pictured Roget shooting him as a trespasser. I could too easily imagine Brian and Chief Constable Heron swallowing some story about Peter coming to rob the place or Roget having to act in self-defense.

It seemed to take forever, but it could have only been a few minutes before Blade and I arrived—I, somewhat out of breath—at the old carriage house. Silently, Blade indicated that we should move to the back entrance, which we did, creeping along the side of the building. There was no sound from inside, but I could see the wavering light of a lantern through the silvered glass of the windows.

We reached a side door, and Blade eased it open, one rusty

centimeter at a time. At each squeak, we froze; but the wind was strong that night, and the old building creaked and groaned with phantom pains.

When the opening was just wide enough, Blade gestured for me to wait, and he squeezed through. I watched him silently cross the sawdust-littered floor to the side of an empty box stall. He crouched down, staring around the corner of the stall. After a moment, he turned to me and gestured for me to come ahead.

Slipping into the musty shadows of the building, I sneaked across to where Blade knelt. Wordlessly, he pointed down the aisle of stalls and tack rooms. It took my eyes a moment to adjust to the uncertain light. At the far end of the building, I could see Roget sitting on a hay bale. He was smoking a pipe, and in the flickering light of the lantern next to him, he looked perfectly relaxed.

But then he had an ace up his sleeve.

I said, forming the words almost soundlessly, "She's in here somewhere."

Blade nodded, and pointed up to the second level. I moved my head in acknowledgement. But if Catriona were lying in wait up there she was not doing a very good job by letting us creep inside the building. Not that I was complaining.

We waited.

The smell of pipe smoke mingled with the faded scents of leather, sawdust, and horse. Overhead, a floorboard creaked once and was silent.

Time passed. I could hear my wristwatch ticking. Next to me, Roy Blade breathed softly, evenly, his muscular shoulder brushing mine. His profile was intent on the front of the carriage house. Feeling my gaze, he turned and smiled at me. I managed to smile back, although I felt much more tension than he apparently did. But then everything that mattered to him was not at stake.

And then the double doors pushed open, and Peter walked in. He seemed to carry the freshness and energy of the night with him, startling in the musty chill of the old building. The lamplight caught the gleam of his hair and eyes, although he stood partly in shadow—and I didn't think he took that position by chance.

"Peter Fox," Roget greeted him. He had a pleasant, cultured voice. "We meet again. At long last."

Peter's thin mouth curled. "Gordon Roget. Or, I gather, George Robinson these days."

"I prefer Robinson, yes. I must say, you look disconcertingly well," Roget remarked. "But then you always did have more lives than a cat."

"Speaking of which, Catriona sends her greetings."

"Does she?" Roget didn't sound too interested in that.

Peter said conversationally, "I admit I'm surprised. I didn't think you'd show."

"You didn't give me much choice," Roget said. "Blackmail is a new line for you, isn't it?"

"One must move with the times. And I move faster when someone tries to kill me."

"That was…perhaps a mistake on my part. I didn't realize at the time you might be open to negotiation."

"Does it mean that much to you?" Peter inquired. "Marriage? The quiet, comfortable life of a country squire?"

Roget shrugged. "Once again you've underestimated me. Now can we get down to business? What is it you want?"

"Fourteen months of my life back. Or, failing that, the Serpent's Egg."

Roget looked pained. "My dear boy, you must know the jewel went long ago to finance any number of lucrative business endeavors. Now if it's money you want—"

"But it's not. Like you, I've done quite well for myself. Well, not quite like you. I never had to betray anyone. Let alone commit murder to buy myself peace of mind."

"Spare me the sermon," Roget said. "I don't have the stone."

Peter seemed to consider him in the hazy light. "I don't think I believe you."

Roget drawled, "That's because you're a romantic fool, and you always were. The fact that you even undertook such a job…" He shook his head in amusement. "In itself, the stone meant nothing to me. But the money from its sale bought me the world."

"That *is* unfortunate," Peter said, "because the stone was the only thing you had that I wanted. And now your world is in my hand." And he made a little motion as though he were emptying his hand.

"What is unfortunate," Roget bit out, and the urbane mask slipped away, "is that you didn't pick some other corner of the world to hole up in." He snapped his fingers, and a tall, slim figure in black rose from one of the stalls. A black cap covered her hair, but as she stood in profile to Blade and me, the body was unmistakably female. She held a wicked-looking little silver gun and it was pointed straight at Peter.

Peter smiled at her. "Why am I not surprised?" he said.

"Nothing personal," she said. The voice carried, flat—and American. *Tracy*, I realized with a jolt.

"It's kismet," Roget said blandly. "We're all the pawns of our destiny. Your destiny unfortunately ends here tonight."

I don't remember moving, but Blade yanked me back hard, and I landed on my tailbone. He continued stealthily down the line of box stalls. Scrambling up from the sawdust, I saw Roget nod to Tracy. But they both froze at the movement on the stairway leading from the loft above.

"I'd think twice about that, old thing." A cool voice with a soft Highland lilt said, "That is, if you want to live to see the sunrise."

We all stared as a tall, slim figure in black, red hair tumbling over slender shoulders, came swiftly, surefootedly down the narrow stairs.

Then Tracy's face darkened; she spun, bringing up her pistol as Catriona jumped lightly to the floor below. Peter dived for Tracy, knocking her arm up. She fired into the ceiling.

Men rushed in through the open double doors—I recognized the dark uniforms of the police—and then I spotted Brian.

"Throw down your weapons!" he ordered. "Police. Put the guns down!"

And there were now multiple guns. Something dull and deadly glinted in Roget's hand. I saw it in the instant before he reached out and knocked over the lantern. The barn plunged into darkness, the lantern rolling across the floor, flickering wildly, before it vanished behind a stall. The taint of kerosene cut the benign barnyard odors.

To the left, I saw a muzzle flash in the darkness, and then there was movement speeding up the aisle toward Blade and me. A dozen flashlight beams began to stab the darkness.

Someone knocked into me with force, tripped, and went hurtling forward. I rolled out of the way. There was a scuffling above me, another muzzle flash, the bang of a shot; and Blade let out a sharp oath.

"Are you all right?" I cried out, reaching for him.

The door behind us pushed open and a shadow briefly blocked the stars. The door slammed shut and leisurely drifted open again.

His voice startlingly near, Peter said furiously, "What the hell are you doing here?" And I was grabbed and hauled to my feet. He began to feel me over with hard, anxious hands. "Are you hurt?"

"I think Blade's been shot," I said.

"He bloody well ought to be!"

"I'm all right," Blade gritted out.

"Jesus! I could shoot you both," Peter said. He pulled me briefly into his arms. I clutched at him in relief and gratitude for his safety, but the next moment he thrust me away and gave me a shake. "What the hell am I supposed to do with you?"

"Is that rhetorical?" I said shakily.

The light came on from another lantern, the unsteady lamp glow fluttering against the rough beams and open stalls. To the side, two policemen were stamping out the tentative flames of the fallen lantern. Brian stood near the double doors trying to hold onto Tracy. She was kicking and wriggling, swearing with a vigor and inventiveness even surprising for her.

"Where the hell did he go?" he shouted to Peter over Tracy's raging.

Peter pointed furiously at the door offset, on its jamb. "Brilliant work as usual!"

"Don't let him get away!" Brian's curses joined Tracy's. He

began to shout orders. Policemen ran out into the night in pursuit of Gordon Roget.

Releasing his punishing grip on me, Peter knelt beside Blade, who was sitting up, clutching his arm. Blood glistened in the dim light, trickled down Blade's black leather sleeve.

"It's just a flesh wound."

"Not for your jacket, mate." Peter's grin was reluctant.

Blade's swearing joined the general profanity around us.

I was looking for Catriona, but I didn't see her anywhere. For one awful moment I thought she might have been hit by the gunfire, but then I realized that she was nowhere to be seen. This was confirmed a moment later when Brian said, "The Ruthven woman—where did she go?"

■■■■■

"I can't believe you went to the police," I said much later that morning, as Peter unlocked the door to Rogue's Gallery.

"I should think you'd be pleased. Isn't that what you're always advising me to do?"

Bells chimed soft and silvery as he pushed the door open. We stepped inside the dim interior and Peter fiddled with the alarm. I looked around. Golden sunlight glanced off the familiar marble bust of Byron, flooded the old maps on the wall illuminating the delicate tracery of long-lost roads and byways.

"And Brian believed you?" I glanced up expecting to see the door of Peter's flat open, expecting to see some sign that Catriona was here—and bracing myself for that encounter. But the door to the flat was closed. And I noticed that the mermaid figurehead— her dark wooden belly repaired and whole—hung suspended once more from the vaulted ceiling above us.

"I don't know if he believed me," Peter said. "I think he was hoping to watch me outsmart myself and fall into his trap. Although he did say something about no one being mad enough to make up such a story."

"He's a good man," I said.

Peter was smiling at me.

"What?"

"Perhaps you didn't notice. Twice he said, 'So *that* was Catriona Ruthven?'"

"Oh, no," I said. "You can't mean what I think you mean. There's no way *Brian* would fall for your psycho ex-girlfriend. She's a villain!"

He just continued to smile in that maddening way.

"It's unthinkable," I said.

He said blandly, "She'd be very good for him."

I was shaking my head, repudiating such a notion. "I don't want to think about it." I was too tired to think about it, frankly, but...I had to admit that during the carriage house mop-up that night, for the first time ever, I'd had the odd feeling that Brian had only been peripherally aware of me.

Starting up the stairway to the flat I said, "What happens if they don't catch Roget?"

"I don't think there's a chance in hell they'll catch Roget." He sounded very weary.

I glanced back, and he said, "It doesn't matter. They've got Tracy, and if last night was anything to go by, she'll spill everything she knows in the interests of a reduced sentence."

"But does she know everything?"

"She knows enough to clear me of any suspicion of murder."

I wasn't convinced of how much talking Tracy would do. Regardless of who had been pulling the strings, it was evident that Tracy had been the trigger woman. According to Brian, Interpol had matched her profile to that of an international hit woman. While she had failed to kill Peter, it looked likely that in a fit of exasperation she had eliminated her erstwhile partners, the February brothers—the night I had revealed that police scrutiny had fallen upon them.

So much for my feminine instinct. The irony was that all those times I had imagined Tracy was making romantic advances toward Peter, she had actually been trying to get him alone long enough to kill him. I suspected she had been a little attracted to him, though, because she had certainly taken her time trying to dispatch him.

We reached the flat; Peter unlocked the door, pushing it wide. Sunlight illumined the long, lovely room. The grandfather clock against the wall, the curio chest before the red leather sofa, the telescope facing out the picture windows that framed the dark woods and purple-shadowed mountains beyond: all seemed untouched, unchanged. I truly felt that I was coming home. But *was* this my home?

"Is that it then?" I asked. "Have we seen the last of Gordon Roget and the Serpent's Egg?" Have we seen the last of Catriona? I wondered.

When he didn't answer, I turned to face him. He was studying me quizzically.

"Is this where the story ends?" I asked, and my voice was softer than I intended.

His mouth curved in a slow smile, and without moving consciously I was somehow across the room and in the warm circle of his arms. He gazed down at me, and his eyes were bluer than the bluest of the lakes.

He said, "Some stories don't have an ending, Esmerelda...."

EPILOGUE

"WHAT'S THIS?" I asked as Peter offered a large, square, be-ribboned box he had fished out from beneath the bed.

It was Tuesday afternoon following the arrest of Tracy Burke—and the escape of Gordon Roget. Peter and I had slept, then woke and talked, made love, and talked some more. And then he had apparently remembered the parcel beneath the bed.

The silver-wrapped box was far too large to contain a jewelry case. I took it and shook it gently. He winced.

"Does every girl get a prize?" I inquired, plucking at the large white bow. "Or have I been especially good?"

His mouth twitched, but something in his eyes told me to—just this once—shut up.

"Open it," he said.

I pulled the white silk bow, and it slipped loose, pooling on the sheet. I gently peeled back the foil paper. The box inside was simple and white. I opened it, moved aside the star-spangled tissue paper. My fingertips found something cool and pointed. I reached in and lifted out what I took at first to be a fragile statuette: Two bisque doves nestled beneath a wire arch of tiny seed pearls, pale pink stones, and silvery velvet leaves.

"It's lovely," I said. "What is it?" And then I knew what it was. I met his eyes. "It's a wedding cake topper." I felt a prickle behind my eyes.

Peter cleared his throat. "Circa nineteen-twenty," he said.

One of the doves held a ring in its delicately formed beak. I freed the ring. It was a delicate twist of gold and diamonds and tiny smoky stones—of cairngorm perhaps. Just the color of the tarns and lakes when the evening sun burnished them.

He took the ring from me and slipped it on my left hand.

"How does that fit?" he asked.

"It fits perfectly," I said, and kissed him.

■■■■■

Grant Sorenson

ABOUT THE AUTHOR

Diana Killian is the author of three other novels in the Poetic
Death series, as well as two more in the new Mantra for Murder
series. As part of The Browne Sisters & George Cavanaugh, she
also performs Celtic music at festivals and concerts across the U.S.
Killian lives in Southern California with her husband, where she
gamely struggles to turn her desert backyard into an English cottage garden.

MORE MYSTERIES
FROM PERSEVERANCE PRESS
💀 *For the New Golden Age* 💀

JON L. BREEN
Eye of God
ISBN 978-1-880284-89-6

TAFFY CANNON
ROXANNE PRESCOTT SERIES
Guns and Roses
*Agatha and Macavity Award
nominee, Best Novel*
ISBN 978-1-880284-34-6

Blood Matters
ISBN 978-1-880284-86-5

Open Season on Lawyers
ISBN 978-1-880284-51-3

Paradise Lost
ISBN 978-1-880284-80-3

LAURA CRUM
GAIL McCARTHY SERIES
Moonblind
ISBN 978-1-880284-90-2

Chasing Cans
ISBN 978-1-880284-94-0

Going, Gone *(forthcoming)*
ISBN 978-1-880284-98-8

JEANNE M. DAMS
HILDA JOHANSSON SERIES
Crimson Snow
ISBN 978-1-880284-79-7

Indigo Christmas
ISBN 978-1-880284-95-7

KATHY LYNN EMERSON
LADY APPLETON SERIES
**Face Down Below
the Banqueting House**
ISBN 978-1-880284-71-1

**Face Down Beside
St. Anne's Well**
ISBN 978-1-880284-82-7

Face Down O'er the Border
ISBN 978-1-880284-91-9

ELAINE FLINN
MOLLY DOYLE SERIES
Deadly Vintage
ISBN 978-1-880284-87-2

HAL GLATZER
KATY GREEN SERIES
Too Dead To Swing
ISBN 978-1-880284-53-7

A Fugue in Hell's Kitchen
ISBN 978-1-880284-70-4

The Last Full Measure
ISBN 978-1-880284-84-1

PATRICIA GUIVER
DELILAH DOOLITTLE
PET DETECTIVE SERIES
The Beastly Bloodline
ISBN 978-1-880284-69-8

WENDY HORNSBY
MAGGIE MACGOWEN SERIES
In the Guise of Mercy
(forthcoming)
ISBN 978-1-56474-482-1

NANCY BAKER JACOBS
Flash Point
ISBN 978-1-880284-56-8

DIANA KILLIAN
POETIC DEATH SERIES
Docketful of Poesy
ISBN 978-1-880284-97-1

JANET LAPIERRE
PORT SILVA SERIES
Baby Mine
ISBN 978-1-880284-32-2

Keepers
*Shamus Award nominee,
Best Paperback Original*
ISBN 978-1-880284-44-5

Death Duties
ISBN 978-1-880284-74-2

Family Business
ISBN 978-1-880284-85-8

Run a Crooked Mile
ISBN 978-1-880284-88-9

VALERIE S. MALMONT
Tori Miracle Series
**Death, Bones, and
Stately Homes**
ISBN 978-1-880284-65-0

DENISE OSBORNE
Feng Shui Series
Evil Intentions
ISBN 978-1-880284-77-3

LEV RAPHAEL
Nick Hoffman Series
Tropic of Murder
ISBN 978-1-880284-68-1

Hot Rocks
ISBN 978-1-880284-83-4

LORA ROBERTS
Bridget Montrose Series
Another Fine Mess
ISBN 978-1-880284-54-4

Sherlock Holmes Series
**The Affair of the
Incognito Tenant**
ISBN 978-1-880284-67-4

REBECCA ROTHENBERG
Botanical Series
The Tumbleweed Murders
(completed by Taffy Cannon)
ISBN 978-1-880284-43-8

SHEILA SIMONSON
Latouche County Series
Buffalo Bill's Defunct
ISBN 978-1-880284-96-4

An Old Chaos *(forthcoming)*
ISBN 978-1-880284-99-5

SHELLEY SINGER
Jake Samson &
Rosie Vicente Series
Royal Flush
ISBN 978-1-880284-33-9

NANCY TESLER
Biofeedback Series
**Slippery Slopes and Other
Deadly Things**
ISBN 978-1-880284-58-2

PENNY WARNER
Connor Westphal Series
Blind Side
ISBN 978-1-880284-42-1

Silence Is Golden
ISBN 978-1-880284-66-7

ERIC WRIGHT
Joe Barley Series
**The Kidnapping
of Rosie Dawn**
*Barry Award, Best Paperback
Original. Edgar, Ellis, and
Anthony Award nominee*
ISBN 978-1-880284-40-7

*REFERENCE/
MYSTERY WRITING*

KATHY LYNN EMERSON
**How To Write Killer
Historical Mysteries:
The Art and Adventure of
Sleuthing Through the Past**
ISBN 978-1-880284-92-6

CAROLYN WHEAT
**How To Write Killer Fiction:
The Funhouse of Mystery &
the Roller Coaster of Suspense**
ISBN 978-1-880284-62-9